THERE WAS ON
THE GUNS TO BE FIRING BLANKS

The teams had to be held in place and kept busy while the Farm traced the signal from the vid cam. Correction—while the Skywalkers traced the signal from the Farm!

Instantly Schwarz whipped out a jamming device to block unfriendly transmissions, but Lyons took more direct action by firing his Colt Python from the hip, the heavy Magnum round shattering the vid cam into a million pieces.

"Rock House, this is the Senator," Blancanales said urgently into his throat mike. "Abort the trace! Suspects were waiting for us to signal you! Repeat, we've been tricked! The X-ships are on the way! Do you copy?"

The only response was the dead crackle of background static.

DON PENDLETON'S

STONY
AMERICA'S ULTRA-COVERT INTELLIGENCE AGENCY
MAN®

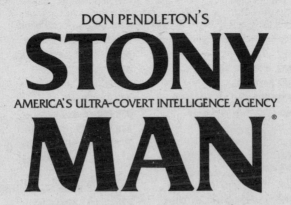

DARK STAR

A GOLD EAGLE BOOK FROM
WORLDWIDE®

TORONTO • NEW YORK • LONDON
AMSTERDAM • PARIS • SYDNEY • HAMBURG
STOCKHOLM • ATHENS • TOKYO • MILAN
MADRID • WARSAW • BUDAPEST • AUCKLAND

First edition August 2008

ISBN-13: 978-0-373-61980-1
ISBN-10:   0-373-61980-4

DARK STAR

Special thanks and acknowledgment to
Nick Pollotta for his contribution to this work.

DARK STAR

*For Sgt. Jason "Scramble" Campbell, U.S. Marine
Corps, 2nd Battalion.
Nice to have you back, buddy.*

PROLOGUE

Compose Island, Brazil

Partially hidden by rising clouds of steam, the huge space shuttle dominated the vast empty expanse of the launch pad. Surrounding the colossal concrete apron was a lush tropical jungle full of wild birds, small monkeys, trip wires, video cameras, proximity sensors and land mines.

"T-minus fifty minutes and counting," an amplified voice announced over the public-address speakers, the words echoing across the island and startling the flocks of colorful parrots in the nearby coconut trees. For a single moment it almost seemed like a rainbow exploded into existence, then the birds separated, each taking off in a new direction, and it was gone.

Standing alongside the colossal spacecraft, the gantry tower was alive with dozens of scientists, technicians, mechanics and astronauts carefully preparing the billion-dollar vehicle for its maiden flight. In only a little while, a new era would begin for Brazilian space travel.

A large crowd of excited people clustered in front of the Vehicle Assembly Building, watched the complex preparations from behind a line of safety barriers. The cream of Brazilian society was in attendance: politicians, billionaires, scholars, famous athletes and movie stars, along with a small army of new reporters, their digital cameras flashing almost nonstop. This was a very special day for the nation, and everybody wanted to be here for the event.

"T-minus thirty minutes and counting," the voice loudly announced once more as the technicians on the gantry started disconnecting myriad cables and hoses attached to the shuttle as a prelude to the launch.

More than simply a new class of space vehicle, the monstrously huge *Skywalker* would be the world's first armored shuttle, fully capable of being armed to defend Brazilian interests in space or to remove enemy military satellites. The brewing war with Colombia over dwindling natural resources was becoming inevitable, and the Ministry of Defense always took the long view and planned for the future. When the hammer fell, Brazil would be ready to defend itself against any possible invader.

Fully aware that the combination of the *Skywalker* and the crowd of high-profile notables was a tempting political target for any terrorist group, the Ministry of Defense was taking no chances today and security was tight. Discreetly armed members of the S2 secret police moved through the excited throng, watching intently for anything suspicious. A full battalion of soldiers was situated in the jungle, and floating serenely off the nearby coast was the massive *São Paulo,* the flight deck of the aircraft carrier full of SuperPuma gunships, and the new AMZ fighter-bombers, their sleek wings bristling with weaponry.

"T-minus ten minutes and counting," the calm voice announced. "Will all nonessential personnel please leave the launch pad immediately. Repeat, all nonessential personnel leave the launch area…. Alert! Red alert! We have incoming!"

The crowd looked at the sky to see something bright streak by overhead, moving faster than they could track. Was it a meteor? A missile? A split second later they had their answer as the truncated cone came to a dead halt in the air above the throng of dignitaries and a hurricane wind brutally slammed them to the ground.

Suddenly a wave of heat engulfed the spectators, followed closely by a thundering volcano of fire, the roiling blast tearing the horrified people apart, arms and legs sailing away like burning autumn leaves. Heads rolled across the cracking concrete and bodies were hammered flat, only to be reduced to ash in mere seconds.

Shocked motionless for a moment, the news reporters on the roof of the Main Assembly Building lurched into action and swung their cameras around to record the ghastly slaughter. But they caught only a brief glimpse of a strange machine hovering above the ocean of fire before the hellish wave of smoke and flame erupted over the edge of the building. Helplessly, the reporters and their equipment were slammed across the roof to tumble off the other side, falling fifteen stories to the hard concrete below.

A low moan sounded just then, rapidly increasing into a strident howl as warning sirens cut loose, the noise nearly rivaling in stentorian exhaust the cone-shaped machine in sheer mind-numbing volume. Bursting out of other buildings across the base, Brazilian security guards stared in horror for only a heartbeat, then pulled their 9 mm automatic pistols and began shooting at the impossible invader. But if the steel-jacketed rounds even reached the machine there was no way of knowing.

Moving sideways, the ten-story-tall cone floated across the parking lot, its exhaust igniting rows of cars, the gas tanks promptly detonating into a staggered series of fireballs. Black smoke rose in dense plumes as hundreds of soldiers burst out of the jungle to start shooting their assault rifles at the intruder. The hail of 5.56 mm rounds throwing off sprays of bright sparks as they ricocheted harmlessly off the armored side of the sleek cone.

A kilometer offshore, an AMZ fighter-bomber suddenly launched from the deck of the *São Paulo,* as a full wing of SuperPuma gunships lifted into the air and assumed a combat formation.

Inside a radar installation, the Brazilian soldiers frantically tried to operate their consoles and get a lock for the SAM bunkers hidden in the distant hills. However, the softly glowing screen only registered the AMZ fighters and SuperPumas, but nothing else. As far as radar was concerned, the sky was clear.

"By the blood of Christ, how is this possible?" a civilian technician cursed, thumping the console with a clenched fist.

"Who cares?" a gruff sergeant growled, crossing the room to yank open a metal locker. Inside the cabinet were neat rows of Imbel assault rifles, stacks of ammunition clips, rows of 30 mm rounds, and one large, bulky fiberglass tube.

Yanking out the Carl Gustaf rocket launcher, the sergeant checked the batteries, zeroed the aft port, then started to rummage for 83 mm shells. Damn it, there only seemed to be armor-piercing rounds designed to take out an APC or hovercraft. But there had to be at least one. Please, Lord, just one, single...*yes!* Sliding the antipersonnel round into the gaping maw of the huge weapon, the sergeant closed it tight, flicked off the safety and grimly strode for the door. A corporal and the civilian tech were already there, working the arming bolts of their assault rifles and thumbing in fat 30 mm rounds.

"Ready!" the sergeant announced, leveling the weapon.

But as the others threw open the door, hell itself exploded into the room, slamming the weapons from their hands and the very flesh from their blackening bones. The delicate equipment short-circuited in a wild display of electric sparks as windows blew out in a glittering rain of glass, then the roof flipped off as the concrete floor cracked, exposing the black box recorder. The resilient device briefly resisted the monstrous onslaught, then it was gone, reduced to red-hot slag and glowing vapors.

Just then there was an unexpected creaking noise as the maze of steel struts supporting the radar array above the installation began to soften and the huge confinement globe started to tilt. Instantly the cone streaked into the sky just in time to avoid being hit by the collapsing tons of advanced electronics.

By now the entire launch facility was in chaos, the soldiers and guards still firing at the bizarre flying machine to no avail whatsoever as hundreds of terrified people ran about screaming. The Main Assembly Building was on fire, and burning cars continued to explode as a spreading cloud of smoke began to completely swamp the base.

Moving above the death and destruction, the cone headed directly toward the *Skywalker.*

Streaking across the sky, the first AMZ fighter banked sharply toward the aerial machine and promptly unleashed a pair of Sidewinder missiles. Incredibly, the deadly heat-seekers streaked past the cone as if it didn't exist and disappeared into the distance.

Cursing vehemently, the pilot began to turn for another try. How was this possible? The damn thing was sitting on a column of flame! he thought. There were no markings on the machine, whatever it was, to announce the country of origin, but clearly it had to be from one of the superpowers.

Suddenly a warning light flashed and the pilot of the AMZ fighter banked sharply to get out of the way of the incoming delta of SuperPumas.

Reaching the *Skywalker,* the cone washed its exhaust across the gantry, sending swarms of burning people flying into the jungle. As the gunships began to fire their 20 mm cannons, the fuel lines attached to the shuttle snapped and out gushed torrents of liquid oxygen and liquid hydrogen. The semifrozen elements instantly combined and ignited. Looking horribly similar to fuses, the burning fuel lines raced up the side of the huge shuttle, then disappeared inside the armored hull. For a long second, it seemed as if nothing would happen.

Then the shuttle bulged slightly just before violently exploding, the blinding detonation spreading across the entire base like the wrath of a prehistoric god. Caught in the titanic shock wave, the gunships and jet fighters were smashed to pieces, the grisly remnants sent tumbling away to splash harmlessly into the gentle waves cresting on the white sandy beach.

As the lambent corona finally faded away, there was no sign of the cone. But standing on the bridge of the aircraft carrier, the captain of the *São Paulo* felt deep in his guts that the enemy machine had not been caught in the massive explosion. Although, how anything could have escaped the gargantuan blast seemed absolutely impossible.

As a second wing of SuperPumas rose from the flight deck to head for Compose Island to start emergency rescue operations, there came a low rumble of something breaking the sound barrier. But the soft noise was lost in the combined roar of the gunship's engines and the horrible crackling of the spreading inferno that completely engulfed the ruined launch facility.

CHAPTER ONE

Washington, D.C.

Passing through the sturdy concrete barrier that encircled the military airfield, three identical limousines rolled across the smooth asphalt and onto the airfield. Separating, each of the armored vehicles rolled toward a different waiting 747 jumbo jet, the huge planes parked on converging runways.

Covering hundreds of acres, Andrews Air Force Base was located close to the capital and was charged with the primary defense of the city. Dozens of Apache and Cobra gunships were parked in orderly rows, ready to launch in a moment's notice. More than a dozen hangars edged the field, the sliding doors pulled aside to reveal ranks of jet fighters and interceptors: F-15 Eagles, F-16 Tomcats, F-18 SuperHornets and even a handful of the brand-new F-22 Raptors.

Riding in the back of the second limo, Hal Brognola snorted at the massive display of firepower and wondered what type of disaster had recently occurred in the world that required his immediate presence. The big Fed had been on a rare fishing trip with his family in upstate New York, but when the President of the United States called he had rushed down here immediately, barely stopping long enough to change out of his old denims into a business suit. As the head of the Sensitive Operations Group, Hal Brognola was only contacted by the Man after the blood had already hit the fan.

As the limo braked to a halt at the foot of an air stairs, the man from Justice waited as a Marine in full dress uniform opened the door and moved aside. Stepping onto the tarmac, Brognola noticed two other men dressed in business attire getting out of the other limousines.

Most impressive, Brognola noted professionally. Things must really be bad for the Secret Service to make such complex security arrangements to mask which jetliner I'm boarding. The man was under no delusion that the precautions were for his benefit, but for the august passenger on the waiting 747, better known to the world as Air Force One.

"Good afternoon, sir," the Marine said, checking a photograph attached to a clipboard. "Password, please."

The honor guard made the request in a friendly tone, but Brognola knew the man's response would be lightning fast and decidedly lethal if the wrong response was given. "Agamemnon," Brognola muttered, for some reason suddenly feeling the urge for a cigar, even though he had given them up years ago.

Nodding, the Marine looked at him much closer now. "Wife's maiden name?"

Puzzled, Brognola tilted his head slightly, only to notice the other men dressed like him at the other planes doing exactly the same thing. Damn, they could even copy his body language? Damn, the Secret Service was good.

"The name, sir?" the Marine repeated in a more insistent tone.

Brognola provided the required information, now very eager to get out of the open and inside the waiting 747. The sky was a clear blue, with scarcely a cloud in sight, yet he felt oddly vulnerable.

Easing his stance slightly, the big Marine motioned toward the air stairs. "Right this way, sir."

Nodding, the big Fed quickly walked up the portable staircase, his sharp eyes checking in every direction. There were snipers lying on the rooftops of the terminal buildings, and several Harrier Jumpjets parked on the grassy strips between the runways, the air in front of them blurry from the heat of the idling turbo engines. What in hell had happened that he didn't know about yet? There had been nothing on the news. But these were the sorts of safeguards normally reserved for a shooting war, not a tense peacetime.

As he reached the top of the stairs, a pretty female Secret Service agent checked his ID again, and Brognola gave the proper answers to her questions as a full delta formation of F-15E Strike Eagles streaked noisily by overhead, the deadly fighters leaving misty contrails behind from the sheer speed of their passage. There seemed to be a lot of contrails up there, crisscrossing in every direction, enough to almost make a smoke screen above the busy military base, which was probably the general idea. Entering the cool interior of the 747, Brognola forced himself to stop making wild guesses. Soon enough he would know the truth.

"Welcome aboard Air Force One," a smiling flight attendant said politely, an Uzi machine gun hanging at her side. "If you'll just hold for a second, sir…"

Standing still, Brognola waited while another Marine used a handheld EM scanner to check him for weapons and explosives. Nobody got close to the President without being scanned, and then scanned again. As part of his job, the big Fed usually carried a 9 mm Glock pistol in a shoulder holster, but that had been left behind in the limo. Over the years, he had created a lot of enemies, but most of them were buried six feet under the ground. However, no visitors got this close to the President caring anything that could be used as a weapon. End of discussion.

"Clear," the Marine announced crisply, tucking away the device.

"Welcome to Air Force One," the flight attendant said, smiling briefly. "If you'll please follow me…" Without waiting for a response, the woman turned to briskly walk down the main aisle of the jet toward the passenger section.

As the Marine closed and locked the hatch, Brognola proceeded down the main aisle of the jetliner, as always marveling that the rich carpeting and polished mahogany panels of the sumptuous interior masked enough state-of-the-art military armor for the plane to be driven through a brick wall.

Catching a movement outside the window, he saw one of the other 747 jumbo jets taxi into position for an immediate take-off. But that was to be expected. The President always traveled in a three-on-three defensive formation, whether it was a 747 or a limousine. Any potential assassins would not know exactly which vehicle he was traveling in.

Passing the stairs to the second level, Brognola reached the passenger section and noted the unusual assortment of people sitting in the comfortable seats. Normally the craft carried a host of government aides, cabinet members, news reporters, along with the occasional member of Congress or the Senate. But this day there seemed to be only grim Secret Service agents, several key members of the Joint Chiefs and a score of Air Force Rangers openly carrying M-17 assault rifles and wearing full body armor.

"Please have a seat, sir," the flight attendant said, a touch of urgency in her voice. "We'll be taking off in just a moment."

Knowing it would be useless to ask about their destination, Brognola took the only empty seat in sight. He barely had time to buckle the seat belt when there came a low rumble of controlled power and the 747 started moving forward, the pressure increasing on him as the front of the jet lifted and he felt the telltale tingling sensation in his gut that meant they had just left the ground. Wow, that was fast. Things had to be a lot worse than he had imagined if the pilot pulled a stunt like that with Eagle One on board. It was almost as if the pilot was taking off under combat conditions and trying to avoid enemy fire.

The angle of assent, maintained for a lot longer than Brognola would have thought necessary, finally leveled out and the rumble of the massive engines faded to a subdued murmur as the colossal plane reached cruising altitude. A light above his seat flashed that it was safe to remove his seat belt. The flight attendant returned.

"Please follow me, sir," the woman said with a smile.

Brognola stood and followed her to the rear of the aircraft.

Walking up to a plain door, the woman tapped a code into a keypad set into the burnished steel frame, then pressed her hand against a glowing plate. There was an answering beep, a light above the door turned green and the flight attendant stepped aside as electromagnetic bolts disengaged and the door slid into the wall with a hydraulic sigh.

"Good to see you, Hal," the President said from behind a large wooden desk in the corner of the room. "Glad you could make it on such short notice."

"No problem, sir," Brognola replied, stepping into the office. "The fish weren't biting worth a damn." Softly, the door closed behind him and resoundingly locked into place.

"Fishing…" the President said with a wan smile. "I haven't done that in ages. You're probably using the wrong type of bait again, my friend. Can't catch catfish with a pop fly, you know."

"As you've mentioned once or twice before." Brognola grinned as he took a seat.

"I'll get you to switch from lures to flies yet."

There was a soft beep from the door. The President pressed a button on the intercom set into his desk and the door opened again, admitting a steward pushing a wheeled cart holding a steaming coffee urn, stacks of cups and saucers and several serving trays piled high with an assortment of sandwiches. Both men nodded politely to the steward as he departed, then completely ignored the food.

"All right, what's so important that we couldn't talk at the White House?" Brognola asked, crossing his legs at the knee. "Has there been an assassination attempt?" He paused in consternation.

"Nothing that simple, I'm afraid," the Man said with a grimace. "And I will not be returning to Washington until further notice. My double is sitting in the Oval office while I stay at Cheyenne Mountain. The Veep is heading for Camp David."

That was unsettling news.

"Okay, what happened?" the big Fed demanded bluntly. "Are we at war with somebody?"

"You tell me," the President replied, pressing a button on the intercom.

Silently an oil painting of President John Adams rotated on the wall to display a plasma-screen monitor. There was a brief strobing effect as the room dimmed, and Brognola found himself looking at the smoke-covered remains of Cape Canaveral in Florida. The Vehicle Assembly Building was on fire, the flames licking skyward for hundreds of feet, the blaze occasionally punctuated by a powerful explosion. Several fire trucks were positioned around the blaze and countless firefighters hosed the structure with steady streams of water and foam.

In the foreground of the screen lay a smashed crawler-transporter. The colossal machine was designed to ferry a space shuttle from the assembly building to the launch pad so that the technicians could work on the vehicle and save days of time for a fast turnaround. With a top speed of one foot per hour, the crawler-transporter couldn't catch a snail, but it was tough enough to roll over an Abrams battle tank without ever noticing. But now the monstrous crawler was deeply bowed in the middle and covered with glowing rivulets of molten metal only partially congealed. The engines were blackened ruins, the armored treads lay broken and randomly scattered. A gigantic pool of hydraulic fluid and diesel fuel covered the ground several feet deep.

Even worse, lying across the top of the crawler-transporter was something that only vaguely resembled a space shuttle. A dozen burned skeletons were sprawled around the crushed wreckage, almost every ceramic heat tile gone or dangling loosely from the warped and badly dented hull. The cockpit was open to the sky, the cargo hatches crumpled like old newspaper. The rear engines were jagged pieces of twisted metal and tubing.

"Son of a bitch," Brognola muttered, leaning closer.

"Wait, there's more." The President sighed.

Slowly the camera panned to the right showing the toppled remnants of two gantry towers, extended over the lip of a huge crater large enough to swallow the crawler-transporter intact. The interior of the depression was filled with a dense gray cloud, tarnished steel rods rising out of the swirling fumes like the desperately reaching fingers of a dying man.

"That was the fuel depot," the President said in a monotone.

With his heart pounding, Brognola gave no reply, studying the scene of destruction closely as the camera took almost a minute to get past the smoking blast crater to finally focus on a relatively undamaged section of the launch facility. Spread out in neat rows were dozens of black plastic body bags, armed soldiers standing guard while medics ferried the still forms into waiting ambulances. Far in the distance, several Navy warships could be seen along the coastline, while swarms of Apache and SuperCobra gunships hovered overhead.

The room seemed to grow still as Brognola said nothing for a few seconds; there was only the muted hush of the jet engines.

"How many people did we lose?" the big Fed asked, controlling his seething emotions. Normally the Cape was as clean as an operating room, washed and scrubbed almost daily. Now it looked like the bombed-out sections of Beirut.

"Eighty-six are confirmed dead," the President reported. "With another hundred missing, including a lot of tourists."

Inhaling deeply, Brognola turned away from the grisly vista of destruction and sat back in his chair. For a long moment he said nothing, lost in dark contemplation.

"Any idea who did it?" he asked.

"None."

"Damn. And we're sure this was not a nuke?"

"Absolutely positive," the President replied, scowling down at the closed report. "Both NASA and the DOD checked for residual radiation, and NSA Keyhole satellites registered nothing out of the usual on the magnetic spectrum."

"All right, if they weren't hit by a nuke, then what happened?"

"We're not exactly sure," the President replied, tapping a few buttons on his desk. "But the NSA was able to retrieve this image from the cell phone of a Mr. Thomas Hutchings who was fishing about a mile off Cocoa Beach."

The monitor flickered, then abruptly changed into a jumpy view of the bow of a fishing boat, and a white line stretching down into the water.

Just then something fiery shot down from the sky like a film of a missile launch played in reverse. Smoke exploded from the Cape, then a series of bright explosions, closely followed by a blinding light flash that extended outward. The corona was dotted with bodies and tumbling cars, and pushed back the choppy waves to create a tidal wave that slammed into the fishing boat and sent it flying. The cell phone was dropped to the deck with a clatter and there were only chaotic images for a few seconds, mixed with the sound of splintering wood before the screen went blank.

"Hell of an explosion," Brognola said in an ordinary voice.

"A hell of an explosion," the President agreed.

"How long did the attack take?"

"Three minutes, fourteen seconds."

"To destroy the whole damn Cape?"

"And escape," the Man said.

Unbelievable.

"Was radar able to track the trajectory of the… whatever it was, coming or going? That could tell us a lot about it's origin," Brognola stated.

"No."

Frowning, the big Fed started to speak, but the one-word answer spoke volumes. This was just incredible, but horribly true. The entire facility had been destroyed, annihilated was a better word, in only a few minutes by something that moved faster than a missile, dropped straight down from the sky, was radar invisible and killed with fire from the underneath.

"Show it to me again," Brognola ordered brusquely. "Slower this time, with maximum magnification focused on the flying object."

The President hit another button on the small console and the monitor came to life once more, the nightmare scene advancing in a series of freeze-frame shots every few seconds.

"Hold it right there," Brognola said as something moved horizontally across the base.

The picture went motionless, and he stared hard at an object momentarily silhouetted by a rising cloud of white smoke. It looked like a cone of some sort. A cone riding a column of fire…

"So it has finally been done," the big Fed said with a sigh, rubbing his forehead. "Somebody solved the power problem and built an SSO."

"Unfortunately that is also the opinion of the Department of Defense," the President said, turning off the monitor. "As well as myself, which is why I immediately called you."

A working SSO, a single-stage-to-orbit rocket. Brognola tried not to shudder. Several years ago he had been present at the maiden flight of the *Delta Clipper,* the first test model of an SSO ever built. If successful, it could have been the first true spaceship in human history, a rocket that launched straight up, standing on its own legs, and landed doing the same thing. Just like in the comic books. A genuine rocket ship. Unfortunately the *Delta Clipper* failed. The vehicle had gained barely a hundred feet of height when it had a massive short circuit in the controls and developed a fuel leak that almost killed the crew. Also, the engines had been pitifully weak, barely able to lift the tiny, thirty-foot-tall X-ship. The test flight was considered a total failure, and the project canceled. It was the considered opinion of everybody involved that the present state of modern technology was simply insufficient to build such an incredible complex piece of machinery.

Which was actually for the best, Brognola noted grimly. A working SSO, or X-ship as it had been nicknamed, would have been a security nightmare of gigantic proportions. Able to launch from a driveway and to land on top of an apartment building halfway around the world, a successful X-ship could have heralded a tidal wave of smuggling that would have engulfed the entire world. It would rise straight up into space, then drop back down again in a steep curve, using the natural rotation of Earth to cover thousands of miles in only a few minutes. Overnight, border guards, harbor patrols, custom inspectors and airport security would have become obsolete. Weapons, drugs—anything—could almost literally be delivered to the front door of the customer. Terrorists would have been able to land right on top of their targets—buildings, bridges, schools— and use the fiery exhaust of the X-ship to do more damage than most conventional explosives. Why carry a bomb when the thundering exhaust of the rocket engines was even more powerful? Unless they got hold of a nuke. A working X-ship armed with a tactical nuclear weapon could destroy any place on Earth, and nobody would be able to stop it. The fantastic speeds involved and the vertical trajectory would make all conventional air defense systems virtually useless.

All that was needed was for some lunatic to also make the things invisible to radar, like a stealth bomber, and you'd have the end of the world, Brognola thought.

Only now it seemed that somebody had solved those technical problems and had just gotten in the first strike.

"Okay, we're facing an X-ship," Brognola said, cracking his knuckles thoughtfully as he digested the impossible information. "Any chance the lab boys at the

Pentagon were able to get an estimate of the size of the SSO from the cell phone video?"

Reaching for a coffee urn, the President poured himself a cup, took a sip, then placed it aside. "Yes, roughly 120 feet tall."

About the size of a ten-story building, Brognola mused. No way that monster was going to be hidden in a garage or car port. Okay, one small point in our favor. It's invisible, but huge. That sounded like a contradiction of terms, but sadly was not.

"Have there been any other attacks?"

"Hal, every other major launch facility in the world has been hit. Edwards Air Force Base, Houston, Compose Island in Brazil, Woomera Base in Australia, French Guyana, Rocket City in Russia, Tanegashima Island in Japan, Sriharikota Island in India…every launch facility capable of putting a shuttle into space has been flattened. Utterly smashed. The death toll for all of the bases combined is monstrous."

"This is why we're meeting here," Brognola said suddenly, tapping the arm of the chair. "A moving target will be harder for them to hit."

"Exactly." The President paused, then added, "Plus each of the three planes have another jumbo jet riding above it as a physical shield."

Damn, that was smart. Once more his admiration for the sheer guts of the U.S. Secret Service was raised. The President would have to stay on the move from now on, never stopping for anything, refueling in midair, until this crisis was resolved.

If it could be resolved. Annoyed at himself, Brognola shook the negative thoughts from his mind. "Mr. President, is there any chance that we know the sequence of the strikes?" he asked hopefully, concentrating on the task at hand.

"Now, I just know where you're going with that question," the Man said, giving a half smile. "And the answer is yes. Compose Island, Rocket City and Cape Canaveral were all hit at the exact same moment, so we're facing at least three X-ships, with possibly more of them being held in reserve.

"Currently, the Army Corps of Engineers is working on emergency repairs of the facilities," the President continued, "but it will take several weeks before we're able to put anything into space again. Maybe a month."

"A month we don't have." Brognola leaned back in the chair. Christ, in a week these things could smash civilization apart. "And I'll assume that I've heard nothing of this on the radio, cable TV or the Internet because the nations involved are trying to keep a tight lid on the matter and prevent a panic."

"Exactly. No police force in the world could control the rioting if the news of the X-ships was released. This matter must be handled covertly, as quietly as possible."

"Agreed, sir. Secrecy is mandatory. Too bad nobody was able to shoot one down. We could have learned a lot from the wreckage."

"Hal, everybody shot at them," the President said surprisingly. "But bullets did nothing and heat-seekers went straight past the X-ships without even slowing."

"But they ride a column of fire larger than the Statue of Liberty! How is that possible?"

"Unknown, and part of your assignment," the President said. Just then, a light flashed on his intercom and the man stabbed it with a stiff finger to turn off the distraction. If it was anything of importance, his secretary would come into the office. "At the moment, Homeland Security is working with the Pentagon to try to come up with some sort of defense, a way to beat the radar shield of the X-ships. From the sheer volume of their engine exhaust, these things must be flying fuel tanks, so a single missile should blow them to hell."

"But a missile can't destroy what can't be seen," Brognola finished. The combination of stealth technology and the vertical flight path of the X-ships made them virtually unstoppable.

"The FBI is checking into the major corporations still interested in trying to build an SSO—Armadillo Aerospace in Texas, Blue Horizons in California, and the like," the President went on, templing his fingers. "The CIA is doing the same thing overseas, with Army Intelligence investigating our known enemies in Europe, Navy Intelligence doing the Middle East and Africa, with Air Force Intelligence concentrating on South America." He paused. "Especially Brazil."

"Understood," Brognola declared. "Just because they were the first place hit, that doesn't mean they're not actually behind everything and just trying to throw off suspicion."

"Precisely." The President frowned. "Now, what I want from Stony Man is for your people to hit the underground, the crime cartels, drug lords and arms dealers."

"Understood, sir. Somebody paid a fortune to build these things, and it will cost even more to maintain them."

"Precisely," the President said, sliding over the sealed manila envelope. "Here is all of the data that we have, copies of the cell phone video, security logs and such, along with all of the information on the *Delta Clipper* experiments."

Accepting the envelope, Brognola noted the security seals were still in place. If it had been opened, the white band along the top would have turned red in only a few seconds.

Damn, it was slim, he thought.

"Yes, I know." The President sighed unhappily. "That's not much to go on, but…"

"It'll be enough," the big Fed stated confidently, rising to his feet once more. "And if not, we'll get the rest from these murdering bastards just before we shovel them into the dirt."

"Move fast on this, Hal," the President said earnestly. "The only possible reason that these X-ships ran a sneak attack on every launch facility was that they don't want us putting anything into space that might challenge them. Because if they manage to hold the high ground…"

"We lose," Brognola said bluntly, feeling a surge of cold adrenaline in his gut. "Plain and simple. We lose the whole goddamn world."

Lifting the telephone receiver, the President waited for only a moment before speaking. "Captain, please head for Dulles airport at once. And I want an immediate take-off as soon as our passenger has disembarked…no, we'll refuel in the air over Pennsylvania…yes, thank you." He set down the receiver. "Twenty minutes, Hal."

Brognola grunted and tucked the folder inside his jacket. Unbidden, the earlier scenes on the wall monitor playing over and over in his mind. It seemed that

World War III had started, and the good guys had lost the first battle.

Now everything depended on Stony Man.

CHAPTER TWO

Stony Man Farm, Virginia

In a rush of warm air, the Black Hawk helicopter set down on Stony Man Farm's helipad. The side hatch was thrown aside and Hal Brognola stepped out clutching a slim manila envelope.

Waiving away the driver of the SUV who would have taken him to the farm house, the big Fed decided to walk the short distance.

By the time he reached the building the door was open and Barbara Price, mission controller, stood on the threshold.

"Here, you better see this," Brognola said, thrusting the envelope forward.

"Already have," Price said, pushing it back. "Aaron and his people are hard at work doing an analysis, and I've recalled both teams from their current assignments."

"Excellent," Brognola said, tucking the envelope away once more. He was not really surprised that the woman was already familiar with the report. Before being recruited into Stony Man, Barbara Price had been a top operative for the NSA. The woman led him into the farm house.

"Are those infrared cameras?" Hal asked as they walked across the spacious room.

Price nodded in acknowledgment. "I don't know if it will give us a warning in enough time to respond, but it's the best we could come up with in an hour."

Reaching the elevator bank, Brognola pressed the call button. "Not bad, but just in case…" The doors opened and they stepped inside.

"I already have several auxiliary video cameras in the barn set to only see in the ultraviolet spectrum," Price told him as the doors silently closed. "Once again, I have no idea if it will help, but…" She shrugged, leaving the sentence unfinished.

"Well, if it works, we can relay the information to all of our military installations, as well as every friendly nation," Brognola replied as the car began to descend. "Unfortunately, any civilian targets these bastards hit won't have that sort of equipment."

"Yes, I know," Price stated. "But Aaron has his people working on a few ideas about that."

"Good to know. The one thing we don't have is a lot of time."

The elevator reached the bottom of the shaft and the doors opened with a musical chime. As they exited into a long corridor, Brognola noted the extra blacksuits standing guard. "Expecting trouble?" he asked pointedly.

"Always," she replied grimly.

As the pair passed a staff room, Brognola could see that it was empty, the break table covered with half-filled cups of steaming coffee, along with partially eaten doughnuts and sandwiches. Mounted in the corner of the ceiling was a flat-screen monitor showing a local news anchor talking excitedly into a microphone and standing in front of a smoky view of Cape Canaveral.

"Damn, the news media has the story," Brognola muttered irritably. "But I guess we couldn't kept it from them for very long."

"I did my best," Price said, not glancing that way. "At least I have most of the news channels convinced it was merely a fuel leak explosion and not a terrorist attack."

"How did you manage that?"

"Had the NASA spokesperson deny it vigorously... before they could ask."

In spite of the situation, the big Fed almost grinned. "Yep, that would do it, all right."

She shrugged again. "It usually does."

Reaching the far end of the corridor, they hurried to one of the electric cars that would take them along the underground passageway that led to the Annex building. Moments later, after passing through security, Price and Brognola headed to the Computer Room.

A hushed excitement filled the large room with palpable force. A soft breeze murmured from the wall vents, the pungent smell of strong coffee came from a small kitchenette, and the soft sound of muted rock music floated on the air. Hunched over elaborate workstations, four people were typing madly on keyboards.

"Damn it, there are too many of them!" Aaron "The Bear" Kurtzman growled, callused hands pushing his wheelchair a little closer to the wall monitor.

"And this isn't even half of them," Carmen Delahunt said, her face hidden behind a VR helmet as her gloved hands fondled the empty air opening computer files on the other side of the world.

"Explain," Kurtzman demanded, turning the heavy chair in her direction.

"A lot of these companies don't have computerized files for me to hack," Delahunt replied. "Some are actually using handwritten ledgers, for God's sake! There is no way that I can ever track down all of the shipments."

"Shipments of what?" Price demanded as she advanced closer.

"Air," Kurtzman said, briefly glancing at her, then turning to wheel back to his workstation. His desk was a mess, covered with papers, CDs, hastily scribbled notes and several books on military history with handwritten corrections in the margins. A steaming mug of coffee stood next to his keyboard.

"Air?" Brognola demanded, crossing his arms.

"Liquid air, actually," Kurtzman explained, locking the wheels into place. "We did a spectral analysis of the MPEG from the cell phone and found out the X-ship was using conventional rocket fuel."

"LOX-LOH?" Price demanded skeptically. "But that's impossible! The combination doesn't give enough energy to power an SSO!"

"Which means they have some way to boost the reaction, but there's no denying the facts," Kurtzman retorted gruffly, tapping a few buttons. "See for yourself."

With a flicker the main wall screen revealed a wind rainbow with a few interspersed black bars.

"See those color absorption lines?" the cyber wizard said pointing a thick finger at the black bars. "That's oxygen and hydrogen, no doubt about it."

"Can they be tricking the sensors somehow?" Brognola asked hesitantly.

Reaching for the mug of coffee, Kurtzman paused to arch an eyebrow. "Trick the visible spectrum?" he asked, sounding incredulous. "No, Hal, the things are using LOX-LOH as fuel. That's a fact. How they get those re-action pressures is beyond me, though. Hunt is working on a few ideas, but has nothing yet."

Hearing his name, Professor Hunting Wethers looked up from his workstation for a moment, then returned to the complex mathematical equations scrolling across his monitor. The side monitors were full of three-dimensional images of rocket engines and charts of shock-diamond explosion pulses inside the exhaust flames.

"It doesn't matter how the terrorists are boosting the engine power of the X-ships," Price said. "What is important is that if they're using regular fuels, then they just refuel after every attack." She paused. "Which means they must have refueling stations hidden all over the world, mountaintops, in the middle of a forest or a desert, anywhere at all. Distance means nothing to these ships."

"That's why you're checking into industrial air plants," Brognola added, his interest piqued. "To try to track down any recent shipments of liquid oxygen."

"Close enough," Kurtzman said. "Only it's—"

"Hydrogen," Delahunt interrupted, her gloved hands brushing aside firewalls and massaging access codes. "There's too many medical uses for liquid oxygen, so hydrogen is much easier to track."

"Anything usable yet?" Brognola prompted.

"No," the woman replied curtly, her frustration obvious. "There are simply too many air plants in the world."

"Roughly a double deuce of them worldwide," Kurtzman added.

Mentally, Price translated the figure. "Twenty-two thousand plants?"

"At least. Lots of uses for compressed air, you know. Hell, we pack munitions in pure argon, and use liquid halogen in our fire extinguishers! And who's to say the terrorists haven't built one for themselves in Borneo or Outer Mongolia."

"Liquid hydrogen…what an interesting possibility," a voice murmured. "Yes, that might just work."

"What do you have, Akira?" Kurtzman demanded, twisting in his chair while setting down his empty mug.

Over at the third workstation, a handsome youth of Japanese ancestry thoughtfully blew a bubble of chewing gum before answering. "I've been considering the inability of the heat-seekers to attack to the X-ships," Tokaido said, unwrapping a fresh piece of bubble gum. Briefly he inspected the sugary piece before sliding it into his mouth. "The only possible answer is liquid nitrogen."

Frowning, Kurtzman was about to ask a question, then his face brightened. "You mean, a defusement pattern, like Looking Glass?"

"Yes, exactly."

"Damn, that's clever," Kurtzman muttered. "Yes, I'll bet that would work as a heat shield. Not for very long, but obviously for long enough. These things travel so fast."

"Speed is the key," Tokaido confirmed, tapping a button before a series of charts flashed into existence on the wall screen.

Price and Brognola looked hard at the diagram. They both knew that Looking Glass was the code name for the 747 jumbo jet used as the mobile headquarters for SAC, the Strategic Air Command, the people who controlled all of the nuclear weapons in the nation's arsenal. The 747 was heavily armed, and the Air Force had boasted for decades that it could not be shot down. Studying the screen, they now knew why. The moment radar registered an incoming missile, Looking Glass would automatically release a stream of liquid nitrogen that chilled the air around the jet engines, momentarily masking their heat signature. With nothing to lock on to, the enemy missile would simply sail right past the mobile headquarters.

"Doesn't Air Force One use something similar?" Price asked.

"Sure, the Secret Service invented the idea."

"How much liquid nitrogen would an X-ship need for this tactic?" Brognola demanded. "Those big engines must be hotter than a hellfire barbecue."

"At least," Tokaido replied, snapping his gum. "I don't know how large a crew they carry, but I'd guess—and it's purely a guess, mind you—that an X-ship is probably only good for two maybe three ventings. After that, they'd be as vulnerable as any ship. Unfortunately…"

"Unfortunately, after the first missile salvo, they take off faster than lightning," Kurtzman said, working a calculator program on his console. "Damn it, we'd need a concentrated strike of ten Sidewinders launching in unison, overlapping two other salvos, to get a definite kill on the first attack."

"Can you set the SAM batteries of the Farm to do that?" Price asked.

After a moment Kurtzman nodded. "Yes," he said hesitantly. "But we'd have to replace the blacksuits with a master computer, and that would take at least a week."

"Useless then." Brognola sighed, grinding a fist into his palm. "But we better send out the word about the overlapping salvos in case somebody else can do it. Maybe the U.K. They have a lot of automation in their defense systems."

"Consider it done," Tokaido said, already typing madly.

"Have there been any demands from these people yet?" Kurtzman asked, reaching for his mug. Upon finding it empty, he pushed away from the workstation and headed toward the kitchenette. "Any requests to release prisoners, transfer money to a Swiss bank account, get troops out of the Middle East, anything at all?"

"No," Brognola stated. "And that's the part that scares me the most."

"Agreed," Price said. "It means that these people are not planning to negotiate for anything, but simply seize what they want. And who can blame them? As of right now, nobody can stop them."

"That is not quite correct, Barbara," Wethers said slowly, leaning back in his chair. "I have been studying the videos of these attacks, and been running some rough calculations. They can't fly."

"Are you kidding?" the woman asked.

"Not at all," the distinguished professor replied, pulling a briarwood pipe out of his shirt pocket and tucking it comfortably into his mouth. Smoking was forbidden in the Computer Room, but he found chewing on the stem highly inducive to the thinking process. "If the X-ships are using a standard LOX-LOH fuel, and we know this for a fact, then they simply cannot generate enough power to fly as fast and as far as we know they do." He shifted the pipe to the other side of his mouth. "Which sounds like a contradiction, but is not. What it means is, they've somehow augmented the combustion."

"Any idea how?" Brognola asked, feeling out of his element. He was a cop, not a scientist.

"Indeed, yes," Wethers replied with a wan smile. "There have been some NASA experiments to increase the power of a standard shuttle engine by boosting the ignition with microwaves. Now these have worked in a laboratory, but failed on the launch pad. A microwave impeller can indeed increase the power of a rocket engine several times, more than enough to accomplish what we've seen."

"So why haven't we done that?" Price demanded impatiently.

"Because the intense magnetic fields would soon kill the crew," Wethers said. "That is, unless there is sufficient shielding to protect them. But that would weigh so much it'd completely neutralize the boosting effect."

"If you boost the engine, the crew dies," Kurtzman said thoughtfully, starting a new pot of coffee. "So either the crews of the X-ships are all suicides, or they have no idea what the engines are doing to them."

"This could give us some critical leverage to turn one of the terrorists when we find the people behind these attacks," Brognola said.

"Personally, I'd rather simply blow off their heads," Price stated. "But it's more important to stop these lunatics."

"How does it kill them?" Kurtzman asked. "Damage to the brain tissue, destroys the nervous system, or invokes artificial leukemia?"

"Leukemia," Wethers stated. "Exactly the same as the

technicians who work on improperly shielded power lines and cheaply built electrical substations, but on a much more intense level."

"Really? How soon would it affect them?" Brognola demanded. "If we're talking years…"

"At the levels of power necessary to boost a ten-story spacecraft, I'd say no more than a few days at the most."

"At least that gives us a place to start," Price said.

"Unless each crew only does one mission," Wethers amended. "Then another team takes control of the ship… no, wait, that would be a logistical nightmare. The terrorists might have hundreds of refueling depots hidden around the world, but to also have each one staffed with a reserve crew is ridiculous."

"Could the ships be fully automated?" Price inquired. "Computer operated with no live crew?"

"Impossible," Kurtzman countered. "Good work, Hunt. Start looking into whatever would be needed to build the microwave…beamers?"

"Impellers."

The man gave a curt nod. "As you say, impellers. Carmen, check into any large purchases of antileukemia medicine purchased within the past month."

"I'll also look for any shipments that have gone missing, or been stolen," the former FBI agent added from behind the VR helmet, her gloved hands rapidly opening and closing files.

"In the meantime, I'll access the logs of the NSA Keyhole satellites to try to find out where the ships first launched from," Kurtzman stated, heading for his workstation. "If we can pinpoint their place of origin, that could tell us—"

Suddenly a printer set against the wall started humming and pushed out a single sheet of green-tinted paper. Changing direction, Kurtzman rolled toward the machine, but Price got there first.

"The FBI was checking the two American companies trying to build SSO transports and found only smoking ruins," she stated. "The working models, blueprints, schematics—everything is destroyed."

Brognola bit back a curse. So far, the terrorists were way ahead of them, with Stony Man playing catch-up and doing a poor job. "What's the official story?"

"That each airfield was struck by lightning, which caused a wildfire."

The big Fed grunted. That was close enough to the truth for the present. But pretty soon somebody was going to figure out the truth and then it would be chaos in the streets. "Were there any survivors?" he asked hopefully.

"Lots. As soon as they get out of the hospital, the FBI will debrief them."

"I'll want a copy of those reports."

"No problem, I'm already in their system," Kurtzman replied, the FBI emblem fading into view on his computer screen. "As soon as there is something, I'll have a blacksuit deliver it to your office."

"Don't bother, I'm here for the duration," the big Fed replied, going to the wall and claiming a spare chair.

"What's the status of the field teams?" Price asked, glancing at the clock on the wall. "It's been over an hour since we sent the recall signal."

"No response yet," the cyber wizard replied gruffly, looking at a submonitor. "Which means they're either in the middle of a fight or have gone silent."

"Or they're dead."

There was no possible reply to that, so everybody in the room continued with their work. But the air seemed a little bit colder now as the people pointedly ignored the clock on the wall, the frenzied typing suddenly sounding painfully similar to machine-gun fire.

CHAPTER THREE

Fayetteville, South Carolina

A cool rain fell across the sprawling military base, washing the red clay dust from the side of the stout brick buildings.

"Here we go!" a burly sergeant shouted, gnarled fists resting on his hips. "You have five minutes, then we leave without you!"

Bursting into action, the elite troop of Marine specialists dived off their bunks and scrambled across the barracks, grabbing duffel bags and yanking on unmarked jackets to cover the handguns riding in their shoulder holsters. There were no sirens to announce the intentions of the combat troops, only a small red light flashing above the exit to signal the call to war.

Through a rain-smeared window, the sergeant could see the brilliant columns of combat searchlights sweeping the stormy clouds, and he knew that a dozen radar globes were probing the sky far beyond the range of visible sight. The balloon had gone up only minutes earlier, but already the gate to Fort Bragg was closed and locked, a full platoon of armed soldiers in body armor standing guard, along with a pair of Bradley Fighting Vehicles. The Bradleys were angled toward one another, forming a narrow channel too small for any truck or car to get through, and spike strips had been laid in case somebody tried to ride a motorcycle through or around the imposing the blockade.

Located near the artillery range were half a dozen long-range cannons, their barrels pointed at the sky. Everything the base had was primed and ready for battle, big antiaircraft shells set to explode at different heights to fill the sky with a deadly maelstrom of shrapnel.

Massive Abram battle tanks were parked on the parade grounds, positioned back-to-back in a large circle for fast deployment. Wearing slickers and "hot com" helmets, grim soldiers walked the flat roofs of the PX and library, carrying Stinger missile launchers and lugging cumbersome, four-barrel, HAFLA multirocket launchers.

"One minute!" called the sergeant, checking his watch. "Move it or lose it, people!"

"About time we finally saw some action," a private said, grinning as he lay his black letter on a shelf. Everybody going into combat was strongly urged to leave a goodbye note for his family in case he didn't come back. That was just standard operational procedure for the U.S. Marines.

"Don't get too excited, kid, until we find out what we're fighting," a corporal replied gruffly.

Whenever some boot heard that they were being trained to fight in space, a specialist in zero-gravity combat, they always started to make jokes about Space Marines as if nobody had ever thought of it before. Nine times out of ten that started a fight, but it was often held behind a barracks or in the motor pool after reveille, where such matters could be settled with quiet and decorum. What the CO didn't know couldn't get you cashiered.

It confused and offended the troops that so many people thought it was odd that America had taken steps to protect its interests in space. A paratrooper was specially trained to fight while falling out of the sky. Commandos did it behind enemy lines, snipers did it from a mile away, scuba divers did it under water and Navy SEALs could fight anywhere, hanging upside down from mountain peaks if necessary. The United States of America had thousands of satellites in low-Earth orbits and a fledging space station in high-Earth orbit, and was planning to expand it, even build another one, before going back to the moon. The same as the Red Chinese. It would be foolhardy for the Joint Chiefs not to make plans to protect those stations with troops.

"Time!" the sergeant announced, throwing open the exit door.

Forming a rough queue, the men walked neatly into the rain. Across the road was a line of nondescript Hummers waiting to take them to Pope Air Force base as the first step in their rapid journey to the Cape. The vehicles were parked near a large bronze statue of General Bragg, the soft rain blurring the features of the officer so that it almost appeared as if he were crying.

Shaking off the unnerving sight, the men of the Special Space Combat Unit started across the road when they paused and began to shudder. Dropping their duffel bags, several of them bent over and started vomiting onto the gravel. Clambering out of the Hummers, the drivers rushed to aid the fallen men when they also started to shake violently, then topple over, foaming at the mouth, streamers of red blood pouring from their eyes.

Utterly horrified, the sergeant standing in the doorway of the barracks took a step toward the rain outside, then changed his mind and turned to sprint for the emergency button on the wall. Smashing a fist through the thin glass, he hit the switch and a strident siren began howling above the barracks. Knowing help was on the way, he went back to the doorway. Fighting the urge to rush outside, he looked over the fallen men, twitching on the ground. What in the holy hell was going on here? he thought. Wild screaming came from all over the base and, squinting against the rain, he could see a gunner topple limply off the roof of the PX, and then another from the library. Bloody hell! If he didn't know any better, the sergeant would have swore that this was a—

Suddenly a sharp pain filled his lungs, and the Marine lunged forward to try to shut the door, but it was already too late. His fingers felt like jelly. The soldier slipped to the floor on boneless legs, his eyesight dimming even as his mind recognized the deadly symptoms of VRL nerve gas. No. Impossible! VRL was banned by every civilized nation in the world.

Struggling to drag in a lungful of air, the sergeant could hear the sirens of an approaching ambulance. Throwing himself forward into the rain, he cried to wave off the others, struggling to shout out a warning. But there only came a horrid burbling from his dissolving throat. Suddenly a terrible cold filled his body and the man felt himself falling forever into an inky blackness darker than space.

Hovering a mile above the rumbling storm clouds blanketing South Carolina, the pilot of the X-ship waited until the canisters of VRL gas were completely empty before boosting the engines and streaking away for a quick refueling on the tropical island of Fiji, and then on to his next target. At last, the preliminaries were over, and now Dark Star could begin its real mission.

CHAPTER FOUR

Beijing, China

A flash of light from above drew the guard's attention just before his world exploded into flame.

Moving along the top of the wall of the People's Maximum Security Prison, the hovering X-ship burned out both searchlights and all three guard towers before anybody had time to react.

A dozen guards burst from the last tower, blowing whistles and desperately loading 5.56 mm Norinco machine guns. As they raised the weapons and touched the triggers, bright red laser beams shot out from the tiny black box clipped under the barrel. For a moment it looked like a burning spiderweb filled the air as the lasers swept along the smooth hull of the gigantic X-ship.

"Fire!" a sergeant bellowed, and the machine guns cut loose with streams of soft lead that bounced off the side of the huge ship.

Just then, a steel door slammed open and a big corporal strode into view carrying a massive machine gun with a long belt of 7.8 mm rounds dangling from the side, a bipod attached to the vented barrel. Working the arming bolt, the corporal aimed the machine gun at the X-ship, then paused in shock as he saw the red dot of a laser pointer resting on his chest. For a breathless moment he waited for the prison guard pointing the Norinco at him to move the beam aside, then in cold realization he understood the beam was angling down from the invading vessel.

Jerking up his head, the corporal looked into a grinning face of a man crouching in a small open hatch in the side of the X-ship, some sort of angular rifle in his hands. Instantly, both men cut loose. The heavy-duty 7.8 mm combat rounds hammered briefly across the adamantine hull of the X-ship, then the guard exploded, guts and blood spraying outward for yards.

The gunner was cut in two. The ragged remains of the torso fell into the exercise yard, while his undamaged legs toppled outside into the freedom of the night.

Quickly turning, the man disappeared from the hatch and a salvo of rockets shot out to impact on the inside of thick granite wall. The noise was deafening, and billowing smoke exploded across the enclosed prison yard.

On the ground, a lone guard threw an arm across his face and braced for the impact of shrapnel, but nothing occurred. Hesitantly, the guard lowered his arm in confusion. But how could that be? He saw the missiles hit! Could they have dummy warheads that only produced smoke and noise? But that would mean...

"Jail break!" he bellowed, running blindly through the dense fumes. "Alarm! Alarm! Mass escape!"

Sirens began to stridently howl as the double doors of the dining hall slammed aside and out poured a howling mob of prisoners, their gray work suits fluttering with prison ribbons. Howling like wild animals, the murderers and rapists spread across the courtyard, grabbing the fallen weapons of the dead guards and firing at the other guards. The smoky air was alive with red laser beams.

Staying safe inside the dining hall, four men poured water over their clothing and hair, then flipped over a table and crouched behind the impromptu shield.

A buffeting hurricane filled the yard as the X-ship descended, the fiery exhaust tearing the prisoners apart, their tattered bodies smashing against the granite wall. The red-hot ammunition in the dropped weapons of the dead guards ignited, generating a fusillade of ricochets as a river of elemental flame poured into the dining hall pushing back the sideways table, charring the thick wood.

Racing away from the monstrous heat, guards sprinted for arms lockers, while scores of prisoners dropped to cover their heads and shout pleas for mercy.

Extending four gridwork legs, the X-ship landed in the courtyard, the steel pads of the legs crushing numerous corpses with a sickening crunch.

As the thundering engines decreased to a low bellow, the four prisoners darted out from behind the burning table, their clothing steaming from the awful heat. Dashing across the courtyard, they reached the landing legs, but a man appeared in the hatchway holding a strange angular weapon that looked like something out of an American science-fiction movie.

"We're here only for you, Chen-wa," he stated in bad Mandarin, and the FN F2000 assault rifle hummed out a brief stream of 5.56 mm rounds, the Teflon-coated bullets tearing apart the astonished bodyguards.

Even as his people fell, Chen-wa scrambled up the access ladder.

"Hold!" a guard bellowed, working the pump-action on a 10-gauge shotgun.

But the man only smiled and the big second barrel of the FN F2000 spoke. But in spite of the laser dot on the guard's chest, the 20 mm round missed and exploded harmlessly on the ground, the concussion slamming the guard aside and knocking away the shotgun.

As Chen-wa gained the top of the ladder, the stranger lowered the sleek rifle to point directly into his face. Chen-wa paused, uncertain, then the rifle moved aside and a helping hand was offered. Without hesitation, the terrorist took it and eagerly crawled through the hatch of the vehicle.

Inside, the craft was cramped with thick pipes leading everywhere, some of them radiating heat, while others were frosty with ice. That badly confused Chen-wa. Ice? How could a ship use frozen fuel? he wondered.

Slamming the hatch shut, the man twisted a lever, engaging a locking mechanism. "We're in!" he bellowed, shouldering the rifle and grabbing a wall stanchion.

Chen-wa barely had time to react when the pipes began to hum. The subdued roar of the engines increased in volume, then a rush of acceleration threw him to the perforated deck. The pressure was horrible.

After a few moments the pressure eased to a more tolerable level.

"Many thanks, my friend," Chen-wa panted in Mandarin, rolling onto his side. Then he recalled how poorly the stranger had spoke the official language of China. "Thanks," he said in English.

"I'm just glad you made it safely," the man replied, holding the FN F2000 through a hatch to the next level. Hands took the weapon. "Come on, we have a chair for you."

Following the man up a ladder, Chen-wa poked his head into a sort of control room with three chairs set along a complex panel that curved along the walls. There were no windows as he would have expected. How odd. There was only a series of video monitors, showing the blue sky above, the horizon to the west and south, and the smoky prison below. It was rapidly dwindling out of sight, the swirling clouds of smoke and exhaust fumes filling the central courtyard.

"I am impressed by your vehicle," Chen-wa said, climbing awkwardly to his feet. "Does it have a name?" He knew for a fact that there was not a sailor, or pilot, alive who did not have great pride in his craft. Asking for the name was a sure way to ingratiate himself to the crew. Secretly, he was badly frightened, but determined to show no fear to these people. That was how he had run a terrorist organization that operated for more than three decades before being caught, and how he had stayed alive in the brutal, inhuman hell of prison. *Show no fear, stand your ground, kill without hesitation.* It was the way of the world.

"Of course, this is the *Lady Colette,*" a burly man replied in perfect Mandarin, glancing over a shoulder. His hands were on a pair of joysticks and his shoes working levers on the floor. "I'm Captain Ivan Nicholi, and these are Overton and Sullivan."

Already sitting at control panels, the other men merely nodded at the introductions as they adjusted dials and threw endless rows of switches. Oddly, some of their actions seemed random, yet upon closer scrutiny, the control boards looked more complex than anything he had ever seen before. Suddenly Chen-wa was highly suspicious that some of the controls were dummies, installed to merely make the operation of the aircraft seem impossible to manage for any passenger or prisoner to forestall any attempts at a hijacking. Grudgingly, he approved of the tactic.

"I am most pleased to meet you all," Chen-wa said honestly, moving to the only empty chair. "When I received your message from the new inmate, I naturally assumed it was a joke, or at best, a trap by the Americans, but then when the ship descended in fire from the sky!" He broke into a gentle laugh, then stopped as there was no response from the others. "A pity about my men," Chen-wa said experimentally.

Both hands busy, the captain merely shrugged, dismissing the matter. The others ignored him.

"I know you are not members of my organization," Chen-wa said slowly, weighing each word carefully as if walking across a field full of land mines. "So clearly somebody has paid for my release. Who was it? Who arranged for my release?"

Suddenly the radar began to emit a rapidly escalating tone, and lights flashed on the console near Sullivan.

"We have company coming," the thin man said calmly, adjusting the dials with fingertip pressure. "Five—no, six J-10 Chengdu-class interceptors. Okay, no danger there…aw, shit." He looked up, his features pinched. "Sarge, there's also a fucking Sky Dragon!"

At the pronouncement, Chen-wa arched an eyebrow,

but did not speak. Sarge? How could a man be a captain and a sergeant at the same time?

"He's jamming our radar," Sullivan said. "Damn, he's good. Didn't know you bastards could do stuff like that."

"I hate my nation's Communist leaders, but my people are excellent technicians," Chen-wa replied, feeling oddly insulted by the slur.

A light flashed on a side monitor.

"Missile alert," Overton muttered, stroking the controls like a concert pianist. "Activating jamming radar. Firing chaff and flares."

"Nitrogen is on," Sullivan added as another missile flashed past the X-ship, much closer this time.

"Nitrogen?" Chen-wa asked.

"Shut up," Nicholi growled.

"Okay, playtime is over," Nicholi said, shoving both joysticks savagely forward. "Give me full power. We're heading for the black!"

Tightening his grip on the armrest of the chair, Chen-wa silently prayed these men knew what they were doing. The Sky Dragon was the Chinese version of the American F-22 Raptor, built from stolen blueprints. It was the fastest jet fighter in the Red Army, and armed like a battleship.

There was a surge of power, crushing the terrorist into the cushioned chair, and the soft tones of the radar screen got louder and louder, then abruptly stopped.

"Clear," Overton announced with a satisfied smirk.

"Did we lose it?" Sullivan asked.

"A side hatch tore off and the piece of shit broke apart from the wind sheer." Sullivan laughed. "Excellent technicians, my ass. I told you guys that the Reds were a decade away from mastering that level of technology."

As the other chuckled assent, Chen-wa bristled but said nothing, marking the fool for death.

Just then the noise of the engines faded and the blue sky changed into the starry black of space.

Filling a central monitor was the slowly rotating blue-white ball of Earth. There were scattered clouds over the Pacific Ocean, and a storm was ravaging the west coast of North America. Chen-wa was astonished. They had only left China minutes ago! How fast was this vehicle traveling? Fascinated, the terrorist stared at the world. It seemed strange to see no borders. There was no way of telling where one nation ended and another began.

"We've left the world," Chen-wa exhaled, amazed and appalled at the same time. "What a truly amazing vessel!"

"Oh, we're still Earthbound," Nicholi replied over a shoulder. "Don't have enough power to break out of orbit, but then we don't have to, eh, boys?"

Suddenly there was a tug from below and Chen-wa felt a rushing sensation in the pit of his stomach. "We're descending already?" he demanded, tightening his grip on the chair.

"And we'll be down in only a few minutes," the captain retorted. "Better hold on, there's a storm over Hawaii. Could get bumpy up here."

"Is that where I will meet your master?" Chen-wa demanded excitedly. He was eager to join forces with these strange people. With a machine like this he could wage war on any government that he wished.

"No, that's where we dump the trash," Sullivan snarled, slashing out with the flat of his hand.

Caught by surprise, Chen-wa only saw a brief flash of

light as bone splinters were driven into his brain, then there was only infinite darkness.

"Is he dead?" Nicholi asked, watching the radar screen. There was already a lot of activity from Paris Island, but nothing dangerous coming their way.

"Of course he is," Sullivan replied curly, unbuckling his safety harness and awkwardly standing.

Hauling the still twitching corpse out of the chair, Sullivan threw the body down the ladder to the main deck, then climbed after it. Stepping over the corpse, he placed a hand on the lever that opened the hatch.

"Ready!" he announced loudly.

There was a feeling of falling for a moment, then the engines surged with power and the sensation ended abruptly.

"Dump him!" Overton shouted from above.

Throwing the lever, Sullivan opened the hatch and a wave of heat poured into the X-ship, along with a reeking stink of sulfur. Dimly seen through thick clouds, below the vessel was a hellish vista of bubbling red lava. Gagging from the pungent fumes, Sullivan grabbed the dead terrorist by the collar and heaved him out of the hatch. The limp body tumbled through the smoky air and vanished inside the mouth of the volcano.

"Clear!" Sullivan yelled, closing the hatch.

Immediately the engines surged with power and the X-ship rose quickly.

As the man started up the ladder, he noted a strong smell of sulfur that didn't fade away, and realized it was coming from his clothing. Well, there was nothing he could do about that until they landed to refuel. There was always spare clothing, foods and weapons at every drop site. Colonel Southerland never missed a trick. Chen-wa being the case in point.

"How's the fuel?" Captain Nicholi asked, both hands working the joysticks. The temperature gauges were almost in the red zone, but as the ship climbed the hull rapidly cooled back to normal.

"Just barely enough for us to reach Mexico," Overton replied, checking the controls. "A double jump is really pushing the limits on this ship."

"Had to be done," Nicholi replied gruffly, already starting the descent. "After this, everybody will be positive that Chen-wa is behind the attacks and waste a lot of valuable time on a worldwide hunt for the wrong man."

"A dead man," Overton corrected as Sullivan climbed into view to reclaim his chair. "And there's no way they'll ever find his body."

"Got that right." Sullivan grinned, buckling on the safety harness.

As the colossal X-ship settled onto the hard-packed sand of the isolated desert, the three men shut down the huge rocket engines and exited the vehicle to start the dangerous refueling process. Now that the decoy had been engaged, they were eager to start the next wave of attacks.

Soon enough, the whole world would be engulfed in the flames of war, and nobody would ever discover what the colonel and Dark Star had really accomplished in three bloody days.

CHAPTER FIVE

The Computer Room, Stony Man Farm, Virginia

"How's it going," Price asked, placing a hand on Aaron Kurtzman's shoulder

"What? Oh, hello," Kurtzman grunted, glancing up briefly. "Everything is fine. So far, so good."

"Why are you watching the Weather Channel?" Price asked.

"It's a wild idea I've come up with, and I'm trying to see if it works."

Grabbing the hard-rubber rims of the wheels on his chair, the man rolled himself away from the workstation. "Meanwhile, Akira is doing a global search for any information on theoretical X-ship designs, while running support for the teams, getting them government clearance, forging diplomatic immunity, erasing their flight plans…the usual stuff."

Both at the same time? Turning her head, Price glanced at the young man sitting at his workstation, chewing gum and listening to rock music. He appeared to be daydreaming, but the mission controller knew from past experience that she'd have to shoot the hacker to get his attention, nothing less would penetrate his iron wall of concentration.

"Fair enough," Price said, almost smiling. "I just saw Hunt outside the staff room. He mentioned a slight problem. So what's the delay with Carmen? We helped develop the firewalls that Interpol uses, so she should be able to access their files at will."

"Normally, yes," Kurtzman replied. "But an X-ship landed on the main file room of Interpol. Their master computer isn't crashed, the damn thing is half melted. Millions of data files are gone forever."

"What about the off-site files?" Price asked. "Those should have been safe." Every major corporation kept a duplicate set of important documents in a secure location miles away from the master files, just in case of a fire or corporate espionage. Governments did the same; the NSA kept their backup files at Menwithill in the UK, while M-I5 kept their files in Minnesota, and so on. Only the Farm did not use that standard safeguard, but it was the sole exception.

"Yeah, the clever bastards got them, too," Kurtzman growled, his face becoming hard. "And you know what that means, Barb."

"Interpol has a mole," Price muttered. "A traitor working for the, as the President calls them, *Skywalkers* inside the organization."

"Or else the hacker for the people behind the X-ships is an absolute wizard at tracing encoded signals."

"Is that possible?"

The man shrugged. "Anything is possible."

"Okay, I just read the FBI reports on Blue Origins and Armadillo Aerospace," Akira Tokaido announced. "Both companies are nowhere near a functional SSO ship. The only useful information the FBI got is that the X-ships have to be singles."

"What does that mean?" Price demanded curiously. "Hand-built or something?"

"No, the ships only have one control system," Tokaido replied. "Take a NASA space shuttle, for example. Those have a complete backup system for everything. In case anything goes wrong, it can continue to fly without loss of performance. On some of the critical systems, there are even three or four backup versions. Control board, air re-cycling, teleflex cables, fuel lines, everything but the en-gines, toilet and crew, comes in a minimum of three."

"I see, and that adds a lot of weight," she said, chew-ing over the new information. "So the *Skywalkers* took out everything not actually needed for flight, which mas-sively cut the weight of the X-ships." She frowned. "No, this doesn't work, because they also have armored hulls. Wouldn't that equal out the same weight as before?"

"Not really. The armor is mostly just heat-proofing, the few hardpoints are an ultralight composite," Kurtzman stated. "But they would still need the microwave boost-ers to put them over the top."

"Which is killing the crews. That beggars the question, do they know, or not care?"

"Unknown."

The woman started to pace. "Okay, if the X-ships have no backup controls, then if we damage one at all, even minor damage, it's down for the count."

"Absolutely. But you've seen how fast they are," Carmen Delahunt said. "Combine that raw speed with their stealth technology, and these things are damn near invincible."

"But not invulnerable."

"Oh no, a standard LAW should be able to blow them out of the sky. But you have to hit them first."

"All right, if speed is an issue, then how about using a PEP?" Tokaido asked out of the blue. "That might do the job."

"What is a PEP?" Delahunt asked from behind the VR helmet, her body language showing the woman's puzzlement.

"A Plasma Energy Projectile," Kurtzman translated. "And no, don't ask me why the Army calls a laser weapon a projectile. I have no idea."

"Yes, I have heard about that. The weapon is a highly advanced form of a deutronium-fluoride laser about the size of a refrigerator," Hunt Wethers added from around his pipe. "But it weighs a lot more, about five hundred pounds. However, with special bracings, it can be mounted on the side of an APC, or even a Hummer."

"So what does it do?" Price asked impatiently. "I know the Army had lasers that could blind people all the way back in Vietnam, but those were declared illegal by the UN, and banned worldwide."

"No, this is a real weapon," Kurtzman stated. "It kills. The beam cycles so fast that anything it hits becomes superheated into a plasma and explodes."

"They do what?"

"Explode. Let me tell you, it's a hell of a blast. Roughly the equivalent to a 40 mm grenade. Only the PEP can chew its way through even tank armor, just by staying focused on one area. The laser is fast enough to take out jets, but strong enough to kill tanks, maybe even sink ships, who knows?"

"The Pentagon planned to deploy them in a few years," Tokaido said smugly. "But I managed to locate a couple of working prototypes at the Pickatinny Experimental Weapons Lab in Pennsylvania, and had them assigned to us for field testing."

"Excellent!" Price said, exhaling. "Send one here, and one to the…no, send both of them to the White House."

"Both?" the man asked in surprise.

"If a SOTA military laser suddenly shows up in the middle of a national park, what would you think?"

"I wouldn't think anything," Kurtzman snorted. "I'd know for a damn fact that was the location of a secret base. Okay, fair, enough, they both go the White House."

"However, we still have to find the X-ships to destroy them," Tokaido added. "They move way too fast for us to respond. We need to be waiting at the target, before they arrive."

"We have to beat the men," Delahunt added, "not the machines,"

"Exactly."

"Unfortunately, we have no idea where they are going to hit next," Price said.

"Barbara," Kurtzman stated, "the impossible can be done."

"With a little bit of luck," Price amended. "And so far, our luck is registering at just below zero. We call the terrorists the *Skywalkers* because that Brazilian shuttle was their first target, but in truth, we don't know anything about these people. Are these attacks religiously motivated or political? What are their ultimate goals?" She turned, and started for the door. "Hell, we don't even know their real name yet."

CHAPTER SIX

Outer Siberia, Russia

The two Dark Star agents shuffled their feet on the frosty ground and shivered in the morning breeze.

The crisp, clear air was bitterly cold, and carried a faint acidic taste of rock dust. Reaching from the dark mountains to a jagged cliff, the desolate landscape was barren and rocky, like the far side of the moon. There were no plants in sight, no grass or trees, not even the slightest touch of green to brighten the otherwise sterile vista.

The man and woman knew there were parts of Siberia that were lush and green, covered with dense forests and fertile fields of wheat, the cities bright and lively with commerce, music and laughter. But not here. Then again, less than a decade ago this section of Russia had been forbidden for anybody to even discuss, much less visit, unless you were a KGB agent, a privileged member of the Presidium or a slave.

Steadily losing the arms race against the prosperous West, the old Soviet Union had been overjoyed to find a motherload of pitchblende in such an isolated area. Hundreds, then thousands, of innocent people were arrested on false charges and sent to the area to slave in the hastily erected mines, many of them freezing to death before starving.

Which was just as well, Colonel Zane Southerland thought humorlessly, stomping his sneakers to maintain circulation. Because the acid fumes used in the process that extracted tiny flecks of uranium from the tons of pitchblende was slowly destroying their bodies. He considered it a much better fate to die from the cold, rather than coughing out bloody chunks of what was once your lungs.

When the mine became exhausted, the Soviets had started to convert the labyrinth of tunnels into an underground fortress, then the government ran out of money, and then out of power. These days, the barbed-wire fences were long gone, the one road smoothed until it once more merged with the shifting dust of the desolate landscape as a modern Russia tried to erase the crimes of the old USSR. Abandoned and forgotten, the uranium mine had been thoroughly wiped from the pages of the history books.

Which should have made it the perfect location for a refueling cache, the colonel raged furiously, buttoning closed his collar. Except that the expected tanks of liquid nitrogen and hydrogen were not there!

Less than an hour earlier he had been warm in South Africa bombing the capital building. Now he was freezing to death, but he knew the attack had been well worth the price. Formerly the head of Internal Security, Southerland had been thrown out of power when Mandela led the revolution. Now a wanted criminal around the world, the colonel stayed constantly on the move, always one jump ahead of Interpol and their ridiculous charges of war crimes. Bah, he had been merely protecting his homeland. He was a hero, not a monster!

Glancing over a shoulder, the colonel stepped closer to the hulking transport, savoring what little heat there was coming off the rapidly cooling engines. In spite of the hostile weather, Southerland was dressed in only a lightweight, camou-colored ghillie suit and sneakers, with a Webley .44 revolver strapped about his waist, but no spare ammunition. Although they operated at maximum efficiency, the X-ships consumed fuel at a prodigious rate, and weight was a matter of prime concern. His teams carried only what was necessary for their next mission, and nothing more.

Although a relatively short man, Southerland was solidly built, appearing to be made of only muscle and bone, similar to a closed fist. His hair was cut in a severe military style, and there was a long scar on the left side of his face that marled the left eye to a dull white orb. Long ago, while questioning a traitor, Southerland had felt pity and offered the chained man a glass of water. It had been gratefully accepted, then smashed against the stone wall, the jagged edge slashed across his throat and face.

Knocking aside the makeshift weapon, Southerland had grabbed the prisoner around the throat and squeezed until the bones cracked, killing the man on the spot. Which was probably exactly what the rebel had hoped for in the first place—escape from the brutal torture to reveal the location of a hidden weapons cache. The doctors at Johannesburg had offered to repair the scar, but Zane refused, preferring to keep it as a grim reminder to himself to never again offer another person mercy.

"If only we had some fuel," Southerland muttered, scowling into the distance. "Where are those fools?"

"Just arriving now, sir," Sergeant Davidson said over the comm system. The pilot had stayed in the control room of the X-ship to monitor the pressure in the fuel tanks during refueling.

"And look what the idiots are carrying," Major Theodora "Zolly" Henzollern drawled, lowering her binoculars.

Standing well over six feet tall, the major was a Nordic beauty with soft, curly blond hair that cascaded gently to her shoulders. Diagnosed as a sociopath as a child after burning her parents alive, Henzollern was sent to an insane asylum, but escaped as a teenager and roamed the streets robbing rich tourists, until being caught and forced to join the army.

In boot camp, her special talents were soon discovered, and the young woman was promptly put to work in the underground torture rooms for the Ministry of Defense, then into the field as a counterinsurgent for the Ministry of War, and finally recruited as a personal bodyguard for the legendary Colonel Southerland.

Seemingly impervious to the cold, Henzollern was also wearing a ghillie suit and sneakers, but carried a wide assortment of weaponry. A coiled garrote hung from her shoulder epaulet, an Italian stiletto was sheathed at her hip, an American switchblade knife tucked up a sleeve, and a French police baton was holstered at the small of her back. Holstered directly in front of her stomach was a brand-new, Heckler & Koch MP-7 machine pistol. Larger than a standard Colt .45 automatic pistol, the superfast HK could fire 950 rounds per minute, creating a wall-of-lead effect, the oversize clip containing 4.5 mm rounds of highly illegal, case-hardened steel penetrators that were capable of going straight through NATO-class body armor.

"Air tanks," Southerland stormed, clenching his fists. "Those are conventional air tanks, not liquid air containers!"

"Yes, sir, they are," she replied, brushing back her riot of curls with stiff fingers, her hand brushing against the coiled, plastic garrote on the way down. "It seems that O'Hara was right. He said not to trust these people. Guess the little bastard was correct."

"So it would seem," the colonel stated, forcing open his hands and clasping them behind his back in a martial stance.

Bouncing and shaking at every irregularity in the rough ground and coughing blue smoke, the battered old truck came to a rattling stop only a few yards from the colonel and major, smack in the shadow of the huge X-ship. Turning off the sputtering engine, the incredulous driver was unable to look away from the gigantic ship, but the fat man in the passenger seat seemed unimpressed. A missile was a missile; they were all the same. Big, noisy and expensive. Merely toys for governments, and not a proper weapon at all. Ivan Kleinof had made his fortune in the mean streets of Prague, Minsk, and finally Moscow with only an ice pick, nothing more. Even the old KGB had been afraid to cross the path of Icepick Ivan, the red czar of the Soviet underground.

"Greetings, my friends!" Kleinof boomed in a deep bass voice as he climbed down to the ground. "I have your shipment. Where is my money?"

"Inside my ship," Southerland said woodenly. "But I don't see my shipment. Is it hidden among those useless tanks of compressed air? Or perhaps it is lashed under the bed of that…well, let's call it a truck, shall we?"

The smile vanished from Ivan's face, and the driver behind the wheel put his hands out of sight below the dashboard.

"What are you babbling about, old man?" Kleinof shot back. "That is exactly what you ordered, a hundred thousand yards of oxygen and hydrogen, and right on schedule, too!"

"No, you're over an hour late," Southerland replied, bending his head slightly forward like a bull about to charge. "I order a hundred thousand gallons, not yards, fool, and those are compressed air cylinders, not liquid air tanks! Don't you know the difference?"

"Bah, all oxygen is the same." The man snorted, waving a hand to dismiss the claim. "My people stole these from a hospital. It is the very best oxygen and hydrogen. I should charge you more, so such quality, but a deal is a deal, eh?"

Pursing her lips, Henzollern noted the numerous splatters of blood on the outside of the air tanks, but that did not concern her. How these people got the fuel was not important. Only that they had brought the wrong stuff.

"As you say, a deal is a deal," Southerland said, turning sideways. "And you have reneged on it completely."

"What? I don't know that word…renig?"

"Renege. It means to fail," Southerland said calmly, turning his head slightly. "Zolly, please kill these idiots, but don't hurt the truck. We may need that later."

Suddenly grinning, Henzollern whipped forward the

MP-7, the weapon firing into the cold ground, it stitched a path of destruction straight into Kleinof and up his body. Caught in the act of pulling an ice pick, the criminal's face took on a strange expression as he broke apart and toppled to the ground in segments, wisps of steam rising from his internal organs.

Snarling a curse, the driver jerked up a pump-action shotgun and fired, but Southerland and Henzollern had already separated, and the hail of buckshot rained harmlessly off the hull of the X-ship.

As the driver worked the pump, Southerland came out of the roll on one knee and fitted the Webley, a foot-long lance of flame stabbed from the barrel. A hole appeared in the windshield of the truck, and the driver jerked backward as he sprouted a third eye. Moving his mouth as if talking, he convulsed, and the shotgun discharged, blowing a hole in the floorboard. A rush of pink gasoline chugged out of a severed fuel line, the cool liquid hissing as it hit the hot exhaust pipe. Southerland and Henzollern retreated quickly as there came a whoof from under the truck, and a few seconds later flames engulfed the vehicle, setting the corpse ablaze and licking out from around the hood. Keeping their distance, the man and woman waited until the shotgun shells cooked off from the heat, the random spray of buckshot finishing the job of shattering windows, flattening a tire and blowing off a door before stopping.

"Pretty," Henzollern whispered softly, watching the growing conflagration.

Casting a glance at the killer, Southerland holstered his weapon and touched his throat mike. "Davidson, did you see?"

"Yes, sir," came the crisp reply. "And I've already worked out the calculations. We can travel about fifty miles on what is remaining in the auxiliary tanks and fuel lines. But after that we're dead on the ground."

Unacceptable. Whipping out a cell phone, the colonel tapped in a long number, then listened carefully for eight clicks as the call was relayed twice around the world via satellites.

"Yes, Colonel, was there trouble?" Eric O'Hara said as a greeting.

Southerland detected a faint sneer in the hacker's voice and accepted the unspoken reproof. He had been wrong, O'Hara right. He couldn't fault the man for feeling smug. That was only human. But if the hacker had said anything out loud, he would have killed him.

"We need an alternate source for fuel," Southerland stated bluntly, looking over the barren landscape. There was nothing in sight but mountains and rocky desert. "Is there anything we can use within fifty miles?"

"No," came the prompt reply. "But I'll guess that Davidson did the calculations for a crew of three. If only two of you go, that'd extend the range to a hundred fifty miles and…" There came the pattering of fingers on a keyboard. "Okay, there is an air processing plant only seventy miles away. Here are the coordinates."

As a string of numbers flowed across the screen, Southerland tapped a button to lock them into storage.

"They will have enough liquid oxygen and hydrogen to fill the main tank halfway," O'Hara finished. "I'll divert the local police, and do what I can to pave the way. But expect some resistance."

"Understood." Southerland snapped closed the lid of

the cell phone. Tucking it into a pocket of the ghillie suit, he touched the throat mike. "Davidson, come down immediately. You will stay here while I do an emergency fuel run."

"Sir?" came the puzzled reply.

"The ship can't fly far enough to obtain fuel with all three of us, and I go nowhere without the major."

Still watching the fire, Henzollern stood a little straighter at those words, but said nothing out loud.

"Of course, sir," Davidson replied hesitantly. "I'll...come right down."

As their carbuds went silent, Henzollern rested a hand on her MP-7. "Sir, will we be returning for Davidson?"

"Yes," Southerland retorted sternly. "Dark Star never leaves a man behind."

Nodding in agreement, the woman tore her attention away from the burning truck as there came a metallic clang and the hatch swung open to reveal Davidson. The pilot paused uncertainly for a moment, then put his back to the others and climbed down the ladder to the ground. The blackened soil was soft around the great ship, but as the man got farther away it started crunching under his sneakers.

"We won't be gone more than thirty minutes, an hour at the most," Southerland said, patting the man on the shoulder. "The fire should keep you warm for that long. But even if it dies early, stay in plain sight and wait right here for us. We're already behind schedule and I do not wish to waste time hunting for you among the rocks."

"Yes, sir," Davidson replied, snapping off a salute. "And if Interpol, or NATO, should arrive before you return?"

Already starting toward the ladder, Southerland stopped to turn and stare hard at the pilot. "Throw yourself off the cliff," he ordered in a perfunctory manner. "People often flinch at the second when shooting themselves in the head, and are only wounded. The bastards must not learn anything of importance from you. Understood?"

"Yes, sir! Hail the Motherland!"

Placing a sneaker on the bottom rung, the colonel gave a grim nod. "God bless South Africa," he said in reply, starting to climb.

"Sir!"

At the top of the built-in ladder, Southerland climbed into the X-ship and dogged shut the hatch. Heading directly to the control room, he found Henzollern already strapped in and adjusting the dials. "Preburners on," she announced, flipping a switch. "Reaction chamber is reaching operational levels...ready to go, sir."

"Launch," Southerland commanded, strapping on a safety harness.

There came a deafening roar and crushing acceleration slammed the man into the cushioned seat. He watched the world drop way below them, then move sideways as the X-ships descended from the mountains. Keeping a sharp watch on the fuel gauge, Southerland was starting to become nervous when the mountains finally gave way to rolling foothills and then a jagged coastline.

Minutes later a small factory town came into view on the monitor. There were row upon row of small wooden houses laid out in orderly streets. Thick black smoke poured out of tall brick chimneys of the main plant, and the dockyard was busy with cranes loading and unloading cargo from a fleet of vessels.

"Busy place," Henzollern commented. "What is it called?"

"I could not care less," Southerland retorted, studying the monitors for their goal. "All I am concerned with is…there! See it there, just to the west?"

"Yes, sir," she replied, working the joysticks. "Starting descent now."

The air plant was situated off by itself, well away from the town and public roads in case of an explosion. The building was long, the flat roof edged with hundreds of small windows in an obvious effort to try to control the damage of a blast, and off to one side were some bare steel exhaust vents covered with ice and surrounded by white mists.

The colonel started to point at them, but the woman was already heading in the correct direction. The legs extended, a red light began to flash as the X-ship landed on the pavement, the material cracking from the tremendous weight.

"We must have had a lot less fuel than O'Hara figured," she reported. "We barely made it here, sir!"

"Good thing for him we did," Southerland said dryly, rising from the chair. "If I die on a mission, he dies."

Licking her lips, Henzollern ached to ask how it was arranged, but restrained herself. The colonel would not be the man he was without taking any, and all, necessary precautions to safeguard his return. He will make a fine king of South Africa, she thought.

As the man and woman undogged the hatch, they found a crowd of astonished workers gathered around the vessel. Without hesitation, Henzollern began to sweep the people with the MP-7. A dozen workers died before the

rest registered the slaughter then scrambled away, screaming in terror.

Ignoring the rabble, Southerland and Henzollern
climbed down the ladder and stepped over the twitching
corpses to enter the plant. There were no divisions or
walls inside the structure, the entire building one single
massive room. Hundreds of tall steel bottles were lined
up neatly, the bronze nozzles attached to pressure lines.
Somewhere big pumps were thumping, steadily forcing
two-thousand square feet of gas into the six-square-foot
cylinder. While constructing the X-ships, Southerland recalled seeing an oxygen tank fall over, the bronze nozzle
snapping off against a concrete block. Instantly, there
was a hurricane as the volumes of gas inside rushed out
and the cylinder shot along the floor, then up into the air,
zooming about madly like an unguided missile, smashing apart men and machinery, until punching through the
cinder-block wall and disappearing into the distance. Surrounded by so much explosive material, there was a sud-
den tingle in his gut similar to the rush of combat.

"Watch the feeder lines," the colonel directed, pointing. "Green is oxygen, red is hydrogen. We need the insulated tanks. Those will hold the liquid gases."

There came the sound of running boots and several
burly men in denim jumpsuits appeared from around the
row of air tanks, brandishing long wrenches and iron
bars. One fellow in a suit was holding a fire ax. Obviously,
that was the owner of the plant, or at least the foreman.
Knowing to discharge the Webley this close to the charging lines might blow them to hell, the colonel pulled out
a knife and jerked his wrist.

Across the floor of the plant, the man dropped the ax

and staggered backward, the handle of the knife jutting from his throat. As red blood began to gush between his spasming fingers, the workers lost heart and ran away frantically, casting aside their makeshift weapons.

"Cowards," Henzollern sneered, pressing the release button on the French police baton. The coiled sleeve of steel extended to a full yard, and locked into position. Eagerly, she tapped the deadly bludgeon against her leg, looking for prey. But there was nobody in sight, only the jerking hoses and thumping machinery.

Retrieving the gory blade, Southerland saw a side room full of refrigeration tanks and heavily insulated conduits. Opening the door, he was hit with a bitterly cold wave that chilled him to the bone. "This is it!" Southerland cried, reaching for a pair of safety gloves lying on a convenient table.

Having done something similar hundreds of times before, it took only a few minutes to run a pair of flexible hoses to the X-ship and start the pumps. In short order, the refrigeration tanks had been emptied, and the Dark Star operatives disconnected the lines to simply cast them aside. Returning to the control room, Southerland took command this time and started the engines, frowning deeply as the fuel gauge only registered a quarter full. Damn, just barely enough.

The colonel sent the X-ship soaring skyward, the fiery exhaust igniting the feeder hoses, the flames rushing back into the plant as they climbed high into the sky.

Streaking back toward the mountains, Henzollern saw the huge explosion rip the plant apart. As a roiling fireball covered the building, hundreds of black shapes began darting around within the blast, punching through the walls, and roof, then spiraling off into every direction. Mother of God, those had to be the air bottles!

Like a salvo of missiles, the steel containers dispersed randomly, a handful reaching the town to smash through buildings, spreading a wave of destruction throughout the homes and factories, and even reaching the cargo ships moored at the wooden docks.

"Our next stop will be Tasmania," Southerland said, working the joysticks. "After that, we go back to home base."

"But, sir, what about Davidson?" Henzollern asked uncertainly.

The man grit his teeth. "Unfortunately, we don't have enough fuel for three, so he must stay behind."

"I'll take care of it, sir," she said, pulling out the MP-7 and checking the clip.

"No, a commander must handle such things himself," the colonel countered, gliding sideways toward the old uranium mines. "It is a matter of honor."

"I'm sure he would appreciate the gesture."

"Oh, I doubt it highly," the man chided. "But as a soldier, he would understand the necessity, and that is enough."

The dark plume of smoke rising from the burning truck made an excellent guide back to the landing site, and the X-ship hovered over the area for only a few seconds, before streaking upward into the starry black of space.

CHAPTER SEVEN

London, England

Ethereal mist moved over the Thames River like a living thing, the ancient stones lining the shore weather to the consistency of polished marble from the endless decades of wear. Far at the bottom of the river, covered in layers of silt and mud, the decaying pieces of German war planes warmly rotted alongside the remains of the vaunted Spanish armada from another century.

Rising majestically over the murky waters, Tower Bridge was an imposing Victorian edifice. The massive Cornish granite blocks had been intricately carved by master masons from another era, and the two great Gothic towers that stood on either side of the center span resembled something from legend, beautiful, dominant, eternal.

High overhead, the perpetually gray sky rained slightly, then stopped, merely to start once more as if it had forgotten what happened just moments earlier. On the busy sidewalks crossing the ancient bridge, only the tourists cried out in annoyance, or dashed about struggling to open their newly purchased umbrellas. The locals simply ignored the drizzle, the same as they did the blaring car horns from the streaming traffic, or the thick reek of diesel fumes from the fleets of double-decker buses.

"Ah, just like home!" A tourist smiled, deeply breathing in the smog. "God, I miss New York."

"Are you insane? How can you think about Manhattan when we're standing smack in the middle of London!" his wife gushed happily, both of her hands full of shopping bags from Harrods department store. "I mean, look at this, Harold! We're actually standing on London Bridge!"

"London Bridge," he said slowly, tasting the words. "As in the old song, 'London Bridge is falling down…'?"

"Exactly! Isn't it exciting?"

"London Bridge," the man said slowly, smiling.

Several of the people passing by tried to hide their amusement at that, but an elderly barrister stopped alongside the gawking couple. Lord love a duck, bloody Americans didn't know a lorry from a lavatory!

"Excuse me, old chap," the barrister said, resting his umbrella on the sidewalk with a flourish. "But this is most certainly not London Bridge." He flipped the umbrella upward to point at the two massive structures at either end of the span. "See those? This is Tower Bridge."

"Not London Bridge?" the wife asked, hoping this was some sort of joke.

"No, ma'am, honestly, it is not." The barrister used the umbrella again to point upstream. "See there? The next bridge is London Bridge."

"Are you sure?" the husband asked warily.

"Absolutely." He smiled tolerantly.

Just then the clouds parted and fire descended from the sky.

Realizing what was happening, the SAS operative posing as a barrister started to go for the gun under his jacket, then changed his mind and shoved the two tourists over the side of the bridge in a desperate effort to save their lives.

The shocked husband and wife were still falling when the X-ship arrived to hover above the bridge, its exhaust washing over the granite slabs to ignite people and vehicles. Screams and explosions filled the roadway, the SAS operative trying for his weapon just before vanishing in the incandescent fury of the rocket engines.

On the roof of the South Tower, an iron-bound door slammed open and a dozen Special Forces soldiers charged into view, working the arming bolts of their Enfield L85 assault rifles. Rushing to the parapets of the castelated tower, the troopers took aim and fired streams of 5.56 mm hardball bullets upon the huge ship below them. But the hail of bullets only bounced harmlessly off the steeply sloped sides of the smooth hull.

Desperately, the soldiers raked their gunfire along the scarred, white hull, searching for a window, or a hatch, anything that might yield a vulnerable point to the flying mountain. But the seamless X-ship seemed to be a single homogenous artifact, immutable and indestructible.

Seeing the futility of the assault, the lieutenant swung up an XM-18 grenade launcher and started pumping high-explosive rounds at the giant machine. But again, the 40 mm shells ricocheted off the smooth hull before detonating, doing no damage at all.

"Get clear!" a sergeant bellowed, swinging up a

Stinger missile launcher. The brains in Whitehall had deduced how the X-ships were protecting themselves from the heat-seekers, and new software had been hastily written and loaded into the minicomputer of the antiaircraft Stinger. It was no longer a guided missile, but a deadhead, a simple rocket that would fly true until it ran out of propellant. All he had to do was to get close and—

"Bugger me!" the sergeant snarled as the distance to the X-ship appeared on the viewfinder. The damn thing was too close! The tower was two hundred feet tall, but the X-ship was well over a hundred itself, and hovering several yards off the bridge. A standard Stinger needed a hundred yards to arm the warhead and the X-ship was less than one third of that distance!

Gamely trying anyway, the soldier fired the rocket, and it slammed into the side of the X-ship only to shatter into pieces and fall tumbling into the ocean of boiling flame covering the bridge.

The unit's lieutenant stared hatefully at the steel invader. Then he paused. Was it made of steel? A chap from the RAF said that space shuttles, and the like, had a sort of heat-proof glass shield covering the nose as protection. By sheer necessity, the material was rough and tough, built to take incredible punishment. However, it was breakable.

"Aim for the nose!" the officer bellowed over the unimaginable noise of the engines. "Bust the heat shield and it'll melt trying to lift off. That's the weak spot! The top!"

Focusing their attack on the crest of the cone, the British soldiers got off only a few bursts before the X-ship incredibly started to rise and a monstrous wave of volcanic heat-searing fumes poured over the parapet, stealing the air from their lungs.

Coughing hard, the soldiers were driven back inside the South Tower and hastily slammed the ancient iron door shut.

"Mother of God," a corporal wheezed, barely able to form the words, while another man bent over the iron railing at the top of the granite stairs and nosily lost his breakfast. Struggling to pull in a breath, none of the others blamed the poor sod a bit. That was the closest any of them ever wanted to get to hell. A few more seconds of that and they all would have keeled over.

Suddenly the streams of heat came from around the thick door, eased away, and a great silence filled the tower.

Never pausing in the reloading of their weapons, the troopers listened hard, but they could only hear the piteous wails of the wounded and the crying civilians mixing with the crackling of the burning cars and trucks.

"Did it leave?" a private asked, thumbing a 40 mm shell into the grenade launcher of his L-85 assault rifle.

"Bleeding hope so," another man snarled, then hawked and spit in the corner. "God, I can still taste the stink!"

"Silence!" the lieutenant snapped, pressing an ear to the warm metal of the door. Instantly the men went quiet, but still he could hear nothing from outside. Nothing at all. Strange…

"What is it doing, sir?" the sergeant asked, loading another Stinger missile into the spent launcher.

"Not a damn thing that I can tell," the officer muttered hesitantly. Then in sharp comprehension of what was happening, the man turned and charged for the old stone staircase. "Retreat!" the lieutenant shouted at the top of his aching lungs. "Run for your lives!"

Surging into action, the platoon stormed down the

winding stairs having no idea what was happening out-side. Were the terrorists planting a bomb? Disgorging troops? Taking hostages?

Reaching a small landing, the sergeant fired a burst from the Enfield to shatter a stained-glass window and steal a fast glance. The accursed white hull of the X-ship was only feet away, and a refreshingly cool breeze wafted into the tower. It was a delightful change from the awful heat…

"Oh fuck, move it or lose it, boys!" the sergeant shouted over a shoulder, dashing across the landing to start down another spiral staircase. "The bastard is venting!"

Venting? That could only mean one thing, the X-ship had landed and was releasing its deadly supply of liquid nitrogen. Not to mask the hot engines from a heat-seeker, but to crystallize the bridge, making the Cornish granite and steel beams as fragile and weak as an old man's bones.

Grimly, the soldiers tried to redouble their speed. They had only seconds now. They would be safe in the tunnel below the river, but the tower was two hundred feet tall, and there was an additional fifty feet before they would reach underground.

"Sir…lieutenant!" a private gasped, almost stumbling on the granite. "Any…chance the walls are…thick enough to—"

"No, they're not!" the lieutenant yelled. "Now, keep running!"

Just then, a wave of bitter cold came from the solid stone wall and sparkling ice particles formed along the handrail and stairs. Instantly, the lieutenant slipped and went flying to hit the next landing with a painful crunch. Awkwardly standing, the man's arm dangled impotently, blood dripping off his fingers.

"Keep going!" he commanded, shoving the sergeant to the lead. "I'll cover the rear!"

Their breath fogging in the air, the frowning soldiers obeyed just as a deep groan sounded from all around them, closely followed by a terrible crackling noise as if a million autumn leaves were falling.

Frosted with ice, the lights winked out, the slippery steps under their boots cracked, and there came a low rumble from outside as the X-ship lifted off once more.

Instantly the air was warm and the ice vanished, but the stone blocks started crumbling, softening, melting away to reveal the fiery exterior world. Two of the men threw themselves down the melting stairs, but the rest trained their weapons on the deafening column of flame only yards away.

However, run or fight, it made no difference. A single heartbeat later their world seemed to implode as the upper stories of the South Tower came crashing down onto the shattering base, the megatons of stone hammering a brutal path through the platoon to reach the crystallized support beams. Built to last forever, the riveted array of Victorian steel exploded into sparkling ice crystals.

As the South Tower collapsed inward upon itself, the entire bridge visibly trembled. Then with a low, stentorian groan the mighty Tower Bridge began to sag in the middle, pieces breaking off to plummet into the Thames River. Tilting badly to the side, the North Tower twisted off the walkway, shattering hundreds of windows and spilling a score of screaming people into the choppy waters. Then the base loudly cracked apart and the tower dropped backward, split power lines crackling, and great gouts of hydraulic fluid arching into the air like blood from a ruptured artery. The braided support cables snapped off like cobwebs, and the North Tower slammed onto the roadway, throwing out a corona of broken stone blocks that tumbled and rolled along the city streets, crushing dozens of cars and rescue vehicles, the drivers and passengers screaming in terror for only a brief moment.

Crackling and moaning, like some sort of horrible disease, the destruction spread along the bridge, shattering granite lentils and flipping dead bodies high, black dust spreading out like a death shroud to finally mask the scene of destruction.

Staying above the swirling cloud, the X-ship hovered defiantly in the sky, then shot upward and vanished into the clouds.

Seconds later a salvo of Tomahawk missiles arched over the horizon. But finding no targets, they spiraled and moved out to sea where they could detonate harmlessly.

"The bleeding bastards planned this!" a BBC news reporter snarled, panning his video camera across the scattering of corpses floating in the choppy river. It looked like a scene from Cambodia or Laos. "These bastards knew we'd expect them to attack the wrong bridge, and that we'd depend upon the granite to protect our troops, yet they landed there anyway to…to…"

"Slaughter us like sheep," a constable growled, lowering her empty handgun. It had been a futile move to shoot the airborne goliath, but what else could she do? "They slaughtered us like Solstice sheep, and the bridge is gone. Tower Bridge is gone!"

The words sounded ridiculous to them, and hung heavy in the air like a palpable force. The bridge was gone, and jagged mounds of wreckage blocked the Thames. Street traffic could be diverted to the other bridges, but now it was impossible for any ship to enter, or leave, the city. The military would have to send in demolition teams to clear the vital waterway, or else there soon would be food shortages and gas rationing.

"At least they didn't hit during rush hour." The reporter sighed, yanking out a filled disk and shoving in a fresh one. "This could have been a lot worse."

"Could it? Yes, I suppose so," the constable replied, itching to do something, anything, for the people in the river.

Still tearing itself apart, the broken stones of Tower Bridge splashed into the murky water somehow making the river seem darker than usual.

"Thank God, it's over, eh?"

Glancing upward, the constable watched a full wing of RAF interceptors streak upward in hot pursuit of the X-ship. "Over? Oh, this fight isn't over, mate," she said softly, a terrible sense of foreboding filling her guts. "I'd guess that this war hasn't even really begun yet."

Pelican Bay Supermax Penitentiary, California

THERE WAS NO WINDOW in the small room.

The walls were composed of prestressed concrete blocks overlaid with firebrick. The floor was steel-reinforced terrazzo tougher than tank armor, and the ceiling was a single, seamless slab of unpainted steel. There was only one door. It had six locks, five hinges and no knob. There was an air vent located high in the corner of the ceiling, and the grille was welded into place from both sides. The only light came from a steel mirror set behind a stout wire mesh.

Sitting in the middle of the room was a tired-looking

man chained to a steel chair whose legs were sunk deep
into the terrazzo floor. Directly in front of him was a bare
steel table, the legs bolted to the floor, making it totally
immobile.

The loose gray uniform of the man was scrupulously
clean, but wrinkled, his feet covered with soft slippers. His
fingernails were short, chewed to the quick, his hair wiry
and chaotic, uncombed and unkempt, sticking out in every
direction. With his head bent forward the long hair fell forward and covered his face like a mask, but every inch of
exposed skin was covered with homemade prison tattoos,
many of them distorted by new scars overlaying the old
ink.

Aside from the steady breathing of the prisoner, there
wasn't a sound to be heard, no ticking clock, no hum from
the air vents, no echo of distant footsteps, no laughter, no
birds, even though the prison was set in the middle of a
huge forest. But there were so many buffers and barriers
between the outside world and the man it might as well
not exist.

Located in northern California, the Pelican Supermax Penitentiary was hidden from the public deep
within midst-shrouded mountains, 275 acres of concrete and steel surrounded by multiple walls of electrified concertina wire, proximity sensors, pit falls,
video cameras and automatic machine-gun emplace-
ments. Pelican Bay was a tomb for the living, the unwanted men cast out by society for their monstrous
crimes. Each cell only held one man, and the prisoner
lived alone, washed alone, ate alone, died alone in his
cell, without ever talking to anybody, not even the
guards. All of the doors were controlled electronically

and under constant video surveillance from guards located outside the facility. In case of an extreme emergency, the whole prison could be shut down and flooded with gas from a safe distance.

The starkly brutal facility was considered inhuman by some, but Pelican Supermax was the most secure confinement institution in existence for one specific reason: the prisoners never left the grounds for any reason. Every prisoner was in for life. In crude jailhouse humor, the guards called Pelican Bay, "the Roach Motel," because men checked in, but they never checked out. The prisoners simply called it Hell.

Slow minutes passed in thick silence as the prisoner sat motionless in the interrogation room, his mind reveling in the small delight of being out of his sterile cell for the first time in a decade, even if it was only to be ferried to just another windowless cube. But what could not be changed, had to be endured. That was the way of the world. As immutable as the passage of time itself.

Without any warning, there was a low hum as the magnetic door lock disengaged, then the heavy clank of the mechanical bolt being drawn back. The prisoner did nothing. The long years had killed his curiosity, his sex drive, his hope, until he was reduced to an organic machine for converting food into feces, and nothing more. Formerly the leader of a huge terrorist organization, Akaam Zamir already considered himself dead, and was simply waiting for his body to agree and end his eternal term of confinement. Once, very long ago, Zamir had harbored hopes of being declared clinically insane and getting sent to an institution. Doctors would have been much kinder, and much easier to kill, thus enabling his escape into the world once more. But this was his sixth, and last, prison: Pelican Supermax. The end of the road.

With a low hum of electric motors sunk deep into the walls, the heavy door swung aside. There came the sound of three sets of shoes, a pause, and the door cycled shut to lock tight once more.

Setting down folding chairs, the three visitors formed a line between Zamir and the door and sat. He continued to look at the floor. It had been years since his last visitor, and the memory was not a happy one. So who was it this time? More reporters asking for the details of his life? Or some religious fool trying to save his immortal soul. He was already in hell. Why should he fear death?

Incredibly, Zamir heard a sound absent from his life for countless years, the telltale crackle of a pop-top can being opened.

"Care for a beer?" a voice said.

An electric tingle coursed through the terrorist at the sound of the familiar tones, and he slowly raised his head as if it weighed a hundred pounds. The three visitors were all dressed in civilian clothing: sneakers, loose pants, Hawaii shirts. One of them was holding out a frosty can with white suds dripping down the sides. The nearly forgotten smell of beer seemed to fill the room, and Zamir almost started to reach for it when he caught their eyes and knew the truth. These men were soldiers.

Perhaps, an assassination squad? Zamir could only hope.

The first man was handsome in a rough way, with intelligent eyes and laugh lines around the mouth. The next man had the salt-and-pepper hair of middle-age, but his stocky frame seemed to radiate physical strength. Oddly the fellow sat in almost the exact same position as Zamir, feet flat on the floor, hands draped over the knees, shoulders hunched against the weight of the chains and manacles. What was this, some form of mockery? Zamir seethed at the implied insult, then rationalized that the second man was merely an expert in social camouflage, an expert in infiltration. He could probably chat with millionaires on the French Riviera, and joke it up with Hells Angels at a strip club, with equal aplomb. This man was truly dangerous.

Then his heart skipped a beat at the sight of the last visitor, a huge blond man with close-cropped hair and eyes of cold arctic blue. The big man seemed exactly the same as Zamir remembered when the cop shot him in the neck on the roof of the Super Bowl stadium and ripped the detonator of the hidden bomb from his hands. This was the hated enemy who had successfully tracked him down where so many others had failed, and sent him into this cage forever. Carl Lyons.

And here he now sat offering Zamir a beer as if they were old friends.

"So you want a drink or not?" Lyons asked.

"No…" Zamir rasped, his voice sounding like a rusty machine. He had not spoken to another living soul in many years, and the bullet that ripped out his larynx had done considerable damage.

"Fair enough," Lyons said, taking a sip himself. "Let's talk."

"Talk, leave, I don't care," Zamir muttered with a sneer. "You will learn nothing from me."

"Wrong as usual," Lyons stated, raising the can to

chug down the brew, the excess flowing across his cheeks and soaking his shirt.

The smell was maddening to Zamir, but he forcibly restrained himself. This was a standard interrogation technique, nothing more. Honestly, he would have expected better from the cop.

Finishing the beer, Lyons loudly crumpled the can just as Herman Schwarz pulled a small box from within his shirt and pointed it at the ceiling. He pressed a button on the top, there was a low hum, but nothing else seemed to happen.

"The video cameras and hidden microphones are now receiving a recorded conversation of us talking about the Super Bowl fight," Schwarz said, tucking away the device. "We have about five minutes of privacy before they realize the trick and bust in here with guns drawn."

"So make your choices fast," Rosario Blancanales added, holding out a hand. Lying in the palm was a small, double-barrel derringer.

A gun! Zamir felt himself stop breathing as he stared at the tiny weapon. If it was a fake, it was a very good one. No, he corrected, it was excellent! Every detail was precise, and he could see the dull gray lead of a bullet inside one of the stubby barrels, the other black and empty. Freedom lay within the weapon. Not from Pelican. That was impossible. A hundred locked doors stood between him and the outside world, and more armed guards than he had ever been able to accurately count.

Rubbing the old scar on his neck, Zamir felt an almost sexual thrill at the thought of holding a gun once more. In spite of everything else, the derringer was still the key to freedom. Freedom from the chains, and the boredom, and the silence, and the guards, and the….

"Fuck you, cop," Zamir snarled in torpid hatred at the obvious ploy. "Am I a fool to believe that you smuggled a loaded weapon into Pelican?" Give the dog a treat, then offer freedom from the leash if he did a trick. Bah, did these cops think that he had become weak over time, that solitude and privation had broken his will where truth drugs and beatings from the prison guards could not? It was pitiful.

"Oh, the gun is real, and so is the offer," Lyons said, slipping the flattened beer can into a pocket. "Tell us what we want to know, and it's yours."

"Bullshit."

"There's only one way to find out, asshole."

Leaning back in the chair, Zamir chewed that over. Suddenly, the prisoner was very sorry that he had refused the beer, and there were no more in sight. "All right, out of curiosity, what is it that you wish to learn?"

"You know exactly what we want," Lyons said, studying the prisoner carefully.

"What, you still haven't found the last of the microwave beamers yet?" Zamir asked in dark delight. "How very amusing."

"You stole enough equipment to build ten," Schwarz stated bluntly. "We have recovered six."

"Perhaps I destroyed them," the terrorist demurred. "Or sold them to some other freedom fighters."

"Freedom fighters? You killed women and children!"

"No, I removed the enemies of humanity."

"Damn it, you already knew that nobody had found the stockpile of weapons," Blancanales said slowly. "Probably because we haven't laid a hundred more crimes and murders at your doorstep."

Impressed, Zamir narrowed his eyes. Yes, a most dangerous man, indeed.

"Perhaps what you say is true," he said with a shrug. "Or perhaps not. Has there been some sort of incident with people dying in the streets for no known reason?" The prisoner's voice ached with the strain of speech. "Yes, I can see the anger in your faces. Microwave beamers are involved in a mass murder, and so you came to me." For the first time the terrorist laughed, an inhuman groaning croak. "Things must be desperate for you to try such a ludicrous gamble. Who died, some fat movie star? Or a gutless politician waging war on the downtrodden mass?"

"Cut the shit, you're no more a Communist than I am," Schwarz snorted, checking his watch. Three minutes and counting…

"Terrorists hit a government installation," Lyons said. "They killed thousands, mostly civilians."

That was not exactly a lie, more like a combination of the truth. The X-ships had killed thousands of people, the microwave beamers were merely a piece of the machines, albeit the piece that made them so powerful. This madman was Able Team's best bet to track down the *Skywalkers* and time was running out fast.

"Thousands dead? And they did all of that with my beamers?" Zamir asked, a smile cresting on his scarred features. "Well done. I really should send them a note of congratulations…."

Reaching out, Lyons laid the derringer on the table between them with a low click-clack of metal on metal. Unable to look away, Zamir stopped talking, all of his attention focused on the gun. There was no elegance in the weapon, except for the purity of function. This was a machine designed to kill, nothing more. But that made it the most beautiful object in the world to him.

"Are you threatening me with death if I refuse to talk?" the terrorist asked.

"No, I'm offering the gun if you talk," Lyons corrected. "And upping the ante. You can either shoot me, or go kill yourself."

That took a minute, but slowly the amusement drained from Zamir's face. "You lie," he countered suspiciously.

Picking up the derringer, Lyons thumbed back the hammer. The gun was now primed, six ounces of pressure on the trigger and it would fire the .44 Magnum hollowpoint round. "Tell us where your base is located, and it's yours," he said. "A straight deal. I knew there wasn't anything else you wanted that we could honestly offer. You killed too many people to ever go free, and escaped too many times to ever get moved to a less secure facility. Death is all that we can offer."

"Interesting, if true," the man murmured thoughtfully, staring at the deadly weapon, watching the reflected light gleam on the polished barrel.

"Personally, I think you should have been killed years ago," Schwarz stated gruffly. "A sane man guns down a mad dog. Putting them in a cage forever is not being kind, that is just being a coward."

Almost against his will, Zamir nodded in agreement. At least one of them understood. Life was pain. All a man could do was learn to stand tall and suffer in silence.

"Look, if you're not interested…" Lyons said, starting to rise.

"I'm thinking," Zamir replied petulantly, even though

the decision was already made. "What assurances can you offer that I will get the gun after this interview?"

"After the information proves useful," Blancanales corrected.

Zamir snorted. "No, now," he declared forcibly. "I talk, and you give me the weapon. That is the deal. Nothing else is acceptable."

Exactly what they wanted to hear.

"Accepted," Lyons said, offering a hand.

The prisoner jerked back. This was a gesture he had not encountered in decades. Hesitantly at first, he extended a chained hand and gripped the hand of the cop who had gunned him down and sent him to hell, but now offered a key to paradise.

"There is a strip club on Route 66 near Barstow," he wheezed, massaging his throat. "Chollo's. In the basement, behind the furnace is a locked door. Do not touch the lock! The fifth row of bricks down from the ceiling you will find a firebrick among the common house bricks. You know the difference?"

Lyons nodded.

"Good. Press the brick and wait, the door will eventually open."

"Any traps?" Blancanales demanded.

"The lock of course. Touch it and the mechanism engages for an hour." He smiled. "To keep out the innocent, you understand. Plus there are pressure plates in the floor that trigger a Claymore mine, and touching the light switch releases a spray of napalm from the ceiling."

"Anything else?" Schwarz asked, feeling the pressure of time.

Zamir hesitated.

"Everything, or no deal," Lyons growled, pulling the derringer closer.

"The computer is packed with H-3 high-explosive slurry. You turn it on stroking the mouse. Do not touch the off button, or try to insert a disk into the burn unit, or else…"

"Why composition H?" Blancanales asked with a puzzled expression. "I'd have thought C-4 or thermite would have been a better choice."

"That is true," Zamir said, glancing sideways. "But at the time, some damn fool cop was breathing down my neck and it was all I could acquire."

"Glad to hear it," Lyons replied, standing, using his legs to push back the chair. It scraped across the bare terrazzo with a squeal.

Rising without comments, Blancanales and Schwarz went to the door, threw the lock and walked into the bare corridor beyond. Softly, there could be heard a howling siren and men shouting in the distance.

"Well, you've kept your part of the deal, so I will mine," Lyons said, lifting the gun from the table.

"Truly? But there is no way to know that I have told you the truth," Zamir said hesitantly, braced for the men to withdraw the weapon. Briefly hope flickered in his heart. The pain was almost unbearable.

"I know," Lyons said, passing over the gun.

The derringer was small and cool and heavy, the curved grip fitting his palm perfectly. It said Remington on the side. As his finger touched the trigger, Zamir instantly swung it up to point at Lyons, a smile spreading across his weathered face.

"There's only one bullet," Lyons said, turning away

and starting for the open doorway. "You can have revenge, or freedom, but not both. Make your choice,
Zamir."

For a long minute there was only the hushed sound of
heavy breathing, then a gunshot exploded painfully loud
in the confines of the windowless cube, closely followed
by splatter of brains on the far wall and the clatter of a
dropped gun. But there was no thump of a falling body,
the stout chains merely rattling as they refused to relin-
quish their hold on the prisoner even in death.

Never looking back, Lyons walked out of the interrogation room and closed the door with a soft click.

CHAPTER EIGHT

Barcelona, Spain

A warm sun shone down upon the white sandy beach, while gentle waves crested along the scenic shoreline.

Past the pink coral breakers, a shark fin cut the water, the deadly mankiller swimming back and forth along the net wall seeking some way inside to reach the bounty of flesh frolicking in the surf near shore. Again and again, the shark attacked the resilient barrier, but designed to stop incoming torpedoes, the titanium net did not yield. Then without any warning, the shark vanished from sight.

A few moments later a big man in swim trunks rose from the waves on the other side of the net. Sheathing his bloody knife, David McCarter slowly waded toward the beach, carefully noting the location of everybody in sight. Getting rid of the shark had been the easy part. Now things got a little tricky.

Lounging among the black rocks of an old lava field was a baker's dozen of men in swim trunks and loose white shirts damp from the salty spray. They were chatting and smoking cigarettes with AK-108 assault rifles slung across their muscular backs. Way past the beach was a paved parking lot, and another dozen guards rested lazily against a caravan of luxury cars parked out of the hot sun in the cool shadows below a raised tent of striped canvas. These men wore similar clothing, but carried compact 9 mm Steyr TMP machine pistols hung at their sides.

Professionally, McCarter noted that none of the guards had unbuttoned their shirts in spite of the heat, and from a few odd lumps and bumps under the cloth he guessed that they were wearing some form of body armor. If things went wrong, those would be the first to die.

Situated on wooden towers, lifeguards kept a careful watch on the celebration, their binoculars ever moving through the crowd to try to keep an accurate tally of how many people went into the water and how many came back out again.

There were easily a hundred chaise longues dotting the long section of private beach, but most of them were empty, the laughing people dashing in the shallows, splashing and laughing. The few who remained were almost entirely beautiful women in micro-thong bikinis that covered virtually nothing.

Knowing full well that they were under close scrutiny by most of the men in sight, the scantily clad women were sensually massaging suntan lotion into their dark skin, trying to make the job as erotic as possible by concentrating on their inner thighs and lower bellies. A couple of the ladies had succumbed to the heat and dropped their tops to lie facedown on the lounge chairs, their full breasts peeking through the woven strips like rosebuds hiding in snow.

Nearby, a score of men and women in assorted swimwear and sunglasses were playing a boisterous game of volleyball that seemed to have no rules aside from hitting the ball very high and trying not to let it touch you. Over by a sandstone cabana, large men with thick arms sat perched on tiny bar stools and leaned toward each other to talk softly, the tropical drinks in their scarred fists seemingly untouched.

Reaching the shallows, McCarter scooped up a wiggling young woman and tossed her into the air. She screamed in mock fright, and he caught her in his powerful arms.

"Again!" she implored. "Higher this time!"

Still walking toward the beach, McCarter politely obliged, but upon reaching the sand, he set her down and administrated a playful smack on her buttocks. "Sorry, gotta go. Business, you understand."

"Making money more important than me?" She laughed, stroking fingertips along the hard muscles of the stranger's thick arms. "Stay, please."

There were a lot of promises in those simple words, but McCarter gently removed her hand and gave it a kiss. "Later, I promise," he lied with a smile.

"I'll be waiting," she purred, then turned to walk away, swinging her hips suggestively.

Not made of stone, McCarter watched her leave for a few seconds, before heading for the volleyball game.

"So was that the contact, Chief?" Calvin James said over a hidden earbud. "I think you should stay and do a through cavity search for contraband."

Lacking a throat mike, McCarter was unable to reply, and forced himself to keep a straight face.

In the far distance, rows of swaying palm trees nearly hid a large, modern-style mansion that dominated the top of a wide hill. A winding gravel road led down to the beach, and then a foot-path of wooden boards extended directly to a small area of neatly raked sand surrounded by a low stone wall. At a small private beach set inside a large private beach, a hirsute goliath sprawled in obscene comfort on an oversize chaise longue.

Angling around the volleyball game, McCarter stopped at the bar to grab two drinks, then casually ambled across the hot sand toward the lone man.

Unknown to most of the law-abiding world, Emile San Saun was famous to every major law-enforcement agency in existence. Although long past middle-age, the giant was in excellent health, the daily exercise routines in the private gym maintaining his Olympian physique. His skin was tanned a deep bronze, his hair sun-bleached to a muted shade of gold. Jeweled rings adorned most of his fingers, and a platinum Rolex Excalibur watch was wrapped around his left wrist, which was a fake and actually an EM scanner that checked for listening devices planted by any of his many enemies.

Emile San Saun was an arms dealer, one of the largest, and most successful, in the world. He sold anything that killed: assault rifles, battle tanks, submarines, jet fighters, and he gave volume discounts to repeat customers. And unlike so many others in his dubious line of enterprise, he never "lost" a shipment that had been paid for, or sold inferior goods. Among the merchants of death, he was known for being basically honest, a somewhat dubious distinction that was offset by his infamous acts of revenge on those who cheated him. Interpol agents told the joke that the surest way to commit suicide was to short-change San Saun a nickel.

Another odd quirk was his steadfast refusal to deal in drugs or sex slaves. Oh, the Frenchman was quite aware of how huge the profit margin was in slaves, but after the recent annihilation of a Sardinian cartel by NATO, he had wisely withdrawn all of his financial support and concentrated solely on weaponry. Somehow, taking a life seemed so much cleaner than breaking the will of a young woman. It was these tenuous human attributes that kept the arms dealer off the Stony Man kill list.

Knowing he was under constant surveillance by the guards, McCarter stepped over the stone wall and walked over to San Saun, shaking the drinks to make the ice tinkle.

Lazily, the giant opened an eye. "I didn't ask for a drink," the arms dealer snapped churlishly.

"Shut the fuck up, or you're dead," McCarter said with a friendly smile, offering a glass.

Startled by the whipcrack tone, San Saun jerked backward. "You must be insane," he growled defiantly. "One word from me and my guards will…" Then the man paused at the appearance of a bright red dot dancing among the contents of the tropical drink.

"A laser does not mean there is a sniper," San Saun said smoothly, accepting the frosty glass as if it were a ticking bomb. "Nor that they are any good over extreme ranges."

Instantly, something hummed past his face, the breeze of the passage felt on his cheek, then the sand kicked up a little geyser, throwing the white particles onto the low wall. Holding his breath, San Saun waited, but there was no sound of the rifle over the laughter of his guests or the cresting surf.

"All right, I believe you," San Saun commented, clearly thinking out loud. "Now, obviously, you do not want me dead, or else we would not be having this pleasant conversation. And you could never trust anything I promised to do, or pay, under such odious duress, so that leaves only information." He took a sip and nodded in approval. "Well, since I am temporarily at your mercy, what do you wish to know?"

In spite of himself, McCarter had to admit that the arms dealer was much smarter than expected. San Saun had never gone to school. He had been educated on the mean streets of Paris, yet when Kurtzman had run his theoretical IQ it was well over 160 points, near the genius level. That was both good and bad.

"Laugh when I stop talking so that the guards think I told you a joke," McCarter directed, spreading his hands and making vague gestures in the air.

Throwing back his head, San Saun roared with laughter and pretended to wipe a tear from his eye. "Enough games, what do you want?" he demanded, titling the glass in fake congratulations.

Off to the side, the arms dealer saw that his bodyguards were starting his way with hands on their weapons. Very conscious of the laser dot in his drink, San Saun brushed back his hair with his left hand making sure they saw the signal to retreat, but stay alert. Without nodding or showing any sign they had gotten the message, the guards returned to their former positions, but now all of their attention was focused on McCarter.

"You recently made a sale of VLX gas," McCarter said

bluntly, squatting on his heels. "I want to know who, and where they are. Along with anything else of importance, physical description, the Swiss bank account number, if they paid in cash, what country did it come from, whatever you have."

This was a gamble, but a well calculated one. There were very few people who dealt in nerve gas, and this man's name was at the top of the list. If he proved innocent of this particular crime, then Phoenix Force would visit the next man on the list, then the third, and so on until they hit pay dirt.

"Interesting, very interesting," San Saun muttered, twisting the glass about to watch the play of the laser beam among the ice cubes. "You must have no idea who you're looking for." He took another small sip. "And if I refuse?"

Saying nothing in reply, McCarter took a handful of sand and let it slowly trickle out between his fingers. A split second later two more red dots appeared on the arms dealer's flat stomach.

"Who bought the nerve gas?" McCarter insisted, slightly increasing the flow of the sand.

Inhaling sharply, San Saun seemed confused by the sand, then suddenly understood. That was his life running out of time like an hourglass. Grudgingly, he admired the technique. It was very good. Whoever had trained this man really knew his job.

"Sorry, but I do not deal in such items," the arms dealer began. Then a thunderous explosion erupted from behind him. Tumbling out of the chair, San Saun spun to see black smoke and burning debris flying up from what had once been a multimillion-euro mansion. Then a second blast ripped apart the solarium.

"Thank goodness there was some sort of gas leak in the place before it went up," McCarter said casually, seeming to concentrate on the cascading white particles. "That chased out the servants, and your dogs. Dobermans, right? But your art collection…wasn't that worth millions? Ah well, such a pity."

Screaming loudly, everybody on the beach was running around and pointing, the men digging for car keys, the women hastily donning more clothing. Only the guards remained calm, moving in a steady formation to form a protective circle around San Saun and his guest.

"My home…" San Saun whispered, rising slowly to his bare feet. Completely forgotten, the drink in his hand tilted sideway, disgorging the fruity contents onto the white beach and staining it dark. My… I had a Picasso, you fool! An original Picasso, and two Renoirs!"

"Now you don't," McCarter replied coldly, opening his hand to let the last few grains tumble away to vanish in the wind. "Okay, time's up. Talk, or die."

Shaking with repressed fury, San Saun was unable to speak. He was being muscled on his own private beach! Handled like some village store clerk overdue on the vig! This was intolerable!

"Okay." He sighed, both shoulders slumping. "I will talk." Instantly he tossed the empty glass into the air as a diversion, then spun in a fast circle to slash a flat hand at the other man's belly in a killing martial arts. Without losing his own drink, McCarter caught the hand and began to squeeze. San Saun gasped in surprise at the pain and tried to wiggle free, but it was like being crushed in some sort of machine. Who—no, what was this man?

"Last chance," McCarter whispered, increasing the

pressure and draping an arm over the criminal so that it would appear that they were just engaged in some friendly wrestling.

But the guards weren't buying it, and suddenly red dots from their own weapons moved over the body of the Stony Man commando. But McCarter knew they would do nothing until he harmed San Saun or they got the signal to strike. An early move on their part could kill both him and, more importantly, their employer.

"Release me or die," San Saun exhorted, trying not to show his pain.

"Tell me or die."

A minute passed, then two, and McCarter increased the pressure until he thought the man's bones would break.

"Enough!" San Saun gasped. "I...sold the gas to a representative of a group called Dark Star. They're freelancers who work out of Belgium!"

Mercs, eh? He had never heard of Dark Star, but that meant nothing. "Give me a name," McCarter demanded, applying more pressure until tears of rage formed in the eyes of the man. "And an address."

"O'Hara, Eric O'Hara!" he said through gritted teeth. "No address! Internet sale, the goods were shipped to an abandoned stone quarry in Luxembourg!"

"Yeah?"

"Yes!"

Clever. An X-ship could land for the goods unnoticed once the delivery gang was gone. "They pay in cash?"

"Wire transfer! Shoot if you want, but that is all I have!"

Unfortunately the man seemed to be telling the truth. "Thank you," McCarter said, then spun the arms dealer around to confuse the guards and he dived to the ground.

Unable to get a clear shot past their boss, the bodyguards hesitated for a moment, when a sharp whistle sounded from the sky and small black objects started to drop all over the beach.

"Grenade!" a guard yelled, throwing an arm over his face a split second before the U.S. Army stun grenade cut loose, generating a noise louder than artillery and a flash ten times brighter than the sun.

Deaf and blind, the guards stumbled around helplessly. Uncovering his face, the one unaffected guard swung up his AK-108 and started to aim at McCarter when his chest exploded, most of his vital organs, and a good length of spine, blasting out his back and flying for yards before wetly landing on the warm sand.

A full second later, there came the telltale report of a high-power sniper rifle from the distant hills.

More grenades erupted, the noise and light mixing with thick volumes of reddish smoke. In the parking lot, a bodyguard ripped open the trunk of a Cadillac and reached for the Steyr SSG-70 sniper rifle inside. His head vanished, and the torso rammed into the trunk. As before, a moment later, there sounded a faraway boom of a sniper rifle.

"Fuckers got themselves a Barrett!" a guard snarled, twisting to point his Kalashnikov at nothing in particular. "What should we do, sir?"

"Undala, Jones, cover the boss! Lazzaro and Cain, take the Hummer and get the son of a bitch" the chief guard commanded, brandishing a pistol. "Take the back road and circle around from behind! We'll stay here and try to give you… Shit!"

A fiery dart lanced down from the green hills and

slammed into the Hummer. The LAW rocket hit with devastating force, and the two guards went flying as the armored military vehicle flipped over onto a limousine. The impact smashed every window before the Hummer burst into flames.

"Get those guys!" the chief bodyguard roared, firing his AK-108 at the hill when the reddish smoke from the second volley of grenades wafted across the parking lot. A strange expression contorted his face, then the man limply sat on the pavement still clutching the assault rifle. Weaving slightly, he made a crooning noise then toppled over like a pile of dirty laundry and began to snore.

As the crimson fumes merged with the dark smoke of the flash-bang grenades, more people fell over, asleep, guns dropping from limp fingers. A couple of the men at the cabana poured their alcoholic drinks over napkins and held the crude masks to their mouths, but they only got a few yards before they started to move slower, and slower, as if encountering an invisible wall of glue, then simply lay down on the sand to occasionally give a twitch.

An expert in munitions, San Saun recognized the effects of BZ gas, a stabilized form of LSD. But that was used exclusively by the Americans! So the Yanks and the Brits were both in this, eh?

Realizing his mistake, San Saun lurched away from the wall just as a .50-caliber round from the Barrett arrived to plow through the ancient stones as though they were dusty playing cards. Diving over the chaise longue, the arm dealer took cover behind the next wall, trying to keep the drink cart between him and the distant sniper. Then the cart jerked hard and the wall shook, but there was no penetration. The small refrigerator full of ice had done what a brick wall could not: deflect the massive incoming 750-grain, steel-jacketed thunderbolts.

Safe for the moment, San Saun hurriedly glanced around to estimate the situation. It was difficult to see because of all the smoke, but he could dimly make out dozens of bodies strewed across the beach, some of them guests, some his bodyguards, but none of them was walking or shouting, or doing much of anything except lie there asleep.

Spotting a body sprawled nearby, a guard whose name he could not recall, San Saun saw a machine pistol still holstered at his hip. Yanking the Steyr free, he thumbed off the safety and worked the bolt to chamber a 9 mm round, then looked around for any sign of the big bastard who had almost crushed his hand.

Momentarily, his vision blurred as the red smoke wafted his way. But it had been thinned by the salty spray from the cresting waves, and San Saun managed to stay conscious, although breathing was rather difficult and his thoughts became discordant and jumbled.

Standing foolishly upright, the arm dealer staggered across the sand, weaving among the unconscious people and trying not to trip on them. Spent brass shells from the guards lay everywhere, glinting in the sand like pirate's gold, and he giggled at the comparison. Get hold of yourself, Emile, there are assassins all around! he admonished himself.

Forcing the grin off his face, San Saun headed for the parking lot, then remembered hearing the cars explode, and turned to start for the mansion when he recalled that was also destroyed. What was he to do now?

Unable to think clearly, the man rubbed his sore hand

and simply sat hard in the sand. Looking around drunkenly, the arms dealer broke into a happy smile at the sight of a shapely backside, the young woman lying facedown on a beach towel.

Chuckling in appreciation, San Saun reached out to give her rear a little pat, when a thunder rumbled and darkness covered the shore. Looking upward, Emil San Saun saw a column of fire descending and managed a brief scream before his world was filled with incalculable pain and then eternal blackness.

ALREADY NEARLY A MILE AWAY from the private beach, McCarter and the rest of Phoenix Force were riding in a stolen Cadillac convertible, dutifully reloading their weapons.

"Dark Star, eh?" James said, typing the name into a laptop. "Okay, Aaron says his people will have the dossier on them in five minutes."

"That long?" Rafael Encizo said with a grin, breaking apart the MM-1 40 mm grenade launcher and tucking the pieces away under a seat. "He must be getting old." The 12-round weapon was a favorite of the man, capable of laying down a heavy barrage of shells even faster than an automatic mortar. In his expert opinion, people were much more dangerous than a machine.

"Maybe all of that black coffee finally burned out his synapses," T. J. Hawkins added, throwing back his head to savor the feel of the wind on his face.

"Hey, give the man a break," James said with smile. "It takes awhile to hack into the Interpol database. It's not like raiding some French guy's private estate, you know."

The whole team shared a laugh at that. The mission

had gone off perfectly. They had the name of the mercs behind the X-ships, and not a member of the team had gotten so much as a scratch. That was a win in anybody's opinion.

Hawkins spotted something large move in rearview mirror. "Son of a bitch!"

Slamming on the brakes, he stopped the convertible in the middle of the road and turned to scowl at the distant X-ship moving back and forth along the beach, the fiery exhaust annihilating the dozens of bodies dotting the clean white sand.

"But they're not dead, just unconscious," McCarter whispered.

"They're dead now," Hawkins muttered, his hands tightening on the steering wheel.

"Those Dark Star bastards must have wanted to silence San Saun before he could be made to talk," Encizo said, his heart pounding hard. "They just arrived a few minutes too late." There was nothing that could be done now to help the civilians. Their deaths were not the fault of the team, but of the *Skywalkers*. However, the grotesque image of the X-ship burning the shoreline clean of the helpless civilians throbbed in his mind like shrapnel.

In a rush of flame, the X-ship shot into the clouds and vanished.

"If only they had hit while we were still in range," James growled, hefting a 9 mm Beretta. Then he scowled at the handgun and tucked it away with a grimace. "Yeah, and exactly what could we have done, use harsh language? Write them a parking ticket? Might as well for all the good bullets and grenades would do against one of those flying skyscrapers."

"You've got that right, brother."

Softly there came a low rumble of distant thunder as the X-ship broke the sound barrier.

Turning around, Hawkins started the car again, engaged the transmission and drove off. "Okay, Sidewinders can't see them, and they move too fast for a LAW or HAFLA to track."

"The same for a Carl Gustave or Armbrust." McCarter grunted. "I'm not even sure a Barrett could do enough damage to hurt one of those giants, unless it hit something vital inside, and that's a million to one shot."

"Literally!"

"An electric 40 mm Vulcan minigun might work," James said. "Load it with fléchettes, and we could open one of the things like a can of tuna."

"Unfortunately, the damn X-ships are radar proof, so we'd have to target by sight alone."

"Tricky," Hawkins noted, taking another curve. "More than that, it'd be damn near impossible!"

"Not to mention a Vulcan is about as man-portable as an indoor swimming pool," Encizo added. "Hey, what about using Apache gunships armed with Vulcans?" The man frowned. "No, too slow, damn it. Jet fighters have trouble keeping up with the damn things, a helicopter would be left behind in the dust!"

"Well, we better figure out something fast," McCarter returned, pulling a shirt from a gym bag and sliding it on. "Because the next time we meet, these things will be coming after us, and we better have something in the hopper by then or else the blood will really hit the fan!"

Moving along the winding coastal road, the men of Phoenix Force continued to discuss the complex problem, never noticing the minuscule black shape hovering in the clouds overhead. Suddenly it darted forward to maneuver ahead of them and began to quickly descend....

CHAPTER NINE

Central Park, New York City

Stepping out of the shadows, Hal Brognola coughed twice to be recognized then slowly approached the group of people standing near the boat house.

"Stop right there," the woman commanded, both hands clasped behind her back. "Identify yourself." Her tone was not friendly and carried an implied threat if not obeyed immediately.

Dressed in business casual, a somber dress that went to her calves, a short jacket and a scarf, the woman was rather pretty, but wore little cosmetics and no perfume or jewelry. The Mossad agent reminded Brognola of Barbara Price, all business, and he could easily spot the pistol tucked under her jacket from the slight disruption of the lines. Small, and compact, a Beretta Brigadier, or perhaps a Remington.

"Marcus," Brognola said clearly, keeping his hands in plain sight. He knew most of the other people. They were fellow members of the law-enforcement community from foreign nations. The top cops of the world. Or rather, the secret top cops. There was enough covert Intelligence here to start a university for spies. They also seemed a tad jumpy, but that was not surprising for a clandestine meeting in the middle of the night.

"Aurelius," the woman replied, easing her stance slightly. Then she smiled and her features brightened dramatically. "I find the reference to the ancient philosopher king of Rome most amusing. I assume you were thinking of his 'guardians in the night' speech?"

"What else?" a slim man muttered around the stem of the briarwood pipe in his mouth. Rising from the park bench, he stepped forward to shake hands with Brognola. "It has been a very long time since we last met, Harold," he said, making the name two syllables. "Not the best of circumstances, eh?"

"No, Gaston, it is not," the big Fed replied grimly. "Does everybody know each other?"

"No, we do not," the Mossad agent replied, her smile vanishing. "Introductions are in order, and under the circumstances, if any of us catches another in a lie, I suggest an immediate termination."

"I agree," a burly man stated, his bald head gleaming dully with the reflected light of the halogen lamp set along the shore of the Central Park Lake. The effect was that of a halo, like the ancient god Helio from Greek mythology. He was in casual clothing, slacks and loafers, his arms thrown wide across the back of the bench, showing that he was unarmed. "This is not the time, or place, for half measures."

"Accepted, my friend. All right, I shall start the process. I'm Jeremy Braith-Waite, officially the political liaison for the British Ministry of Trade in America, but in truth…" He smiled and all of the pleasantness vanished. "I am a field operative for MI-5, counter-intelligence."

"Alexander Korolev," the bald man revealed. "FSB, Russian national police."

"Gaston LeRoux," the slim man said, removing the pipe from his mouth. Daintily, he tapped out the cold ashes into a palm before tucking it away. "French Secret Service, special branch."

"Which does exactly…what?" the Mossad agent asked suspiciously.

"Oh, this and that." LeRoux smiled with as much warmth as a glacier in winter. Assassin.

"Debra Stone, Mossad," the pretty woman announced. Then unnecessarily added, "Israel."

"Yes, dear, we know. And I am Jen-djeh Dee," the elderly man said with a weak smile.

"You are also the assistant head of the Red Star in America," Braith-Waite added pointedly, twitching his mustache.

"Unofficially," Dee added, bowing his head in respect.

The old fellow seemed like such a harmless soul, Brognola was surprised at his high rank in the Red Star, but then just for a second, Brognola saw a flash in the old man's eyes and knew he was actually dealing with a cold-blooded killer. A genial, smiling grandpa who could slit your throat while ordering a cup of tea and never think twice about the death.

"No, it's official," Brognola retorted, taking a gamble. "We've seen the communiqué. So cut the shit, Dee, and let's talk straight."

With a low hiss, the old man glared hostilely, his true

personality fully exposed, then he beamed a smile again like Father Christmas about to bestow gifts to happy children.

"Damn, it's unnerving when he does that," LeRoux said, curling a lip.

"Harold Brognola, Justice Department, Special Operations," Brognola stated. "Which these days deals entirely with the *Skywalkers*."

The others took the not-so-subtle hint. The niceties were over, time for business.

"I heard about Fort Bragg," Stone said unexpectedly. "My deepest condolences on the loss of your scientific staff."

Since the incident had never made it into the news media, the big Fed took the declaration as a boast of her capabilities, and leaving out the real function of the Marines was a gesture of friendship. She knew the truth, but would keep her mouth shut. But then, the United States and Israel had always gotten along well. He did not know her personally, but Brognola knew her type of agent, and felt himself warm to the stern woman.

"Are you referring to the so-called Space Marines?" Korolev asked bluntly. "Until today, I had always thought they were a joke, but if these *Skywalkers* take them seriously, then there must have been a cogent threat. Perhaps my government should start a similar project."

"We already have." Dee smiled. "If you get into trouble in space, just call China, and we shall gladly rescue your people. Free of charge."

"And a billion dollars' worth of propaganda."

"What an absurd notion! The freedom-loving people

of China would never think of taking such advantage of others!"

"Tell that to the students at Tiananmen Square," LeRoux muttered, then went absolutely still, his eyes darting to the left.

Suddenly everybody in the little clearing was alert, and slipped hands inside their clothing, including the supposedly unarmed FSB agent. A few seconds later a group of men in rough clothing walked out of the trees to stop at the edge of the bright pool of halogen light, the thick shadows masking their numbers.

"Bad night to be out taking a stroll, assholes," a young man said, sneering. "Now you gotta pay. Toss over your fucking wallets and jewelry, and maybe we let you get out of here alive."

"Yeah, maybe," another teen echoed, whipping out a sawed-off shotgun. There closely followed a chorus of metallic clicks from the surrounding darkness.

For a moment nobody spoke as the two groups faced each other, the tension rapidly mounting. The street gang was starting to get a bad feeling about the mugging. Normally, people screamed in terror at the appearance of the gang, while some begged not to be harmed, and the smart ones ran, tossing away their valuables to try to buy off the gang. But it never worked, and the gang always caught the person and took everything, then beat them unconscious for running. Unless any of the women were pretty. Those were hauled into the bushes for a private party. If they performed well, some were even left alive afterward.

However, this was rapidly going wrong. None of the tourists seemed frightened. The five people just stood there unflinching, as if debating what to do, their eyes steady with what a couple of the older teens recognized as the "hard stare" you learned to survive in prison. Could they be armed? That had happened once before. But there were ten muggers, and only five victims. Easy pickings.

"Come on, this is just a mugging," the leader of the gang said with a straight face. "Nothing bad is going to happen, unless you get stupid and refuse. Toss over the goods, and blow."

"Leave or die," Brognola said, hunching his shoulders slightly. "This is your last chance."

"Wrong place, wrong time," Korolev added grimly.

"Bullshit, old man, we own this lake!" the teenager retorted hotly, pulling out a nickel-plated .357 Magnum Glock. The shiny gun was very pretty, as if polished daily, but the checkered grip had a worn appearance as if used many times before.

"Foolish child, you forgot to take off the safety." Dee chuckled in a creaky voice, gesturing with his abnormally thick cane. "That gun won't fire!"

As the teen glanced for a split second to see if that was true, Dee triggered the 12-gauge shotgun inside his cane, exactly as the other intelligence operatives fired their weapons from inside their clothing, the fabric exploding as bright lances of flame stabbed out into the night.

Falling backward, five of the muggers cried out as their throats erupted, red blood spraying outward. Startled for only a second, the rest of the street gang pulled their weapons and fired back. But the operatives had already shifted positions, darting among the trees or diving into the bushes. Masked from sight, the intelligence pros sent back a withering hail of hot lead, and the street muggers were torn apart by a hammering barrage of Talon armor-piercing bullets and HEAT rounds.

In spite of the fact that modern-day bullet-propellant was totally smokeless, a stabilized form of fulminating guncotton, there was still a definite cloud of muzzle fumes blurring the air for a heartbeat before the diesel-scented breeze from the city wafted over the scene of death.

Leaving the spent brass on the ground, the group moved away from the lake and deeper into the artificial forest, reloading their assorted weapons on the way.

"Attacked in a public park," LeRoux muttered scornfully, holstering his 9 mm FN pistol.

"As if the south bank of Paris is any better?" Dee asked, yanking open the hot breech of the cane to eject the spent cartridge. Reaching into his vest, he extracted a fresh one and slipped it into the cane, the polished wood smoothly closing to a low click.

"No, it is not," Korolev stated, holstering a huge bore .357 Magnum Rex. Then the man gave a humorless chuckle. "In fact, it is nearly as dangerous a place as your own Liverpool."

"Oh, not quite that bad," Braith-Waite replied, tucking away his Browning Hi-Power.

"And exactly how many suicide bombers do you people get every year?" Stone asked rudely, slamming home a fresh clip in her .40 Jericho. "Brognola, why did you choose this absurd location to discuss what can be done about the *Skywalkers?* Surely you must have known about the prevalence of street crime?"

"But I didn't ask for the meeting," Brognola repeated, feeling the hair on the back of his neck start to rise. "Gaston did."

"No, I was summoned by the charming Miss. Stone,"

LeRoux began to say, his voice trailing away, only to come back as a curse. "*Mon Dieu,* this is a trap!"

In unison, everybody pulled their weapons again and moved deeper into the woods. But it was already too late. The dark sky overhead brightened slightly with a reddish glow that rapidly expanded to fill the night with thundering flame as an X-ship dropped into view. Splaying across the site of the rendezvous, the volcanic exhaust hurtled the bodies of the street gang away like leaves, the boathouse exploding into burning kindling. The trees withered and caught fire as the pavement began to melt and bubble, the decorative cast-iron bench softening to melt like candle wax.

Snarling curses in their native languages, Stone, Korolev and Dee raised their weapons to fire at the machine, but Brognola grabbed their arms and pulled the agents deeper into the city park. An idea was already forming in his mind, and it required fast action on their part or it wouldn't work. The others hesitated, then acquiesced and quickly retreated into the cool safety behind a decorative boulder.

Staying low, the five Intelligence operatives strained to see the towering giant blocked by the leafy branches. As the leaves died and fell in droves from the awful heat, they got a clear view of the X-ship for almost a full minute before the roaring engines pulsed with power and the craft vanished into the sky, a ghastly wave of heat sweeping across the landscape, setting a dozen more small fires.

"The fools," Braith-Waite said, tracking the progress of the ship with his service pistol. "They thought the muggers were us!"

"Just a group of armed people at the right place and time," Brognola replied, squinting against the growing volumes of smoke. "Can't blame them for not getting an accurate head count. Then again, who's to say we did not bring assistants or bodyguards?"

"All right, the terrorists think we're dead," Stone said, waving a hand in front of her sweaty face. The heat was becoming stifling. The fires were combining to spread fast. Soon this entire area would be engulfed in flames. "This is a tactical advantage to be sure, but what would be our next…ah, of course. The traitor."

"Exactly! Somebody arranged for this ambush," Dee said, coughing slightly from the thickening smoke. "Someone in the Intelligence community who knew how to get to each of us."

"It was a bold move," LeRoux added, his gun still in hand. "With the five of us removed, any effective search for the *Skywalkers* would be seriously hindered." As if suddenly realizing the Browning was there, he looked at the gun and tucked it away once more.

"But now the hunters have become the prey," Korolev added with a note of satisfaction. The bald Russian seemed impervious to the mounting heat and smoke.

Just then, the wail of approaching fire trucks could be heard in the distance, then the sirens of ambulances and the two-tone bleating of police cars.

"We have to leave," Brognola stated, angling away from the destruction. "Leave and stay hidden. If there is a mole in our community, then we cannot take the chance of contacting any of the usual people in our organizations, anybody at all."

Scowling, Dee started to speak when there came a ragged flurry of gunfire. The operatives tensed, then relaxed, understanding it was only the ammunition in the guns of the street gang cooking off from the rising temperature of the conflagration. Flames were licking high into the air now and a thick plume of dark smoke spread out to cover the parkland.

"*Oui,* we have only this one chance to catch the traitor," LeRoux stated forcibly, "and extract from him…or her—the identity of their master."

"And then we strike," Stone declared.

Resolutely, the others voiced their agreement to the plan and slipped into the darkness to vanish from sight. When an army of police, firefighters and EMTs arrived moments later, they found only the flaming destruction of the boathouse, along with an unknown number of corpses, burned beyond all possible recognition.

Stony Man Farm, Virginia

PRICE WAS MAKING some tea in the kitchenette, and Delahunt was conducting her invisible orchestra opening and closing files at lightspeed, while Tokaido seemed to be asleep, which meant he was hard at work. The only signs of life were the throbbing music seeping from his earbuds, and a single finger stroking across a mousepad. Kurtzman and Wethers were typing furiously, their workstations alive with flashing images from the monitors.

"Eureka!" Wethers announced with obvious satisfaction, leaning backward in his chair.

"What'd you find, Hunt?" Kurtzman asked, not looking up from his console. His monitors were covered with engineering blueprints, a side monitor scrolling with mathematical equations.

"This was extraordinarily difficult, Aaron," the professor replied, removing his pipe and gesturing the stem at the monitor. "Dark Star seems to be protected by an expert hacker who surfs the Internet destroying any reference to them. A most efficient fellow, indeed. But I managed to ferret out a few things."

Saying nothing, Price carried her mug to a visitor chair set near the four consoles. Knowing the diligence of the professor, she couldn't imagine what kind of effort the task had to have entailed for him to admit it required any extra effort at all.

"Go on," Kurtzman prompted, finally turning away from the flashing screen.

"Dark Star is an elite mercenary group run out of the Grand Marnix hotel in Brussels. The titular head of the group is a General Zane Southerland. Not much on him aside from a few cryptic references in the Mossad and CIA files. KGB lists him as dead, and ANSI, the Australian New Zealand intelligence agency, never even heard of the man. Basically, Southerland is a ghost. He owns nothing, buys nothing, comes from nowhere. There are no records of his fingerprints, footprints or dental records, anywhere in the world."

"Southerland could be a fake name," Price said thoughtfully, taking a sip of her tea. "But then, why not call yourself general, rather than colonel?"

"Logically, the assumption would be that it is his real rank."

"Which strongly intimates that Southerland is also his real name." Price added, holding the mug in both hands to savor the warmth. "All right, since we know where Dark Star is located, send somebody in to sweep the place. If the mercs have anything to do with the X-ships, they'll be long gone or dead. However, we might find something useful at their former headquarters."

"NATO will have an investigation team there in a few minutes," Kurtzman replied, releasing his keyboard.

"So soon?" Delahunt asked, turning her helmet slightly.

"Belgium is their home turf," Price replied.

The redhead nodded. "True enough."

"And in the meantime, I've done a quick inventory of all the local shops to see if any odd purchases were made after Dark Star first began operations," Kurtzman continued.

"Find anything?" Price asked curiously, taking a sip and setting aside her mug.

Kurtzman grinned widely. "The day after they took over the building, the liquor store on the corner got a standing order for a case of Raven Stout a week. It was always paid for in cash. Now, in case you don't know, Raven Stout is a home-brewed beer that comes exclusively from Mitchell's Pub in South Africa."

"Could just be a coincidence," Price said, then gave a hard smile. "But probably not. Okay, they're from South Africa. Or, at least, one of them is. Southerland, most likely, considering his name. They might be former military, or even counterintelligence operatives, thrown out after the revolution."

"Absolutely. As each African nation purged itself of military dictators and their thug army, the outcasts invariably turned to crime."

"Anything from the Johannesburg records on a Southerland?"

"Nothing. Most of the Cape Town files were destroyed before Mandella took over. What few computer files ex-

isted were recently attacked by a top-notch hacker."
Kurtzman grimaced. "This guy altered everything across
the board—criminal warrants, police records, medical
benefits, retirement, insurance, purchases, requisitions,
death records—everything! There's no way to tell what
he was after. A very professional job, I must say."

Price looked askance. "You almost sound impressed."

"That's because I am," Kurtzman said honestly. "If
the guy was legit, I'd offer him a job here at the Farm."

Starting to rise, Price paused. "He's that good?"

"Unfortunately, yes."

"I've been tracking his work for a while. He is exceptionally good," Tokaido said slowly, opening his eyelids,
but otherwise not moving. "My guess is that he's using a
Double Deuce. A conjoined IBM Blue/Gene supercomputer for offense, and a Dell Thunderbird supercomputer
for his defensive software. A powerful combination of
brute force and raw speed."

"Dark Star must be extremely well funded to have two
supercomputers."

"Have to be, wouldn't they? Space ships don't grow
on trees like apples."

"Wonder where the money is coming from?"

"With an IBM/Dell combo?" Tokaido scoffed. "Their
hacker could be draining Swiss bank accounts the same
as we do."

So that was a complete dead end, Price thought. "Okay,
how do we stop him?" Price asked bluntly.

The man shrugged. "Aerial bombing?"

"Bullshit, they may be loaded for bear," Kurtzman said
with a humorless smile, "but we are going to bust his ass.
Get on it, Akira."

"I am," Tokaido replied, closing his eyes and starting to softly type with one hand, while maneuvering the mousepad with the other.

Price prayed that they'd be able to stop Dark Star and the X-ships. Unfortunately, this Colonel Southerland had to have been stashing away fuel containers for years, maybe decades. Possibly even since the fall of the white South African government? That was more than possible. The two supercomputers could steal him billions if necessary, but he would have needed millions to buy them or to steal them in the first place. But then, who could possibly know how much he'd stolen from the nation before being ousted from his position of authority?

"Has anybody checked any of their refueling spots?" Price asked.

"Of course," Kurtzman replied gruffly. "The FBI, British SAS, French Secret Service, Mossad, Japanese Imperial Intelligence, Russian FSB, the Australian Bushmasters…we all have looked. But there was nothing left for forensics scientists to look at under their microscopes. The exhaust of these things is hotter than a blast furnace, and leaves only ash and slag behind. They land, top off the tanks, grab some supplies and leave, utterly destroying the cache."

She'd expected as much. When working with the NSA, Price had been allowed to visit Cape Canaveral and witness a night launch of a shuttle carrying a new type of spy satellite. The viewing stands were a mile away from the gantry, and the exhaust still knocked some of them to the ground. It wasn't so much a launch as it was more of barely controlled explosion.

Add to which, the colossal X-ships could land anywhere. The first NASA space shuttle was hailed as the marvel of the ages when it was able to glide down from orbit and land on a standard airfield. But X-ships did a vertical descent, which allowed them to land anywhere they wished. The damn machines could even hover and move sideways to hide from military satellites if necessary. They were 127 feet tall, but the machines could still slip inside a fair number of natural caves and dormant volcanoes, or even take refuge inside the steel framework of an office building under construction. Or just throw a tarpaulin over one and from space it would resemble a house being tented for termites.

The one point in Stony Man's favor, the woman noted, was that the X-ships could not have a refueling station in orbit; they barely reached LEO. A HEO orbit was absolutely beyond their range, but that seemed to be their only limitation. Even if a Keyhole or WatchDog satellite found one on the ground, all they would see would be a metal circle fifty feet wide, which could be anything from the roof of a water tank to a grain silo. The job was impossible! Delahunt was right. They had to defeat the men operating the machines; they were the only weak point of an X-ship.

This was so frustrating! Price fumed. There had to be a pattern in their attacks. Once they figured that out, Stony Man could get ahead of them and meet the next X-ship with enough concentrated firepower to blow the damn thing back into its component atoms. The use of a tactical nuke was not out of the question, if it got the job done, and she knew that Brognola could supply the teams with suitcase nukes within less than twelve hours. However, if these were purely random attacks, with no order or specific purpose, then… Suddenly a musical chime broke her dark chain of thought.

"About time," Kurtzman said eagerly, reaching out to tap the keyboard. His computer screen flashed a series of aerial photographs before going blank. "Damn it, another negative," he muttered unhappily. "Just a cargo ship on fire in the Solomon Islands."

"Those are photos from a Keyhole satellite of possible missile launches," Price said slowly, studying the screen. "I see what you're doing. Clever. You're trying to find the location of the initial launch site of the X-ships. Should be easy enough, the three of them taking off must have lit up the thermal scans like a—"

"An apartment building on fire, or a small forest fire, or a large grasslands blaze," Kurtzman said, ticking off the items on his fingers. "Or how about a legitimate missile test, plenty of those around the world, or the thermal venting from natural steam eruptions in a hundreds locations, artillery practice in Australia, Spain and Russia, a practice bombing run in Canada, a small war in Angola, the burning pits in Dafur, that rather large war in Iraq you may have heard about, a volcanic eruption in Peru, a dozen different factory explosions…

Angrily pushing himself away from the console, he started rolling his wheelchair toward the kitchenette. "I wrote a program to filter out the obvious things, but then I put them back in, just in case I miss something important."

"You mean, in case the *Skywalkers* disguised that first launch under the cover of an airplane crash or a monsoon."

"A tropical rain storm?"

"Wouldn't that defuse the heat signature enough to mask what it really was?"

"Interesting. Yeah, I think it might." Damn, a monsoon. He hadn't thought of that. "Could work for a hurricane, or even a tornado, too."

Crossing her arms, Price frowned in displeasure. "Do you think it's really possible we could find anything from that spot? Surely checking their point of origin is an obvious move on our part."

"True, but we have to check, anyway," Kurtzman stated, braking to a halt at the kitchenette. "People do make mistakes." Grabbing several sandwiches from a pile inside the small refrigerator, he placed them on a plate, put it on his lap then poured a large mug of black coffee.

"Want some?" he asked.

"No, thanks."

Kurtzman turned and rolled back to his workstation.

Studying the wall screen map of the world, Price tilted her head thoughtfully. "So you're going through every heat anomaly on the entire planet?"

"Is there any other way?"

"Maybe there is," Price said thoughtfully, pulling a high-tech PDA from the pocket of her jeans.

"What are you talking about?" Kurtzman demanded suspiciously, placing a sandwich on Wethers's desk. Without comment, the professor started eating, never pausing in his work.

"Give me a minute," she said, thumbing the tiny keys to double-check a few cross-references.

"The NATO team just reported to HQ in Brussels," Delahunt reported without preamble. "They didn't find a thing at the Marnix Hotel. It was surgically clean, not even a bent paperclip in the wastebasket."

"Expected as much." Kurtzman sighed, finishing off his mug.

"There has also been a recent X-ship sighting in Central Park, New York," Delahunt added. "That's odd, why attack a park?"

"Must have been somebody there they didn't like. Or else it was a demonstration of power to rattle the city. Any fatalities?"

"None mentioned in the police report."

"Maybe we'll have better luck this time," Price said, lowering her PDA. "Run a thermal scan on longitude, ninety-one minutes, zero seconds, and latitude twenty-five minutes, thirty seconds."

Tossing the other wrapped sandwiches to Delahunt and Tokaido, the cyberwizard returned to his workstation and punched up the requested grid. The wall screen shifted views in a fast series of short jumps.

"That's northeastern India," Kurtzman said puzzled. Then he was interrupted by a buzzing alarm. A scroll appeared on the bottom of the screen and began listing missile launches from the area only hours before the first wave of X-ship attacks.

"Got them!" he cried. "Heads up, people, we've found the launch site!"

"Where were they?" Wethers demanded, blinking to focus on the wall screen. "Meghalaya? Never heard of the place."

"Barbara, how did you know?" Delahunt demanded, pulling off the VR helmet. Her makeup was badly smeared, eyes red, her normally bouncy curls flattened with sweat.

"I didn't. But I checked to see what was the most cloudy place on Earth," Price replied. "What better location to hide the work of building the X-ships from spy satellites? Seems I guessed right."

"Akira, keep after that hacker," Kurtzman commanded brusquely. "Hunt, do the hospitals and city morgues. Carmen, check the police, and I'll do the military!"

Nobody spoke, but the team bent to their tasks. Several minutes passed in tense silence.

"All right, Meghalaya is an extremely mountainous district of India known as the 'land of clouds,'" Wethers read off a submonitor. "It is the rainiest part of the world, and almost always under cloud cover."

"How almost?" Price asked.

"About ninety-five percent of the time."

"Sounds like England," Delahunt said, pulling up a topographical map of the hidden landscape and throwing it on the wall screen.

"Meghalaya makes London looked like the Sahara Desert," Wethers rejoined grimly.

Kurtzman adjusted the zoom on his console to a tight focus on the mountainous region. There was nothing to see except swirling rain clouds.

"No wonder the bastards chose that area," Delahunt commented, wiping out the damp inside of her helmet with a premoistened towelette. "Might as well be at the bottom of a salt mine in Poland."

"Any terrorist activity in the area?" Price asked, committing the topography to memory.

"Tell you in a minute…" Kurtzman said, speed-reading from a scrolling submonitor. "No, nothing important. The Ministry of Defence at New Delhi reports some political minor unrest—it is India, after all. But no real acts of terrorism. No bombings or beheadings."

"However the local hospital reports show an unusual increase in civilian deaths," Wethers added, his hands moving across the keyboard like a concert pianist, files opening and closing.

"From what causes?"

"Oh, the locals can be quite creative at times in coming up with explanations. There are wild tigers in the area, as well as abandoned British bridges that wouldn't hold a hamster these days. That's in addition to the colossal amount of sheer cliffs you can fall from and never be seen again." He paused to smile. "Plus, there are numerous rumors about yetis."

"Abominable snow monsters?" Price asked, arching an eyebrow in disbelief.

"As I said, merely rumors," the professor said.

"Tall tales to entice the tourists into paying for expensive guides is more like it," Delahunt snorted, donning the VR helmet once more. The gloves followed and she slipped back into the cybernetic world, only dimly aware of the conversation happening around her.

"What about the police?" Kurtzman snapped, narrowing his eyes to slits. A submonitor was flashing with military code.

"There are no unusual deaths according to their public records," Delahunt said, stroking the air, and the figures appeared on the side monitor. "But the Most Secret reports sent to New Delhi claim there have been over thirty deaths in the past year, with no recorded deaths before that for over twenty years."

"Are you sure?"

"One moment…yes, double-checked and confirmed."

That was more than suspicious. "Did the deaths occur in any specific location, or at numerous spots?"

"A few here and there, but mostly in the Rompa River Valley."

"Okay, overlay the NSA map of the three heat sources onto the topographical map," Price directed. It was done, and she smiled grimly. Whatever had caused the three big heat flashes came directly from the middle of the Rompa Valley. "Any chance of a direct visual? Maybe by switching to infrared or ultraviolet?"

"Won't think so, but I'll give it a try," Kurtzman said, flipping a few switches on his console. The downward view of the clouds changed colors, becoming thinner, more translucent, but the ground never came into focus.

"Wouldn't have helped much, anyway," Delahunt added, her hands fondling the empty air. "This is a mountainous region with a lot of rainfall, so I decided to check for any caves or caverns in the area." The left-side monitor on the wall came alive with a geology map of caves and underground caverns. "The Rompa Valley is surrounded by a warren of tunnels and caves. It'd take Phoenix Force a month to check them all."

"What's their location?"

"Just landing at the Barcelona International Airport."

More than a thousand miles away.

"Okay, anybody local we can use?" Price frowned, crossing her arms. "Does NATO have a peacekeeping force in the area?"

"No, but the India army has a Special Forces training facility only a hundred miles away," Kurtzman replied. "Probably for the exact same reason that the terrorists would like Meghalaya so much, the protective cloud cover."

"What kind of Special Forces are they? Recon, infiltration or search and rescue?"

"Antiterrorist."

"Excellent! How soon can they be there?"

"About an hour."

"Let's hope they're good enough," Price said grimly. Just then the screen flickered.

"What was that?" Price demanded.

"I was checking for any more heat sources, to see if they had more than three ships. Well, there was a fourth heat flash from the Rompa Valley in Meghalaya only a few minutes after the three X-ships launched. But a lot bigger than all of the rest combined, and it lasted for minutes, not just a couple of seconds."

"They ignited the fuel dump," Price stated as a fact.

"Spectrum analysis says high concentrations of oxygen, hydrogen and nitrogen…yes, it was their fuel dump. There was also a lot of weird stuff, too, iron and aluminum…thermite! They melted the place with thermite bombs!"

"Then it's going to have even less than the Marnix Hotel. At least they left that standing."

"Afraid so. There's not much remaining of the Rompa River Valley except a smoking hole and a lot of flattened trees."

Another dead end. Turning, Price walked to a nearby wall phone. She had to inform Brognola immediately about the mole. Interpol had several liaison offices in the United States, and one of them was smack in the middle of Georgetown, D.C. Impatiently, she waited for the signal to be scrambled and relayed off the comsat orbiting above the Farm. The traitor did not have to be overseas. He could be right next door to the White House, which might explain why the capital hadn't been hit yet by an X-ship. If Colonel Southerland was a real military officer, then he would not want to kill one of his own men unless it was absolutely necessary.

However, exposing the mole would make it necessary, and might result in an immediate attack on the White House, she realized, tightening her grip on the receiver. She'd have to do something about that. There came a click and Brognola answered.

"Hello, Hal? We have a new problem…." she started, but then a tone interrupted, announcing a recorded message.

"Hello, Barbara," Brognola said. "If you are hearing this message, then I have not been in direct contact with my office for over six hours. In this line of work, you know what that means, old friend." There was a short pause. "When the current situation is resolved, please activate protocol four. Contact the President directly, and he will make Aaron the new head of the Sensitive Operations Group. I have to keep this brief. You've always done a hell of a job, Barb, and it has been an honor working with you. Goodbye." The line disconnected.

CHAPTER TEN

Christmas Island, Australia

Grinning skeletons dotted the field of grass, their handguns and rifles reduced to only rusty lumps of metal. Most of the white skulls had a neat hole in the back of the head, but a few were intact, their bony hands still wrapped around their necks as the deadly gas flowed across them like a plague from ancient Egypt. But this one killed everything it reached; men, women, animals, even the worms in the dirt had died that terrible day of rage and betrayal.

Surrounding the unburied dead was a collection of ramshackle buildings, the splintery wood tilted slightly as if trying to compensate for the push of the mountain winds. A dirt road ran through the middle of the old mining town, the rain gullies overgrown with weeds, a young tree growing tall and strong from a particularly large pothole, although some might have referred to it as a blast crater.

On the edge of town, a sagging water tower bore the faint name of Anthill, an amusing moniker at the time when gold had been discovered in the hills a hundred years earlier, and greedy men rushed in like the ants to dig and slave, and work, and steal, and kill, for a share of the rich bounty. But in only a few weeks the gold was gone, the small vein completely exhausted. Days later, Anthill was deserted, the dozens of patched canvas tents vanished in the night, all of the ambitious projects of a paved road, a sewer line, a saloon and a bordello were abandoned and forgotten. Over the relentless years, the rain and weeds slowly reclaimed what had once been their domain, and now the place was barely discernible from the air, and virtually invisible on the ground. Even the bridges were gone.

Surrounded by a deep river chasm with impossibly steep sides, the only way to reach the isolated mountain plateau had been by a natural landbridge of stone, and later by a wooden box trestle designed to support trucks and ore wagons. But the wooden bridge had been burned down and the natural bridge blown to pieces with high explosives. Now there was no way in, or out, of Anthill except for the clear blue sky.

Sitting inside the old gold mine, Edmund McGregory was humming gleefully as his quick hands pulled the feathers off a dead parrot. Dressed in tattered rags, the toothless man cackled happily over the rich bounty of meat. Meat! He could barely believe it! After so many months of barely subsisting on nuts and berries, McGregory had at last discovered how to make a trap for the pretty birds. There was no fire, so he would have to consume it raw, but there was meat for dinner!

Ironically, Christmas Island was a holiday resort for many Aussies, and only a hundred miles away on the famous pebble beach were hotels, restaurants and an amusement park. Sometimes in the night, McGregory thought he could hear the people and smell the fried food. It drove him mad, and once in a fit of depression, he ran toward the cliff to throw himself off to end the loneliness. But that would have denied him the chance for revenge. Yes, that was more important than anything. He had to have revenge!

Bursting into a bawdy song about women and beer, the hermit felt himself start to smile, then abruptly stopped at the sound of muted thunder. Eh?

Rising painfully to his bare feet, McGregory shuffled to the mouth of the cave and blinked at the sky overhead. There were no storm clouds in sight. Could it…after all of these years…had…had they finally come back?

Casting the food aside, McGregory rushed out of the cave and into a clearing. Squinted upward, he muttered prayers under his breath, then shrieked in delight at the sight of fire in the sky rapidly descending. Hallelujah!

Rushing inside the cave, the hermit grabbed a rock off a ledge and smashed apart the band of dried clay sealing an old steamer trunk. Inside was a piece of slate with a small candle on top, the wick only slightly consumed. Many years ago McGregory had lit the candle and closed the lid so that the tiny flame would consume all of the oxygen inside the container and keep the contents fresh and rust free. *Please, God, please let it still be intact!*

Tossing away the candle and slate, the raggedy man gingerly took hold of a stiff sheet of canvas and eased it back to reveal his precious arsenal, an Uzi machine pistol, two full clips of ammunition, a bandolier of knives and two grenades. Rescued from the dead in the field, the weapons had been lovingly disassembled, oiled and re-assembled before going into storage to make sure they would be in perfect working condition for this moment.

Lifting the machine gun, McGregory slipped in a clip and worked the arming bolt, the metallic clicks and clacks music to his ears. Some time ago, he had been part of a convoy hired in Perth to deliver a couple of huge refrigerator containers to the deserted mining town. But as the convoy dropped off the cargo, that son of a bitch Southerland had blown both of the bridges while his bitch Zolly had raked his crew with a machine gun. Caught totally by surprise, the men died in droves, then some albino bastard with wire-rimmed glasses used an M-18 grenade launcher to fire a dozen projectiles across the chasm. The 30 mm rounds burst apart to flood the plateau with a yellow gas that made the few people still alive start coughing out blood, then chunks of their lungs, and then they went motionless forever. Recognizing mustard gas, McGregory had thrown himself into a trickling creek, and stayed submerged until his lungs were about to burst. Water neutralized mustard gas, but if McGregory raised his head too soon…

But the gods were with him that day, and the deadly gas had dissipated, leaving McGregory stranded on a remote mountain plateau with no way off, or to signal for help. The radio in the truck had proved to be a fake, only a front with nothing inside for him to try to repair. Just an empty box.

But the cargo remained, the two massive refrigerated tanks attached to a small solar-powered generator that kept cycling on to do…well, something to whatever was in the tanks. And McGregory knew that meant Southerland and his pet bitch would come back for their goods, whatever it was, and he would be ready, alive and armed to give them a special greeting from the bowels of hell. There was a place he had set up in the trees where a man would be stretched like rawhide between two trucks, utterly helpless to move and completely at the mercy of the madman who no longer laid claim to the emotion of mercy. There was only hatred in his heart, and a burning need for revenge. McGregory had spent many a long night planning what he would do to Southerland and that busty bitch who worked for him. The old man felt his face burn with lust. Oh yes, he had some very special plans for her!

Several times he had gone to the cold containers and started to open the outer housing to see what was inside, his fevered mind full of delusions of beer and frozen food! But every time, McGregory had forced himself to stop and leave the big tanks alone. If Southerland saw that they had been tampered with he might leave before McGregory would get his chance at vengeance. That could not be allowed to happen, so the man had stayed away from the pressurized tanks, and waited, patiently waited, slowly going insane as he prayed for a single minute of revenge.

A strong wind shook the tall grass, rattling the bones of the dead and sending the skulls rolling into the trees. The exhaust of the X-ship *La Orient* burned the ground clear just before the support legs touched soil. As the engines died, the ship sank several feet into the soft dirt before coming to a stop, then hydraulic rockers adjusted the pitch and yaw of the X-ship until it was resting on an even keel.

Skulking in the bushes outside the gold mine, McGregory closed his fist around the pistol-grip safety of the Uzi, feeling it disengage. As soon as Southerland stepped into view, all he would need to do was touch the trigger and—

The side hatch swung open and there stood a short man wearing a black cap and a grizzled expression. There was a weird-looking assault rifle hanging at his side, and he pulled out a small box to fiddle with the controls.

Caught in the act of aiming the machine pistol, McGregory paused in surprise. Who the fuck was this guy? Where was Southerland and Zolly?

"Good job, Gordon!" he shouted back into the vessel, checking the GPS device in his hand. "We're smack on target! The fuel tanks should be...yep, there they are!" Over by what used to be the Australian government assayer's office was a large canvas mound, the ends lashed down with nylon ropes.

Staying low in the bushes, McGregory balked at that. Fuel? The containers held fuel? Why would anybody go to such measures to hide gasoline? That made no bloody sense!

"Mighty warm place to hide liquid oxygen," John Tripp replied, stepping into view. The tall, lanky man also carried a similar weapon, his hair a wild afro from a bygone age.

For just a moment a wave of nausea flowed through his body. That had been happening more and more often lately. After so many years of detailed planning, it was probably just too much excitement from finally starting the noble mission. Yeah, sure, what else could it be?

"But then, I guess when you're talking about a thousand degrees below zero," Tripp went on, "it really doesn't matter what's the outside temperature. A balmy sixty is just as good as minus thirty."

"More importantly, after Siberia everybody will be looking for these fuel dumps," William Fawcett said, tucking away the GPS device. "And they'll be concentrating on cold places, not warm spots."

"Colonel Southerland is mighty smart," Tripp said with a grin, swinging around his assault rifle and working the arming bolt on the side. "Rule number one in any battle is stay where the bullets ain't." He finished the sentence softly, his eyes focused on the thick growth of plant life surrounding the ghost town.

"Trouble?" Fawcett asked, working the arming bolt on his own FN 2000.

Moving backward slightly so that his entire body was not in the open doorway, Tripp said nothing, his sharp eyes studying the rustling trees and bushes for a long time before he finally relented.

"Guess not, Chief," he said, lowering the weapon's fluted barrel. "Must have been just the wind." There was something faintly disturbing about the little ghost town, almost as if they were being watched. He had gotten the same feeling when doing merc work in Angola and the Sudan. Both times he had been right. Everything seemed fine, but down in his gut he could feel that something was wrong here.

"Maybe it was the wind, and maybe not," Fawcett muttered suspiciously. "Gordon, how much fly time do we have left?"

"Less than an hour, Captain!" somebody shouted from inside the huge ship.

"Not enough to reach Tasmania, which means we have to refuel here," Fawcett stated, opening the breech of the stubby grenade launcher and thumbing in a 30 mm shell. "Okay, Johnny-boy, let's check for snipers!"

Suddenly both men triggered their small rifles, the short barrels strobing flame as they sprayed the foliage with a hail of 5.56 mm rounds. Leaves exploded off branches, and tree bark went flying as the men concentrated on the greenery, reloaded and moved to the weeds, then hammered the old buildings, blowing out windows, shattering the slate roof tiles and throwing up a huge cloud of dust.

A flock of birds was startled into flight, but only got a few yards before being torn into bloody gobbets. A rabbit darted out from under a sagging porch and Fawcett caught it in the middle of a leap, the hardball ammo punching clean through the animal and throwing the bloody body yards away to land in a ditch.

Unexpectedly, the men then pumped 30 mm rounds into the old buildings, each one violently blowing apart until the small town was leveled. The only remaining structure was the wooden brace standing over the artesian well.

Staying as low as possible, McGregory marveled at the little weapons as they tore his world apart. Instead of arching out of a side ejector port like the Uzi, the spent brass tumbled down from the end of a tube set on top of the main barrel. That way the spray of shiny brass wouldn't betray a person's location if he was crouching in tall weeds. Smart. Very smart. He grinned evilly. But not smart enough.

Finally satisfied, the two men reloaded their weapons

and each climbed down with the other standing guard. Crossing the open ground, they stepped over a couple of skeletons and went straight for the tanks.

Pulling a knife, Tripp slashed the nylon rope and it jerked away as if under tension. With instincts honed in a hundred battles, Fawcett dived for the dirt as something shiny lashed out from behind the canvas. Tripp shook as it passed through him, then gave a low gurgle as his chest slid off his hips, the man sliced neatly in two.

As the body fell, Fawcett rolled over to a new position and fired a couple of short bursts into the bushes behind the fuel tanks where they couldn't reach while on the ship. The plants jerked and danced from the barrage and an Uzi answered back in staccato rage. Shit! Triggering a long burst from the FN F2000 just to the left of the noise, Fawcett unleashed a 30 mm grenade to the right. The distance was short, but just enough for the warhead to arm and a young sapling was blown in two, throwing out a halo of splinters.

Incredibly, a grenade sailed over the pressurized tanks to land at his feet. Hurtling himself away, Fawcett hit the ground hard only realizing a split second later that the grenade still had the arming lever attached. A trick! Whoever the assailant was he had no wish to use explosives near the tanks of deadly LOX-LOH.

Starting to rise, Fawcett spotted a string stretched between the bushes, the twine painted black to render it nearly invisible. Sending off a couple of short bursts as a distraction, Fawcett warily ducked under the tripwire wondering what in hell was going on here. This was not how Interpol, or NATO, operated. It was more like a fellow merc.

There was no sound, no faint rustle of leaves or snapping of twigs as a warning. But the next second, Fawcett froze motionless as something cold and sharp was pressed hard against his throat.

"Drop the gun," McGregory wheezed. "Then tell me how to find Southerland, and maybe I'll let you live."

"Who?"

"Southerland! Plus, that bitch Zolly!"

"Look, mate, I never heard of these people. We're a rescue mission from the RAAF!"

The Royal Australian Air Force?

"Shut up, motherfucker!"

"Okay, I give, I surrender," Fawcett said loud and clear, holding out both arms, but not releasing the assault rifle. "Don't kill me."

The knife pressed harder into his flesh, blood welling from the razor-sharp steel. "I said, don't move," McGregory snarled. "I've been waiting a long time for you people to come back. I ate bugs and worms to stay alive, and I did!" He cackled insanely. "I stayed alive and waited. Now you're gonna—" Without warning, the dirty man jerked just as there came the loud crack of breaking bones.

As the knife slipped away from his throat, Fawcett stepped clear, and spun to empty the FN F2000 into the reeking man moaning in the weeds.

Looking up, Fawcett nodded in thanks to Gordon, standing in the open hatch, an assault rifle held tightly in both hands.

"You okay, Captain?" Gordon asked over the com link, his face still tight against the telescopic sight on top of the assault rifle.

"Yeah, just scratched a little," Fawcett retorted. "Glad you were listening to the radio."

"SOP, Chief." The man in the ship grinned. "Sorry it took so long for me to switch from a live shell to a soft wad, but I couldn't risk blowing you up."

"And I appreciate that," Fawcett snorted, eyeing the solid projectile lying next to the raggedy man. Designed by the general to punch a hole through a gasoline storage tank when attacking a military base, and thus set the whole place on fire, the soft wad of lead had done a fine job of breaking the back of the hairy lunatic. Then something caught his attention.

Bending closer, Fawcett saw the tattoo of the infamous South African Internal Police on the arm of the dead man. Impulsively, the captain touched his own arm where there was a Dark Star tattoo. The colonel had been in charge of the Internal Police when the white government fell. Had Southerland left behind one of his own staff? A fellow South African? Was the fellow a race traitor, and this had been his punishment? Or had he become unnecessary and was cast aside like spent brass. The possibility of either such event disturbed him greatly, as if a natural law had been proved false, like actions did not equal reactions, or gravity made things float away. Did this mean that Southerland might abandon them?

Glancing at the ship, Fawcett saw Gordon coming over, his rifle sweeping the weeds for any further dangers. Wisely, the captain kicked some loose dirt over the arm to hide the tattoo. When he had a chance later on, this would require some serious thinking, but right now all that mattered was refueling the ship, and getting the bloody hell out of Anthill.

"How's Tripp?" Gordon asked, looking around. He hadn't seen what happened to the man, but there was fresh blood everywhere.

"Dead," Fawcett replied, shouldering the assault rifle. "Cut in half by a bobby trap."

"Fucking nutter," Gordon growled, then hawked to spit on the warm corpse.

"Yeah, well, maybe he had his reasons," Fawcett demurred vaguely, approaching the canvas mound. "Stay on my six, and watch for more traps! I think this bastard had awhile to prepare for our return."

"Return?" Gordon asked curiously, then stopped and slowly knelt into the weeds. A moment later he rose with a knife in his hand and a homemade bear trap apparently made of old car parts—door hinges and rocker-arm springs with needle-bearings for teeth. Christ, that would have taken his leg off!

It took the two of them more than an hour to complete a full swept of the area. Then they did it again, just to make sure.

"Bastard sure had a real hard-on for us," Gordon said with a sigh, tossing away the last trap, another bear trap this time armed with broken glass smeared with what smelled like human crap. Hadn't the Vietcong used something similar against the Americans? The bacteria in the feces made the wounds fester and you died of blood poisoning. That was a mighty bad way to go. Then he realized there were worse ways. Such as being trapped on a plateau with no way off for the rest of your life.

"Chief, if this guy simply wanted revenge," Gordon asked warily, "why not just vent the gas? That would have seriously fucked us over."

"Maybe he did," Fawcett said, pulling on a pair of insulated gloves. Underneath the old sheet of canvas, the terrorist found two huge insulated containers clearly marked, LOX and LOH.

Thumbing the meter to check the internal temperature and pressure, he turned the main release valve, then the outer valve. A loud stream of icy cold blasted from the nozzle to shake a nearby rosebush. Cutting off the stream, Fawcett walked over to the shiny plant and used his gloved hands to break off a blossom. The rosebud shattered in his fingers like antique glass and crumbled away into nothing. Crystallized in less than a heartbeat.

"Okay, we're good," Fawcett declared with a grateful sigh. "Let's run the lines!"

"What's the pressure?"

"Slightly less than…fifty percent."

"Fifty?" Gordon's face fell. "Oh, shit, we're screwed!"

"No, it's still more than *La Orient* can hold," Fawcett stated, rubbing his throat. "Almost enough for two ships."

"Really?" Gordon was astonished. "But these tanks must have been here for…"

"Ages," Fawcett replied proudly.

"Damn, the boss thinks of everything, doesn't he?"

"Bet your ass, he does. Now, get the hose."

"Yes, sir!" Gordon snapped, shouldering the rifle to retrieve the heavily insulated feeder hoses. Made of woven steel, they had an internal diameter of four inches, and would top off the X-ships in only a few minutes.

Dragging the massive hose across the hundred feet of weeds was a two-man job, and the terrorists were panting when they reached the X-ship. The access port was located at ground level to facilitate easy fueling, but the armored cover was inches deep in the soft loam, and the men had to dig it out with their hands before attaching the heavy coupling.

"No more jungle refuels, okay?" Gordon muttered, clumsily using a wrench to tighten a bolt.

"We go where we're ordered, Private," Captain Fawcett snapped, wiping sweat from his brow on a sleeve.

"Yeah, yeah, I know. But let a man gripe a little, okay?"

"Concentrate on the damn job," Fawcett retorted, then added, "Along with how rich we're going to be once the colonel is back in power. Wine, women and song."

Attaching the pipe took some brute strength, and working the wrenches caused him to rip an insulated glove. Going inside the ship, he tossed it away and donned a replacement pair. Liquid oxygen was tricky stuff and deadlier than radioactive cesium.

Throwing the pressure lever, Fawcett stayed at the hose as Gordon went inside to watch the gauges. When the storage tanks were dry, he shut off the valve and started the engine compressor to compensate the temperature and pressure differences. Minutes later, they were ready to launch.

Disconnecting the hose, Fawcett left it lying on the ground and climbed inside to dog the hatch tight. He was climbing the ladder to the control room when he heard the powerful whine of the preigniters, and was barely able to scramble into his seat before the X-ship blasted off.

"Why the rush?" Fawcett demanded.

"Don't like Australia," Gordon replied out of the corner of his mouth, both hands busy on the joysticks. "Never bloody did."

"I thought you came from there."

"That's why I hate it, see?"

Born and raised in white South Africa, Fawcett could understand the sentiment. Home was not a location, but a memory in your heart.

Startled by the unusual honesty, the captain gave a short laugh as he switched on the radio scrambler and waited for the mandatory seven clicks as the signal was relayed twice around the globe before reaching headquarters.

"Report," Colonel Southerland commanded. "What is your status?"

"Leaving Anthill, sir," Fawcett replied crisply. "But we had some trouble. Tripp is dead."

"An accident with the LOX?"

"No, sir," Fawcett said, and told him about the crazy hermit, leaving off the fact of the Internal Police tattoo.

"Somebody was still alive after all this time?" Southerland asked astonished. "My my, those Aussies really do have an overinflated sense of vengeance." It had to have been McGregory, he thought, the big bastard was tough. "Are you sure he is dead?"

"Absolutely, sir, I saw his heart stop beating."

"Excellent. Pity about Tripp, but good men die in a war. That is a rule older than time." He paused. "Any damage to the ship?"

"No, sir, *La Orient* is ready for our next mission."

"Good. Land at the New Mexico cache for a replacement crew member, then proceed directly to target Alpha Zulu nineteen."

"Alpha Zulu?" Fawcett asked startled, reaching for the code book. "Where on Earth is that?"

"Nowhere, Captain," Southerland replied with a humorless smile. "Nowhere at all…on Earth."

Barstow, California

THE STRIP CLUB WAS GONE.

"Things change in ten years," Blancanales said, lowering the GPS device and switching it off with a click. "This was the exact location of Chollo's Cat Club, but now…"

Steering the van onto an access ramp, Lyons could only grunt. A big sign rose a good hundred feet above the hilly landscape and consisted of merely the numbers 76.

The facility was gigantic, stretching for maybe a quarter mile into the blue-green of a soybean field that reached to the horizon. Near the entrance was a parking lot for big rigs, the painted lines resembling some sort of Aztec symbol, the spaces were so large. A dozen or so rigs were parked in neat rows, and one truck stood off in the corner far away from the others probably so that the driver could catch some desperately needed sleep. Not every truck had a sleeper cab, and black coffee would take a driver only so far before they had to get some shut-eye or risk going off the road.

A large restaurant was located in the middle of the truck stop, and past that a small parking lot for ordinary cars.

"A truck stop," Schwartz commented as the van jounced over a concrete strip that marked the border of the 76. "They built a truck stop where the strip club used to be located.

"Gone, all gone," Blancanales sighed, tucking the M-16/M-203 assault rifle into a ceiling compartment. "Zamir's base is buried under a thousand tons of concrete and asphalt." The ordinary-looking van was actually a rolling command base for the Stony Man team, with bulletproof windows, self-sealing tires, armored sides and an arsenal of military weapons hidden behind false paneling. There was even a small electronic lab in the back for

Schwarz in case he needed to jury-rig something special in a hurry.

"Well, maybe it's not gone," Lyons countered, steering the van past a group of men checking the chains on a Fleetwood flatbed. "Have Aaron check the construction blueprints. It's a lot easier to convert an existing building into something new than it is to build entirely from scratch." The battered old flatbed looked like it had helped haul supplies for Hannibal over the Alps, but it was packed high with heavy cargo containers, the steel boxes welded closed for security purposes. They could have contained German bearer bonds, DVD players, microelectronics or tanks of liquid oxygen. There was no way of knowing without cutting them open, and Lyons knew that was an impossible task. There were dozens of the big containers within sight, and thousands of them on the road across the continent at any moment. Songs and movies had romanticized trains, but most of the goods sold in the United States were moved by truck. Diesel fuel was the lifeblood of the nation.

"Cheaper, too," Schwarz agreed, swinging up his U.S. Army laptop and starting to type. "Although, it all depends on what you want to end up with. Can't turn a cathouse into a cathedral."

"Although, that sure would make Sundays a lot more interesting." Blancanales chuckled, mentally comparing the approaching building with a picture of the former establishment that he had downloaded from the Internet. "Let's hope the new owners were happy with turning a strip club into a restaurant."

To his mind's eye, the two buildings looked about the same size, but it was hard to tell for sure. The cinder-block strip club had been covered with flashing neon signs and huge posters of scantily clad dancers, while the new place was made of brick and covered with windows. A friendly island resting in the middle of a sea of pavement, the restaurant had several sections, one of which was closed off by Plexiglas walls and reserved purely for truck drivers, no tourists and their screaming kids allowed. The food served at truck stops was plain and filling, fuel for the drivers.

Aside from food, there were also hot showers available to the truckers, for a small fee, of course, and a special store where they could buy a wide assortment of items: machine parts, sunglasses, music CDs, condoms, folding knives and just about anything else needed to keep them on the move.

Driving past a group of buxom young women in bikini tops and tight denim cutoffs, Lyons checked the draw on his .357 Colt Python. "I heard a country song once," he said, steering the van away from the other cars and into a deserted section of the parking lot. "Can't recall the exact words, but it said that the goods of the world were not moved by ships, planes, or even trucks...but by Rolaids, No-Doz, Visine and Preparation H."

"Amen to that," Schwarz said. "I did a stint as a suicide jockey once in my teens delivering compressed air cylinders to medical supply houses. I did some TSD runs for a courier, too...that's time-speed-distance—"

"I know what TSD is, Gadgets. The sooner you arrive, the money you make as a bonus."

The man shrugged. "Most folks don't. One winter I was cutting through Allentown and read on the CB where a semi had slipped on ice and was lying sideways across the bridge just ahead of me."

"Sideways? You mean, hanging off the sides?"

"Yep, the cab was dangling down and the rear end was over nothing. The police had no idea how to clear the wreck off the bridge, and traffic was backing up for miles. On that day, I learned why all of the other drivers had insisted I buy a CB and learn to listen to it constantly. I slammed on the brakes, stopped on the berm, then drove backward going up a down ramp to cut across the median, and took side streets until I reached the next bridge. Made my time that day, and earned a lot of thanks from the bigwigs for getting the job done."

"How much of that is true?" Lyons asked, glancing sideways as he maneuvered the van off by itself well away from the other cars. In case of trouble, he wanted as much combat room as possible between them and the tourists.

"All of it," Schwarz said, then smiled.

Just then, the laptop gave a low beep.

"Success," Schwarz reported, reading the screen. "They razed the strip club to the ground, but kept the basement and foundation."

"Now we're getting somewhere," Blancanales said, tucking some tools into a nylon bag and zipping it shut.

"Okay, this is it," Lyons directed, braking to a halt and turning off the engine. "Remember that we're going to be ass deep in civvies, and need to keep a low profile."

"You realize the entire building could be rigged to blow," Schwarz said calmly, turning up his collar to hide the throat mike. A flesh-colored wire attached the device to an earbud, the transponder clipped to the embossed leather belt under his loose shirt. "Remember what just happened in India."

"Sure, but we have you along to protect us," Blancanales said with a smile, climbing from the van and hefting the nylon, python-style bag over a shoulder.

"Okay, as long as we have a plan," Schwarz muttered, closing the door and switching on the anti-intruder systems. Anybody attempting to get inside the van would receive a stunning 50,000 volts through the door handle. If he or she somehow managed to get inside, the reward would be a flood of knock-out gas, plus a deadly charge of 250,000 volts in the steering wheel

Ambling toward the restaurant, the men acted casual and took their time, but watched carefully for any hidden sentries mingling with the crowd of laughing tourists. For this soft probe, they were wearing khaki shirts, denim vests, old blue jeans and work boots. Everything was appropriately clean, but stained and worn. Lyons had a chain going from his belt to his hip pocket as if attached to a wallet, Blancanales was carrying a ring of keys and Schwarz positioned a bag of chewing tobacco in his shirt pocket. But each man also carried a bag of some sort that seemed exceptionally heavy.

Rap music blared from a couple of civilian cars, battling it out for supremacy with the classic rock and old-style C&W coming from a score of Mack trucks. At the diesel pumps, an angry driver in a BMW sedan realized that he had gone to the wrong location and started loudly cursing, a passing SUV with Georgia plates played Dixie on its horn, and the air brakes of a GMC semi-tractor stridently hissed. Everywhere, kids were running, laughing and yelling, while harried parents tried to herd them back into the cars with poor results.

"Not sure that we needed to bring the silencers," Lyons

muttered into his throat mike as the team reached the sidewalk skirting the restaurant.

"Carl, that was a joke!" Blancanales noted in mock surprise. "Are you feeling okay, buddy? Do you need to sit down or anything?"

"Shut the fuck up."

"Okay, he's back to normal." Schwarz chuckled, following his nose to the rear of the establishment.

Hidden from sight behind a decorative stone wall were four huge garbage bins, three of them closed, the fourth open and buzzing with flies. There were a couple of doors nearby, one of them locked tight and the other radiating noise and cooking smells. Obviously, that one was the kitchen.

Going to the second door, Lyons and Blancanales stood guard while Schwarz tricked the lock with a keywire gun, shooting the mechanism full of stiff wire. As the tumblers engaged with soft clicks, he turned the device and the door easily unlocked.

Quickly slipping into the darkness, Blancanales played a flashlight around while Lyons locked the door and Schwarz tucked away his locksmith tools. The walls were cinder block boasting a fresh coat of green paint and the floor was old concrete. There was a time clock on the wall next to a rack of cards, and at the end of the corridor was a door marked Store Room. There was also a second door with no sign.

Checking it for traps, Schwarz declared that door clear, and used the keywire gun again to trick the lock. Inside was a short flight of bare concrete stairs that led to a musty cellar smelling of cabbages.

As the team proceeded down, they noticed several

posters adorning the stucco-covered walls that had to have been salvaged from the old strip club. The semi-naked women were always eagerly smiling, their expressions forced.

The basement was full of metal shelving stacked with canned goods of every description, along with spare table-cloths, cutlery, trays, water pitchers and similar restaurant effluvia. Ignoring all of it, the team did a fast sweep of the place until finding the furnace. In the darkness behind it was an old iron door streaked with rust and without a handle or visible hinges.

After carefully chipping away the stucco, the team revealed the old brick wall. Soon the firebrick was discovered, the dark exterior easily discernible among the common house bricks.

Donning on a pair of gloves, Lyons pressed it and heard a dull thud from somewhere. Slipping behind the furnace, he saw that the iron door was ajar, a dull yellow light coming from the other side.

"So far, so good," he subvocalized, drawing his Colt Python and advancing slowly.

"Zamir certainly had enough safeguards to dissuade any casual exploration," Schwarz muttered, putting on a pair of night-vision goggles and pressing a button to power them up. The blackness was gradually replaced with a soft green illumination of Starlight, minimum light amplification.

Doing the same thing, Blancanales paused. "Did you say 'dissuade'?"

"Hey, I read a book once."

"So it would seem."

Setting his own goggles for infrared, Lyons immediately spotted the pressure plate on the floor. It was a cool blue set among the warm crimson of the concrete. Avoiding the trap, he kept a sharp watch for any trip wires, but the hallway was clear of obstructions all the way to another door of plain wood.

"Yeah, right," Lyons subvocalized, gesturing forward with his Colt.

Sweeping ahead with an EM scanner, Schwarz went to the door and ascertained it was clear before dropping to a knee. Swinging around the Army laptop, the man unraveled a slim fiber-optic cable. Booting the computer, he slid the cable under the door jamb. A black-and-white view of the next room appeared on the computer screen. Twisting the cable using a fingertip mousepad, Schwarz switched the view through several different spectrums until finally getting a clear picture. Angling the cable like a snake to try to see into the far corners and underneath the worktables, Schwarz also recorded everything for later analysis.

"That should do it," he said, reeling in the cable and coiling it around a fist. "Interesting, mighty interesting."

"What'd you find?" Lyons asked tersely.

"Well, as you both have already guessed, the whole damn place is a trap," Schwarz said, tucking away the cable. "The place looks legit—there are worktables filled with electronics, and schematics on the wall next to maps of police stations and military bases." Closing the laptop, he slipped it back into the carrying bag. "There is also an AutoSentry hidden in each corner, nice and cozy behind a bunch of sandbags, and more freaking laser beams crisscrossing through the air than a remake of *Star Wars*." Ruefully, he gave a half smile. "And the whole thing is hardwired to a vidcam so that the bastards can watch us get burned and learn who is coming after them, but at a nice safe distance."

"A vidcam," Ironman repeated. "Is it live?"

"Sure, and it seems to be connected to a cellular transmitter."

"Now that's weird," Blancanales said pensively. "They didn't have that sort of tech when Zamir went into jail. Do you suppose…" His voice trailed away, then came back strong. "Them! This isn't a trap set by Zamir, but the *Skywalkers!*"

"Seems like they're still ahead of us," Lyons growled, feeling a killing rage build inside. With a sheer act of will, he forced down the impulse. "They knew that somebody would connect the dots and question Zamir, then come here to check on the microwave beamers."

"So they left a little gift for us," Schwarz finished, swinging the laptop behind his back. "That was stupid, I can alert Aaron and the gang to watch for a radio burst from the vidcam and they can easily track the transmission directly back to the Skywalker's base."

"If they have a main base," Lyons said. "This whole operation might be mobile."

"Damn, I hadn't considered that," Schwarz admitted sheepishly. "Well, only one way to find out. We go in."

"And stay alive long enough for Aaron and the others to get a trace," Blancanales stated grimly, unscrewing the sound suppressor from the barrel of his Colt .380 pistol before tucking them both away.

Holstering his own Beretta, Schwarz shrugged. "Unfortunately, yes. And we have to give them a real show, make the bastards think we're fighting for our lives."

"That shouldn't be too difficult. They have enough concentrated firepower in there to turn King Kong into hamburger," Blancanales said, pulling a bulky M-16/M-203 assault rifle combo from his kit bag. "There are four AutoSentries?"

"Yep."

"Any chance of a master control?"

"Nope, they're all independents," Schwarz replied, removing a FN F2000 assault rifle from his kit bag. Normally the man would have preferred an M-16, but there was only so much that he could carry on a soft probe before starting to clink.

"Four of them. Swell," Blancanales drawled, working the arming bolt on the assault rifle.

His partner did the same to the bullpup. "You got that right."

"Don't like this," Lyons declared, looking up as he holstered the Colt. "There are too many people in the restaurant for this sort of balls-to-the-wall tactic. We need some combat room."

"No problem," Blancanales said, moving back into the basement, only to return a few seconds later. "Okay, everybody should be running for their lives right about now. I hit the fire alarm, then tossed a couple of harmless smoke grenades into a heating duct. We can't hear the ruckus all the way down here, but trust me, that restaurant will be clear of noncombatants in about two minutes flat."

"Then we go in five," Lyons said, reaching into the nylon bag, withdrawing the Atchisson and flicking off the safety.

The men waited patiently, and on the mark, they

opened fire. The wooded door exploded into smoke and splinters from the maelstrom of outgoing lead, the three weapons sounding like three hundred in the enclosed area. Instantly the AutoSentries responded from inside the room, the four weapons burping off dozens of .22-caliber bullets that raked the open doorway and ricocheted off the floor and walls, zinging about in every direction.

Shouting pointless orders to each other in case the unseen enemy was listening, Able Team was hit several times as it poured gunfire into the workshop, but their NATO body armor took the brunt of the attack easily. As Lyons inserted a fresh drum of 12-gauge shells into the Atchisson, Blancanales and Schwarz rolled smoke grenades into the room. As the thick smoke clouded the air, there was a momentary pause as the minicomputers inside the AutoSentries switched from visual targeting to proximity sensors. But that was more than enough for Able Team to dive inside the room and take cover behind a big wooden desk.

Tracking the motions, the AutoSentries retaliated with unbridled fury, but oddly there was no sound of the .22-caliber rounds hitting the stout mahogany.

Strange, how could they have missed at this range? Lyons wondered.

"Surrender, Zamir!" he shouted, putting a burst into the light fixtures hanging from the ceiling. "We have the place surrounded!" As the chain broke on the far end, the fluorescent lights swung down and the tubes crashed into an AutoSentry. The tripod of the machine didn't fall over, but there was a crackling electrical explosion and the weapon stopped shooting.

One down, three to go.

"There's no escape!" Blancanales shouted, expertly riding the chattering M-16/M-203 into a tight pattern along the wall. Dozens of books and technical journals jumped off the shelves, shredded paper flying everywhere like a snowstorm in a library.

Swiveling to the side to focus on the new movement, the AutoSentry burped a short burst, the muzzle-flashes strobing in the dark corner. In response, Blancanales stroked the grenade launcher. The 40 mm antipersonnel bomb vomited a hellstorm of fléchettes, and the vulnerable rear of the AutoSentry was blown wide open, wires and circuit boards falling into view like robotic intestines. Suddenly the computerized weapon began to swivel, firing randomly. Slapping in a fresh clip of 5.56 mm hardball ammo, Blancanales waited until it was facing away once more, then gave it a long burst right in the rear. Thrown off balance, the AutoSentry toppled over with a crash behind the protective sandbags, pointlessly firing a few more times before going silent.

The remaining two AutoSentries started to fire nonstop, the spent brass flying away in glittering arches.

Halfway there, Schwarz thought. Draining the clip of his rifle, he aimed at a big metal cabinet, the 5.56 mm rounds hammering it across the floor until it was in position. Dashing out from behind the desk, the Able Team warrior charged, cutting loose with a barrage at the metal beams supporting the concrete ceiling. The hail of flattened rounds spun down to punch neat holes in the plastic water cooler. The murky fluid gushed out in arching streams to splash across the wall above the AutoSentry, then straight across the machine as the pressure dwindled away. The weapon stopped shooting, but nothing else seemed to happen.

Cursing, Schwarz pulled his Beretta and fired the handgun around one side of the file cabinet, while he triggered the FN F2000 from the opposite side. The angle was bad, but he hit the machine several times, shaking it almost hard enough to topple over, but it still did nothing. Realizing the truth, Schwarz raced around the file cabinet and trained his assault rifle on the last AutoSentry as he dived over the low sandbag wall. Kicking out a boot, the man sent the impotent weapon hurtling into the wall. The sensor array audibly cracked against the brick, and the ammo box burst open to disgorge a long belt of stubby brass cartridges.

Concentrating their firepower on the remaining machine, Able Team kept hammering away from behind the furniture, constantly moving to new positions, until the armored cowling of the sentry was so badly dented it came free. It was still airborne when the men tore the inner workings into sparking trash, the gun giving one last defiant shot before going still.

"Okay, seal this room, I want full forensics!" Lyons shouted through cupped hands, trying to make his voice sound different.

"Oh my God," Blancanales whispered, bending to pick something up from the litter of spent brass covering the floor. "Look at this!"

Alerted by the tone in the man's voice, his partners rushed over. Lying in the palm of his hand was a tiny wad of burned cardboard.

"Oh shit!" Schwarz said, quickly looking around. He had been concentrating on the AutoSentries, but now he could see that the floor was covered with the little objects, dozens—no, hundreds of them everywhere.

"Blanks," Lyons said in a controlled tone. "The AutoSentries were firing blanks? But I was hit twice when we blew the door."

"Me, too," Schwarz said. "And then never again. The first dozen or so rounds must have been live to make the guns seem loaded. After that, the blanks would keep us busy while…" The reason hit the man like a punch from a friend. There was only one conceivable reason for the guns to be loaded with blanks, to hold the team in place, and to keep them busy while the Farm traced the signal from the vidcam. Correction—while the *Skywalkers* traced the signal from the Farm!

Instantly, Schwarz whipped out a jamming device to block the airwaves of any unfriendly transmissions, but Lyons took more direct action by firing his Colt Python from the hip, the heavy Magnum round shattering the vidcam into a million pieces.

"Rock House, this is Senator!" Blancanales said urgently into his throat mike. "Abort the trace! Repeat, abort the trace! Suspects were waiting for us to signal you!"

There was no response, so the man rushed from the workshop and boosted the power to his belt transponder to maximum. "Rock House, respond! They're tracing your signal! Repeat, we've been tricked! X-ships are on the way! Do you copy?"

The only response was the dead crackle of background static.

CHAPTER ELEVEN

Prime Base, Khulukrudu

A cold and blustery wind blew over the barren rocks of the frozen shoreline. A large squawking tribe of King penguins stood about flapping their useless wings and waiting for the tide to turn so that they could go out hunting for more fish. In the distance, whales broke the icy wave caps, shooting water plumes for a hundred feet, before diving back down into the stygian depth of the bitterly cold sea.

The natural harbor was too shallow to handle large ships, so only a handful of speedboats and catamarans were tied to the wooden dock. As he sat on the end, his feet dangling, a small boy tossed table scraps to the seagulls in the air, and what they missed fell into the turgid water, drawing frenzied birds to its surface.

There was only one short street in what was generously called the town, with a neat row of prefabricated houses and a few tents. There were no blaring car horns, sputtering gasoline engines, beeping cell phones, chatting, cursing, laughing, or any of the usual strident cacophony of what humanity referred to as civilization. There were no television antennas or satellite dishes, no traffic lights or even fire hydrants. A blanket of cold lay over the land, thick and inhospitable. Aside from the wind, and the seagulls, it was almost as if the world had forgotten the remote island.

Sitting in the control room of the underground bunker, Colonel Zane Southerland worked the joystick to swivel the video camera in a full circle to scan the farmlands, graveyard, lighthouse and stone quarry. Situated on top of Minto Hill, the highest point of land, he had a clear view of everything, and it wasn't long before he was satisfied that there were no intruders on the diminutive land mass.

What was that old joke again? This wasn't the edge of the world, the colonel thought, turning off the video camera, but you could see it from here.

Even so, purely as a precaution, he had located the master computers as far away from Khulukrudu as possible. That way, in case of trouble, he would have enough time to escape in his private X-ship, the hand-built prototype, *Bellaraphon*. It was less than a hundred yards away hidden inside an old church. There were numerous ways out of the underground bunker, each of them lined with traps, and every one ending in the basement of the Anglican church. If trouble came, and he needed to escape, a string of Claymore mines edged the roof to blow it out of the way, then the ship could leave, carrying him at once to anywhere in the world. Just him, no passengers, although he had not informed his staff about that small detail. Failure was unthinkable. But a wise man always planned for failure and how to turn it around into success again.

Going to a small refrigerator, Southerland got a bottle of Raven stout. Thumbing off the cap, he took a long pull. So far everything was going according to plan, the man noted with pride, looking at a computer-generated map of the planet relayed by Eric O'Hara at Base Zero. Fear of the X-ships was spreading rapidly, the world was tumbling into total chaos, the superpowers were arming for doomsday and small wars were breaking out on every continent. Soon, his own forces would be able to attack Johannesburg and free his homeland from the black rule, and the hated UN wouldn't even notice what was happening until it was long over, he thought. His father had always said that Hitler had a good idea, just the wrong target. There was nothing wrong with the Jews, they made fine scientists, but the blacks had to go. All of them. End of discussion. And the white race reclaiming control of South Africa was step one in the master plan to purify the world of their odious presence.

Suddenly from outside the door came the sound of marching, and the colonel glanced at his wristwatch to check the time. The hourly patrol was precisely on schedule. Most satisfactory. Discipline assured victory!

As the colonel retrieved a second beer, he heard a soft, feminine singing, closely followed by the rush of water. Sipping the cold stout, Southerland tried not to think about his XO naked and soapy in the shower.

She was probably still trying to get warm after their sojourn to Siberia, the man thought. However, the image of her nude form would not leave his mind. More than once the lieutenant had hinted that if he was interested, she was willing to make their professional relationship much more personal. Born and raised a soldier, Southerland disliked mixing business with pleasure, especially among the ranks. It was bad for discipline. On the other hand, Zolly was a fellow officer, so…

A beep sounded from the control board.

Slowly turning, Southerland glared at the blinking red light that signified an incoming message. He strode forward and took a seat at the board, setting the bottle of beer on a small rectangle of corkboard positioned near the keyboard for just such a reason. Flipping a switch positioned under the light, the chief terrorist watched as the center monitor scrolled with encryption, then cleared into a picture of Eric O'Hara wearing a lumpy green jumpsuit.

"Report," the colonel ordered, his throat tight with thwarted lust.

"The trap in Barstow has been tripped," O'Hara reported crisply, the foggy words visible in the air for a few seconds. "The signal originated from somewhere above Virginia." In the background, the two supercomputers audibly hummed, a digital thermometer reading far below zero.

Suddenly all carnal thoughts of his XO were gone. "Was it from the FBI at Quantico?" Southerland demanded.

"Possibly the CIA at Langley. However, there are so many telecom and milsats in orbit, I can't do a precise trace without a second broadcast." O'Hara frowned. "They must have a hacker who is almost as good as me."

"I did not think that was possible," the colonel said honestly. "But very well, go to Plan B, and activate the contingency plan. Remove this threat immediately."

"Yes, sir. Should I have our—just a moment." There was a pause.

"Are you in trouble?" Southerland demanded, a hand going to a keypad set into the surface of his control board.

"Good news!" the hacker exclaimed with a grin. "I'll have that second transmission in just a few minutes!"

Slowly, the colonel withdrew his hand. "Excellent. When you have a confirmed lock, send in all three X-ships and burn the target out of existence."

"Yes, sir! Hail the motherland!" There was a burst of artificial hash, then a crackle of static and the screen went blank.

"Yes, indeed," Southerland muttered, rising once more to head for the shower. "All hail the motherland."

Barcelona, Spain

DRIVING ALONG THE CURVED roadway, T. J. Hawkins was deep in thought, pondering the problem of the X-ships. How could Phoenix Force fight back? Nothing in the conventional arsenal looked like it would do the job, which meant the men had to invent something special for this mission. Or else the bastards would win, the man noted dourly.

A steeply inclined cliff rose on the right for about fifty feet, the face covered in brick as additional support from the summer rains. On the left was a wooden safety rail to help steer drivers back onto the roadway. Past the railing, Hawkins could see the rolling waves breaking on the smooth white beach. Spain wasn't quite as nice as Texas—nothing was, really—but it certainly was beautiful this time of year.

In the rear of the convertible, the rest of the team was packing away weapons for the long drive to a private airfield where Jack Grimaldi was waiting for them in a C-130 Hercules. One of the largest planes in the world, it was fully capable of flying for tremendous distances before refueling.

Unfortunately, Hawkins wasn't sure what their next

target should be. Oh, they had some names, Dark Star and Eric O'Hara, but now they had to find them to make sure those actually were the people behind the attacks and not just dupes used by the real terrorists to hide their identities. It was a brutal fact that a lot of terrorists were smart.

"This is it," Rafael Encizo said, checking a GPS. "Right…now."

Promptly slowing, Hawkins crawled the convertible along the roadway until there was a disturbance in the laurel bushes edging the berm. Instantly, David threw open the side door and Gary Manning charged into view, still clutching his Barrett .50 sniper rifle. The man was wearing a Hawaiian shirt and short pants to try to look like a tourist, the effect spoiled by the military rifle and the bandolier of cartridges slung across his chest.

"Glad you could make it," James said as the man took a seat next to him. "Did you see—"

"Yeah, I saw," Manning confirmed, working the bolt on his Barrett .50-caliber rifle to clear the breech. Taking the huge cigar-size round, he slipped it into a loop on the bandolier designed specifically for the titanic rounds. "I even got off a few shots at the X-ship, but by then it was leaving the beach and at the extreme end of my range. Hell, I was already a mile away from the beach in the first place!"

"Think you did any damage?" asked McCarter over a shoulder.

"Might have scratched the paint," the big man muttered, shrugging off the leather strap of live rounds and folding it under the seat along with several other pieces of military ordnance. Next, he started breaking down the Barrett, each piece going into a cushioned depression inside an ordinary suitcase.

Just then a warm breeze blew over the men, and they scowled, scrambling for their handguns. That hadn't come from the ocean, but straight ahead.

"Son of a bitch!" Hawkins snarled, taking a curve. An X-ship came into view.

Hovering only yards off the pavement, the huge machine was moving swiftly along the roadway, leaving behind a long strip of partially melted asphalt, dotted with countless small fires. Instantly, the Stony Man commandos realized they were trapped, caught between the cliff and the ocean without even enough room to try to turn and run for it. Easy prey for the X-ship. And even if they somehow got past the big machine, the convertible would become mired in the sticky tar, stuck like flies on glue paper, a sitting target for the next pass, which would burn them out of existence.

"Brace yourselves!" Hawkins bellowed, stomping on the gas pedal and twisting the steering wheel hard to the left.

The Cadillac's powerful motor roared in a surge of power, and a split second later the vehicle's chrome grille crashed into the wooden guard rail with the sound of splintering wood. Soaring off the cliff, the convertible arced gently toward the shimmering blue sea below, and the grim Stony Man commandos forced themselves to rise in spite of the crushing acceleration and dive over the sides, spreading their arms to desperately angle away from the jagged black rocks. A single heartbeat later, the car slammed into the ocean with a tremendous splash.

One by one, the men of Phoenix Force hit the waves, knifing smoothly into the water. Foamy chaos filled their world for a few moments while the conflicting forces achieved balance, then they focused on the bubbles leaving their mouths to mark the direction of the surface, tracked the location of the sinking Cadillac, and quickly started swimming away for deep water.

A reddish light came from above, and the water grew noticeably warmer. They could hear a low growl, like some prehistoric beast on the hunt, and instinctively knew it was the sound of the X-ship moving above the surface on a definitive search and destroy.

McCarter glanced backward to see an ocean of roiling flame cover the sea of water, impact waves from the volcanic exhaust churning the sandy seabed, sending blue shell crabs scuttling away, whole schools of fish darting off like terrified rainbows.

Thankful about divesting themselves of the heavier armament, the men hugged the bottom of the sea and took off in different directions. Unlike most battle situations, there was no safety in numbers this time. Each man would have to find his own safe haven, and then somehow strike back at the *Skywalkers* in an effort to help the others stay alive.

HIS HEART POUNDING, AND LUNGS LABORING, Hawkins was startled to feel something touch his foot. Spinning fast with a drawn knife, he relaxed at the sight of a copse of kelp waving gently in the tide. Visibility was poor from the spreading cloud of sand, but he recalled that kelp liked to anchor itself to rocks. Heading that way, he found a crumbling escarpment and swam around to climb the rough sides, cutting his fingers on the sharp coral and barnacles dotting the stone.

The surface overhead was blue, so Hawkins pushed his

face out of the water and gulped down fresh air to super-charge his aching lungs, then spun and swam out to sea. Even from the brief exposure, his ears were ringing from the deafening noise of the thundering exhaust. Obviously, the escarpment was too close to the X-ship. Same thing if he tried for the beach. Hawkins would be easy pickings for the *Skywalker*. The only possible chance of survival lay in staying far away from that X-ships and the lethal jet engines. One slip in this aquatic game of hide-and-seek, and it would be all over for the man.

PUSHING HIMSELF TO THE ABSOLUTE limits of endurance, James reached an outcropping of coral hundreds of yards offshore. Warily climbing to the top, he drank in the salt air while staying almost entirely submerged. The ex-Navy SEAL hadn't done anything like this impromptu dive since basic training on Paris Island, and was glad the old skills were still sharp when most needed. Unfortunately, somewhere along the way, he had acquired a nasty slash along the left leg, and blood was misting the water. Not enough to signify a damaged artery, but quite sufficient to attract any predatory fish in the area.

Yeah, that's all he needed, James noted dourly, to be hunted by sharks under the water while the flying blast furnace tried to barbecue his head!

Forcing himself to start to breath normally, James pulled himself slightly higher and peeked over the rough coral. A hundred yards away, the X-ship was moving over the surface of the water in an ever-widening spiral, churning the sea to a boil in its fiery wake.

The sight gladdened the man. All of the previous attacks had been fierce, but brief, the X-ships used fuel at a phenomenal rate, and could only chase them for so long before endangering the crew. If there was a crew, he thought.

Shaking the water droplets from his face, James felt his heart surge with adrenaline when a hatch on the side of the machine opened and a man stepped into view. Caucasian, average height, brownish hair, no visible scars or tattoos, tan jumpsuit and sneakers. Well, well, at last, the enemy had a face, he observed.

Holding on to a strap, the man leaned out of the machine and started firing bursts from a FN F2000 into the water outside the area directly underneath the machine. Then the grenade launcher spoke, and a shell streaked away to impact on an escarpment, the blast throwing rock fragments and pieces of kelp sky high.

"Bad move, asshole," James whispered, reaching around to pull his 9 mm Beretta from the holster at the small of his back. He knew the range was impossible for the handgun, but he had to try. The opportunity was too good.

Shaking the sea water from the barrel, the man rested the checkered grip on top of the coral, trying to move his body to the rhythm of the waves…then fired a fast three times.

Sparks flew from the metal hull alongside the hatch, then the terrorist jerked back in a spray of blood from a shattered knee. The assault rifle fell away as the enemy dropped to the deck, fumbling for the safety strap. Another man stepped into view and reached for his comrade, and James emptied his gun at them, hoping for a lucky strike. The second man staggered backward, a rip on his jumpsuit revealing some kind of body armor underneath.

But the wounded man had taken a bullet in the face. Mouthing a scream, the man lost his grip on the strap and rolled out of the hatch. The second man reached for him, then decided it was hopeless and retreated to slam the hatch shut.

The body was still falling when the X-ship engines surged with power and it lanced straight up into the sky, disappearing faster than the Stony Man commando would have believed possible.

No wonder they couldn't track these guys, James realized, slipping in his only spare clip. It was like trying to shoot down an arrow by throwing rocks!

Anxiously, James waited a minute to make sure the thing wasn't going to come back, then holstered his piece and started swimming toward the area of water the body had gone into. A corpse can speak volumes after an autopsy.

Reaching what he thought was the right zone, James took a deep breath to dive, when Hawkins and Encizo rose into view, a limp form held between them. The men shared smiles at the small victory, then took off for the shore.

Dragging the corpse onto the beach, Encizo laid the man out, and James stood guard while Hawkins went through his clothing in case there was anything in the pockets that might be destroyed by long exposure to seawater. But there were only the usual items: cigarettes, butane lighter, space ammunition clips, insulated gloves and sunglasses. Nothing more. Even the blood was gone, washed clean by the warm Atlantic Ocean.

Wading onto the sand, McCarter and Manning looked around with their guns in hand, checking to see if anybody was watching them. Thankfully there was nobody in sight. No police cars wailed around the curves, no ambulances howled to the rescue, or news helicopters appeared above the trees. But then, this section of the coast had been specifically chosen by Emile San Saun for its isolation, which served them both well today.

Satisfied, McCarter holstered his Browning Hi-Power, but Manning kept his Desert Eagle at the ready, watching the sky for any suspicious movements. The X-ships hit like lightning, and by the time a man reacted to their presence, they were already burning you into the ground. The only way to stay alive was to out think the men operating the machine, to outmaneuver the pilot. It would take a volley of field artillery to stop one of the damn things in flight.

Pulling out his cell phone, McCarter shook off some water and flipped the lid. Designed by "Gadgets" Schwarz, the communications device could take a lot more punishment than an ordinary phone, and was waterproof. If the seal held. Tentatively tapping in a long sequence, McCarter was rewarded by a fast series of clicks, but then only silence.

"Stone House, this is Firebird," McCarter said tersely. "We have a passenger and need immediate evac." He waited, but there was no response. "Stone House, do you read?"

Feeling a sense of dread, McCarter closed the connection and tried a second number.

"Sky King, here," a familiar voice replied. "Is that you, Firebird?"

"Confirm," McCarter replied. "Just be warned, Sky King, there's an X-ship in the area, and it's hot to trot."

"Well, so am I," Jack Grimaldi replied, the voice of the chief pilot for Stony Man radiating confidence. "I have the 40 mm Bofors primed and ready for action. If they want to chew on some lovely depleted uranium, just send them my way."

"Will do, Sky King," McCarter answered, trying not to laugh at the man's limitless bravado. Grimaldi always talked like he was invulnerable, but then, so did most pilots. Guts was their stock in trade. "Just be warned they are not in a good mood, having recently lost one of their people."

"How nice. From a bad case of lead poisoning, I'll assume?"

"Close enough," McCarter replied, and briefly explained.

"Wow, remind me to buy that man a drink. What a hell of a shot. Even Sarge would have been impressed!"

That being his nickname for Mack Bolan. "I agree, Sky King. Unfortunately we now have 150 pounds of fresh meat that needs some place safe while we run the toes and tips." Most people these days knew that there was an international fingerprint data base to identify nameless corpses, but few knew Interpol also kept a record of the footprints of babies born in every major city. A footprint never changed during a person's life, exactly the same as a fingerprint. A lot of murder cases had been quietly solved with the little known fact ever since the data base went online. "Any chance the freezer in your Sky Wagon is large enough to accommodate such a cargo?"

"Always has before," the Stony Man pilot answered glibly. "Give me your location and I'll be there in ten minutes."

"Make it five," McCarter answered, touching a button to send the coordinates. When he received a confirmation, McCarter broke the connection and redialed the Farm and got the exact same result as before. Static. The cellular signal was going somewhere, and doing something, but nobody was answering from the other end. Which meant they were either busy fighting for their lives, or the Shenandoah hardsite had already been reduced to a smoking hole in the ground.

CHAPTER TWELVE

Stony Man Farm, Virginia

Grabbing LAW and Stinger rocket launchers from a rack, the blacksuits rushed outside the farmhouse to take defensive positions among the trees and bushes. In the background, the woodchipper roared into life, making a deafening racket.

Standing in the middle of the mine field, Chief Buck Greene had a pair of Navy binoculars to his face and was scanning the open sky. A bulletproof vest was draped over his usual attire, and a SMAW rocket launcher slung across his back. The bulky Shoulder-launched Multipurpose Antiarmor Weapon was almost twice the length of a LAW, but the massive 83 mm rocket it carried could easily penetrate the armor of a battle tank. The SMAW should punch a hole clean through an engine before exploding. A definite kill either way.

"Sir!" a voice crackled in his earbud.

"Go," Greene snapped, continuing to scan the empty sky. It looked so blue and peaceful, it was difficult to imagine that death was coming down on them like a thunderbolt from Zeus.

"The park rangers have announced an early closing due to a coming thunderstorm," the blacksuit replied crisply. "We'll have the place clear in an hour."

"Son, we could be dead in ten minutes," Greene responded bluntly into his throat mike. "Just do your best, and get those civvies out of here if you have to carry them out piggyback!"

"Sir, yes, sir!"

"Good man," he softly added, "and God speed."

More blacksuits raced by carrying LAW rocket launchers and Stingers. Lowering his glasses, Greene took heart at the sight of the weapons' markings. A broad red stripe around the end of each barrel signified they had been modified, the series of bright orange stripes denoting to which degree. In a burst of sheer brilliance, John "Cowboy" Kissinger, the chief gunsmith for the Farm, had switched off the heat-seeking guidance systems of the Stinger missiles, turning them into deadheads, then setting a new detonation sequence for altitude. They would explode, sending out a deadly halo of shrapnel at specific heights, just like the old-fashioned flak guns of World War II.

"Everything old is new again," Greene muttered, returning to the skywatch. He had no idea if the X-ships were on the way, but when Barbara Price told him to get the Farm hard, there was no other conceivable reason to do so but for an invasion. The flak rockets weren't much, the timing would have to be hellishly tight to get a kill, but at least they gave the blacksuits a fighting chance against the *Skywalkers*.

Briefly, he reviewed the defenses. The 50-caliber machine guns were manned; the SAM bunkers taken off radar and set to manually launch; the land mines were live; fire control teams were in position; civilians were being evacuated; and the medics had established a burn victim unit in an outbuilding in case anybody survived. Every door was locked, every gun was loaded and the blacksuits were carrying enough LAW, Stinger and SMAW launchers to smash the moon.

And now, they waited, the man thought, shrugging his heavy SMAW to a more comfortable position. The same as countless other soldiers had done before in a million fights since the dawn of time. They stood and waited for the enemy to arrive and the battle to commence.

Unbidden, Greene thought briefly of his family, Thanksgiving and Christmas, river fishing and cold beer in frosty glasses, the smell of a new car and the look in a woman's eyes when she was satisfied.... Shaking off the distractions, Greene grimly pulled the Colt .45 revolver at his side to check the load. This grassy field might be the last place on Earth he ever saw, but that was okay, just part of the job. If his number was up, so be it. No complaints. He closed the cylinder and holstered the gun. But no matter the outcome, those flying sons of bitches were going to know they were in a real fight today!

Okefenokee Swamp, Georgia

WARM BREATH STREAMING from his mouth and nostrils like smoke, Eric O'Hara touched the temperature control of his electric jumpsuit to increase the power, and looked longingly through the window at the marshy swampland only inches away outside. The triple-thick sheets of Luxan military plastic relayed no sound to the man, or the slightest hint of heat, but the steamy view carried ancient memories of being comfortable.

Bright sunlight dappled the dark water of the peaty marsh, huge banyon trees rising from the mud, the pale roots clearly showing the height of the waterline during the spring floods. Fibrous gray curtains of Spanish moss hung from every branch, and a misty fog moved like a living thing across the lily pads dotting the surface of the murky lake. A green turtle slowly crawled along, leaving behind a contrail of prints, and a snake wiggled through the mud with surprising speed. A cloud of mosquitoes out in the stagnant air formed a dark cloud that moved with every breeze, only pausing as the blood-suckers found a new victim to latch onto. An otter swatted the air, then turned and dived below the gentle waves to escape the flying vampires. The mosquito cloud buzzed about, hoping its victim would return, when several dozen of the insects suddenly vanished as a cluster of brightly colored flowers slammed their petals shut, trapping the bugs inside to begin the slow digestion process. High overhead, a black vulture flapped leisurely, looking for anything long dead, and from the distance an alligator bawed a challenge to the entire world.

Desolate was the word, O'Hara thought, tightening the gloves on his hand. All that was missing was Satan himself to complete the vivid picture of Hell on Earth.

Turning away from the illusion of warmth, O'Hara checked the play on the extension cord connecting the electric jumpsuit to the wall outlet, then wearily shuffled over to his elaborate computer console. The three monitors were all scrolling madly with binary code, rows of lights flashing and meters swinging their needles wildly as his mainframes struggled to bust through the resilient

American firewall protecting the little satellite in orbit. They were not through yet, but soon. Very soon. At least he had stopped anybody from using the satellite by having Captain Fawcett throw a Faraday Net around the damned thing. The firewalls were fantastic, amazingly complex and self-modifying, brand-new designs unlike anything he had ever encountered before. If the hacker hadn't seen it firsthand, he would have considered such a cybernetic event impossible. But then, ghosts often did the impossible.

For a very long time, O'Hara had heard rumors that the United States had some sort of a secret police force to handle national defense. Something way beyond Homeland Security, and ten times more secretive than the NSA. He had dubbed it the Ghost Police as a joke. But now it seemed that the ghosts were real, and coming after him. When the SSO: *Royal Prince* had been in Spain, they'd attacked some people talking with the arms dealers, and in a bizarre turn of events, the victims had struck back with lethal force. Goodwin had been badly wounded, bleeding all over the control room of the X-ship, and Rothstein was dead, or worse, captured alive.

But not for long, O'Hara decided, and bent over the console to start typing on the double keyboard. A few seconds later a small icon appeared on the middle screen. Reaching out, he touched it. The icon flared brightly, then faded away.

"Done," he whispered in sadistic pleasure. If Rothstein was still wearing his dogtags as the colonel had ordered everybody to do, then the hacker had just blown off his head with the explosive charge hidden, not inside the tags, but in the links of the chain draped over his neck. Now, let the Ghost Police try to interrogate another ghost.

Going to the lower keyboard, the hacker typed in a brief message, encoded it three times, reduced it to a microsecond beep, then folded into a mixture of access tones made by a dial-up modem phone connecting to the Internet. It was a crude method of communication, an ax instead of a scalpel, but it did work, and a few seconds later he received an acknowledge from Dr. Ingersol on board the *Navicula*.

Such a pity about the picture codes, O'Hara lamented, reclining in his orthopedic chair. Those had been lovely, real works of art. But the Americans had cracked the codes after 9/11. The South African hacker had been so proud of that creation. Too bad it had been ruined by a bunch of rampaging Arabs who knew nothing about psychological warfare and even less about cybernetics. All they had was assurance of insanity. Although to be honest, that had carried them quite a pretty fair distance to date.

Naturally, the hard-ass, hardheaded, Colonel Southerland had demanded a new version of the picture codes, something even more unbreakable. People were always asking him to do the impossible. O'Hara smiled contentedly. But that was probably because he often delivered the impossible, sometimes in less than a day. Especially with the sort of equipment he now possessed!

Reaching out a gloved hand, O'Hara fondly patted the console, not bothering to turn to see the two supercomputers safe behind their frosty Plexiglas walls. The funding for this operation had been limitless, not figuratively, but literally, without limit. Anything he had asked for had been delivered within days. Now he was the master of an IBM Blue/Gene, the most powerful computer in existence, and a Dell Thunderbird, the fastest computer in the world. Using them in tandem, there was no place on Earth that the hacker couldn't penetrate, control or simply destroy. What did men-with-guns matter anymore, when a smart man could steal the world over the Internet and have it delivered to his door with a bow on top.

Darting his eyes to the left, O'Hara scowled at the left screen still struggling with the firewalls of the comsat. I can go anywhere on Earth, except for one. A strange little telecom sat in geosynchronous orbit above a national park in western Virginia. He had traced the signal from Barstow across the globe as it zigged and zagged through a hundred relays. A truly masterful piece of work, he had to admit, and he had been almost thrown clear several times, but finally he had reached the satellite above Virginia, and been stopped cold. Twice, the internal ICE had thrown out his probes in spite of his own unique anti-intruder countermeasures. O'Hara almost smiled as the phrase made him think about the military phrase, anti-anti-missile-missile. It sounded ridiculous, but was an accurate description.

Except that it wasn't working. He was stymied, stalled, slammed into a firewall that could not be broken or subverted. The location of the Ghost Police was just on the other side of the immaterial barrier, and all he had to do was to get through, and they would be burned out of existence by the X-ships. By all three of them if necessary! But first, that firewall had to come down, by any means necessary. Time to get radical.

"All right, playtime is over, Ghosts," the hacker snarled, typing with one hand while stroking a mousepad with the other. "Captain Fawcett, I have new instructions for you, and please follow them with implicit care. This is a rather dangerous maneuver…."

Stony Man Farm, Virginia

NOBODY SPOKE in the Computer Room, the only sounds coming from the bubbling coffeemaker and the soft tapping of fingertips on four sets of keyboards.

"Well?" Price demanded. "Did the reboot work?"

"Negative. Our communication satellite is still down," Kurtzman reported crisply. "Something must be wrong with the relay, or maybe the uplink, but I'll be damned if I know what." His hand reached out to switch to the land lines, but paused. "Barbara?" he asked.

"Not yet, that would reveal our precise location to the *Skywalkers*," she answered brusquely. "We wait for a little longer before committing to the co-axial cables."

Slowly, his hand was withdrawn. "If you say so," Kurtzman said.

"Are you sure the satellite simply isn't being hacked? That IBM/Dell combo is a monster to beat," she stated.

"Yeah, I'm sure," Kurtzman growled, leaning back in his wheelchair and rubbing a hand across his unshaven jaw to the sound of sandpaper. "Nothing can get through our firewalls without detonating the satellite. Not even me. It has to be the uplink. Some new kind of jamming field or scrambler. There's nothing else it could be, unless… Akira, check the diagnostic program on the sat!"

"On it," Tokaido replied, bending over the console to furiously send commands to the Cray supercomputer. "Okay, everything seems nominal…wait a second. The internal temperature is up, and rising."

"How is that possible?" Wethers demanded, furrowing his brow. "Unless, they're… Aaron, they're breaking into the satellite!"

Turning, Price faced the man. "But I thought the firewall…"

"Not hacking in, busting in," Kurtzman snarled, running both hands over the complex controls. "They are actually in orbit, parked alongside the goddamn satellite and trying to force a way inside the hull!"

"You mean breaking, as in breaking into a bank vault?"

"Yes!"

"Incredible," Price whispered, looking upward for no sane reason. It was utterly incredible. Somehow the terrorists had successfully traced the signal to the milsat in geosynchronus orbit directly above the Farm, but then were stopped cold by the firewalls. So they were circumventing those by seizing the milsat and trying to get inside to reach the motherboards that controlled the altitude jets that held the device in place. With those, they'd know the exact location of the Farm to within inches.

"How is this possible? This tactic was considered in the original designs," Price stated roughly. "That's why the sat is three times as big as it needs to be, and has more armor on it than…that's why the internal temperature is going up, they're cutting in with welding torches!"

"Or lasers," Delahunt added. "They weigh less and have finer control for delicate work like this."

"Okay, we have no choice," Price said. "Send the self-destruct code. Blow it out of space!"

"Can't." Kurtzman grunted, slamming a hand on the console. "I've already tried a couple of times and failed. They've blocked the signal somehow. Maybe with a Faraday Net…who knows?"

"Can you scramble the GPS, hide our location? Erase the on-board files or something?" Price asked.

"Negative. The sat is stone deaf to us right now."

"How about using a maser to remote trigger the self-destruct?" Wethers suggested.

"Okay, that's possible," Kurtzman admitted thoughtfully, chewing a lip. "And we can steal access to the Fermi Lab complex in Chicago, but not in a couple of minutes. Barbara, you better call Hal. Let him know we may be compromised soon."

"All ready taken care of," Price lied, unwilling to go into details at just this moment. "And Buck has the Farm harder than a prayer in hell. So it all depends on us now."

With a grunt, Kurtzman accepted that. Unleashing Greene was like turning on a lawnmower, there would be lots of noise and anybody trying to get close would go home in several very small bags.

"Okay, I've redirected our secondary uplink to a CIA spy satellite," Delahunt reported from behind her VR helmet. "It'll throw us out soon, or self-destruct if we go anywhere near the motherboard, but we have access to the Internet for a little while."

"Excellent! What's available for us to hijack?" Price demanded, and a list appeared on a wall monitor of everything in LEO and HEO above North America. The list was long and impressive: Canadian recon sats, NASA weather satellite, commercial telecommunication, cable television relays, hundreds of cell phone satellites, DOD Watchdog, NSA Echelon, DOE environmental sensors… "Are there any Hunter/Killer satellites in the area that we can send to attack the *Skywalkers?*"

"Checking," Kurtzman responded, working feverishly. "Damn, nothing that could get there in time."

"However, I can piggyback ride a homing trace from

NASA and get into the Hubble telescope," Tokaido announced calmly.

"What good will that do?" Price demanded.

"This," he replied, flipping a switch.

The screens at the front of the room swirled in a kaleidoscope of colors, then turned black. The stars were like diamonds in space, hard and still. The twinkling effect came from seeing them through the atmosphere. In space, everything was reduced to harsh reality. It seemed that dreams stopped at the edge of the atmosphere.

Zooming back and forth, the telescope finally focused on a white object that grew in size until it dominated the wall screen. In cold hatred, the team looked at the enemy. An X-ship was parked along a lumpy globe of burnished metal, bright sparks flying away as somebody in a spacesuit applied an electric grinding wheel to the satellite.

"Dark Star." Price snarled the name as if it were the most vile curse that existed.

The team could see that a whole panel of thermal tiles had already been removed from the satellite, and the terrorists were cutting into the inner metal shield. After that, there were some thin aluminum bracings, then only some wiring between the terrorists and the motherboards.

"Okay, we have no choice," Price decided. "Switch to the land lines and call the Navy. Blow our satellite out of the sky!"

"Terminating primary uplink," Delahunt said, gripping empty air with her VR gloves and ripping it apart.

"Going to the cables," Kurtzman added, lifting a small clear plastic cover and reaching for the toggle inside. But before he touched it, the three screens at the front of the room flickered and went dead.

"Damn it, the bastards got inside, we lost the satellite!" Kurtzman reported, flipping the toggle. A moment later, the wall screens pulsed with light, then brightened to show scrolling binary code.

"Okay, we're on the land lines now," Kurtzman confirmed, throwing switches like crazy. "Hunt, tell the teams the Farm may be compromised soon, and not to trust anything we say without the proper prefix, suffix and ident. Carmen, burn those idents out of the Cray! Akira, confirm that missile strike with the Pentagon, NORAD and PacCom! I'll try to reestablish contact with the Hubble again to let us see what is happening in space."

Nobody spoke; they just moved. As Price watched, the triptych of wall screens became garbled with encryption, then cleared into Top Secret government Web pages. She ached with the urge to do something—anything—but it all depended on the cybernetic team now. A split second later, the individual consoles came alive again and the hackers flipped through screen after screen, accessing files and issuing commands.

"What are the chances the terrorists will find the right motherboard, extract the chips, and escape before the ASM missiles arrive?" Price asked in forced calm.

"Damned if I know," Kurtzman said honestly, typing madly. "But we should find out in just a couple of minutes…."

CHAPTER THIRTEEN

USS: Bunker Hill, Pacific Ocean

Casting a line off the port side of the cruiser, Captain Joshua Henderson started to reel it back in when he felt a definite tug. It could only be the shifting currents, but something deep down in his gut told the officer that he had just hooked a fish, and a damn big one, too!

Giving the line a little extra play, the captain waited for the next tug, and when it came he sharp-jerked the rod upward to set the hook in deep. Gotcha! Instantly the line went taut and started whizzing to the left, and then the right, at impressive speed.

But suddenly, the alarm began to howl and the PA speakers cracked into life. "Red alert! Red alert!" the voice of the executive officer boomed across the cruiser. "This is not a drill! Repeat, this is not a drill! Captain to the bridge! Code Zulu Alpha. Repeat, Zulu Alpha!"

Startled, the captain paused. Zulu Alpha? By God, if this was some sort of a joke, heads would roll, that was a promise! Starting to cast the fishing pole into the sea, Henderson wasted valuable seconds to pull out a pocketknife and slash the line. Already taut, it instantly vanished. Satisfied, he turned and bolted for the bridge. At least now the fish would have a fighting chance for life. Anchored to the fifteen-foot fishing pole it would have been as good as dead to the first predator it encountered. As a sailor, he could do no less. But as a U.S. naval officer, he could do no more. Zulu Alpha...that was the code for a nuclear strike!

Sailors hurriedly got out of the way as the grim captain raced up the metal stairs and burst breathless into the bridge. Unfortunately, one glance at the faces of his executive officer and all of the other men and women in the room removed any possibility this was a joke.

"Captain on the bridge!" an ensign barked sharply.

"At ease," Henderson snapped, doffing his cap and taking a chair near the chart table. "XO, do you have a confirmation on the launch codes?"

"Yes, sir," the woman replied, offering a sheet of Top Secret paper edged with red stripes.

Taking the sheet, Henderson gave it a cursory glance to confirm it was legitimate, then tossed it aside. Details and questions could, and would, come later. He had never received the code before, but a Zulu Alpha was an emergency launch, and the faster the better. "Good enough, XO. Load the coordinates into the firing computer."

"Yes, sir," she replied, stepping to a small keyboard and hurriedly tapping in a long sequence.

As the numbers appeared on an overhead repeater, Henderson darkly scowled. Unless he was very much mistaken, that was over the eastern coast of North America! Virginia, or perhaps Washington, D.C.

"Are you sure you have the right... Son of a bitch, it's

them!" Henderson growled, brandishing a clenched fist. "The *Skywalkers!*"

"Sir?" the XO asked, looking up from her work.

"Sound the alarm," Henderson commanded. "Raise the hatches!"

Set above the bridge, and just below the radar globe, a deafeningly loud Klaxon began to blare. Immediately, everybody on the aft deck scrambled out of the way as the rows of armored hatches loudly unlocked and snapped open to expose neat rows of missiles nestled into the military honeycomb.

"Arm nine through fourteen," the captain ordered, reaching for a small safe set into the bulkhead.

"Armed and ready, sir!"

He twirled the dial and yanked open the door. "Disengage safeties."

"Safeties off!"

Pulling out a plastic tag marked with the month and year, he cracked it open and readied the zero code inside before its oxygen-sensitive ink faded from view. "Romeo, four, Baker, Charlie, nine, Adam. Repeat!"

"Romeo, four, Baker, Charlie, nine, Adam!"

"Fire nine and ten," Henderson said in a deceptively calm voice.

"Aye, aye, skipper!" the XO stated, and pressed a large red button.

Two of the aft honeycombs blasted white smoke upward, then the pointed noise of an ASM rose into view, rapidly increasing in speed until it vanished into the clouds overhead.

"Birds on course, sir!" the radar operator announced over the beeping of the glowing screen.

Henderson nodded. "XO, launch twelve and thirteen!"

Fourteen would be kept in reserve in case of an emergency, or a mistake. Although, any mistake dealing with an X-ship would be a world-class FUBAR.

"Yes, sir!" More white smoke, and the antisatellite missiles leaped for the sky, rattling the ship with the sheer force of the double launch

"Flush out the cells and reload," Henderson ordered. He had just initiated a nuclear strike. It was a damn odd feeling. Not good, or bad, just…momentous. Sort of like leaping off a cliff and trying to enjoy the view on the way down.

"Sir?"

The officer broke from his reverie. "Yes, lieutenant?"

"What now, skipper?" she asked too softly for the rest of the bridge crew to hear. "Do we wait for further orders?"

"No, we run, and pray," Henderson conceded, leaning back in the chair. "If those missiles miss, we're going to have visitors real soon, and they will not be happy campers."

"Aye, aye, sir," the woman said, then swallowed hard.

"Helmsman, full power to the turbines! Navigator, hard to port! Bosun, ready the antimissiles! Sparks, watch that radar! Ensign, get the Vulcan hot, and I mean now, mister!"

While the crew lurched into action, Henderson reached up to haul down a hand mike. "This is the captain," he said, pressing the thumb switch. "Battle stations! Repeat, battle stations! Close all water-tight hatches! Damage Control crew, to your stations! Medical, prepare for wounded! Gunnery crews, man the .54-caliber machine guns and prepare to repel boarders!"

Low, Earth Orbit

TINY STABILIZER JETS briefly hissed from numerous locations over the bulky Russian jetpack keeping the Dark Star terrorist firmly in position alongside a rather dull-looking comsat.

The X-ships were not designed for the delicate maneuvering of working in space, so with no other choice, Captain Laura Silverstein had issued a jetpack to the mechanic in her three-man crew and launched him out the airlock. As the man puffed and hissed across the scant few miles between the transport and the enemy satellite, the X-ship had dropped back into the gravity well of the world and soon vanished from sight. The X-ship was built to make short jumps, so if the *Royal Prince* had stayed with Goodwin, the fuel tanks would soon run dry. Then it would be unable to land, a helpless target for the enemy below.

Back, it's coming back, Goodwin told himself for the umpteenth time. The colonel wanted—no, needed—this circuit board. The American Space Marines were dead, and with the neutralization of the secret police, there would be nobody left to stand in their way. Victory for his people, for the entire white race, was only a few inches away, protected by the hull of stubborn metal.

Now all alone in a low Earth orbit, Goodwin sweated and cursed inside his NASA spacesuit, trying to put some muscle into the task and make the portable cutting wheel grind deeper and faster into the resilient hull of the satellite. However, unlike most comsats, this one was actually armored. It had to be the CIA. Who else would armor a satellite? he thought.

Careful not to cut the Faraday Net wrapped loosely

around the satellite like gossamer swaddling, Goodwin moved the grinding wheel along, marveling at the cleverness of the colonel. Weight was at a premium onboard the X-ships, but there were always a few tools for fast repairs at each fuel cache. There had been one lone spacesuit stashed aside for emergency repairs in vacuum and it had a severely limited service life. The Faraday Net was originally meant to cover a prisoner to make sure any surgically embedded transponders did not give away his location while he was being…questioned, and the cutting wheel was for freeing a fuel line that had become frozen to the X-ship. Simple enough items, nothing special, but when used together, the Dark Star operatives now had the mixed-race mongrels in the CIA howling in terror!

As another section came loose, he gently shoved it away to float off into space, and moved to a new position, then paused at the sight of his goal. There it was, the motherboard! The angle was difficult, so Goodwin made some room with the cutting wheel by slicing apart anything in the way, bracings, wiring and some electronic equipment that he could not identify. But that didn't matter, only the chips in the motherboard mattered. Come on, baby, come to daddy….

"Got it!" Goodwin cried in triumphant, lifting the board free from the lifeless comsat. "I got it, sir!" But since he was also covered by the Faraday netting, there was no response.

Suddenly there was a flurry of motion below his boots and the terrorist looked down to smile at the steadily rising X-ship. Right on schedule! At this distance it was like a tiny firefly, but swelling fast in size to become a match head, a candle flame, a… Pausing in his jubilation, Goodwin squinted into the distance. What were those other things coming his way?

Rising from a dozen different locations around the globe, swarms of tiny flames were streaking upward. The Dark Star operative tried to count them, but then one exploded in a bright flash of light that rapidly expanded for what seemed like miles. In spite of the incredible range, the flash hurt his eyes, making them sting and the universe went dark.

Startled, the terrorist turned his head around inside the helmet of the stolen NASA spacesuit, but there remained only absolute impenetrable blackness. Then the truth of the matter hit the man. There was nothing covering the faceplate; he simply could not see a damn thing! That had to have been a nuclear explosion! The mongrels were throwing dozens of nukes at the X-ship, a firewall he had heard the maneuver called once, and he had caught a full burst of the raw light directly in the face. Which meant he was now permanently blind.

Shrieking curses, Goodwin clawed frantically at the Faraday Net, trying to rip it away to warn the crew of the oncoming *Royal Prince,* then something slammed into him hard and everything became jumbled in the chaos of pain.

Slowly the terrorist regained his senses. Okay, still breathing, which meant there were no holes in the suit, but there was a definite sensation of movement in his gut. Was he falling into the atmosphere to be burned up like a meteor?

However, as the long minutes passed and nothing seemed to be getting warmer, Goodwin knew better, and the only thing that came to mind was that he had to be traveling in the other direction, away from Earth. The telecommunication satellite had been orbiting far beyond the outermost layer of air, so the spreading cloud of ionized plasma from the nuke must have reached just high enough to shove the satellite out of orbit, but without smashing it to pieces first.

Then it slammed into him like a billiard ball, breaking God alone knew how many bones.

There was no pain, only a sort of general numbness in both of his legs and left arm. But if he was this smashed up, why wasn't there any pain? Maybe he wasn't that badly hurt, only stunned! Or maybe he had a broken spine. For some reason the terrorist broke into hysterical laughter.

"Okay, I'm blind and crippled, but I still have the motherboard!" Goodwin shouted defiantly, tightening his right glove on the plastic rectangle covered with computer ships. His eyes could not see it anymore, and there was no feeling through the thick glove, but he was absolutely positive that it was still there, firm in his grasp. "You fucking nuked me! But I still have the motherboard, and that means I win! Do you hear me, scum? I win!"

Whooping and laughing in victory, Goodwin gloriously allowed the growing madness to fill his mind like a soothing balm. Some tiny part of him still sane understood that in a few hours his suit would run out of canned air and soon after that his body would cease to function. But it did not matter. Goodwin had beaten the mongrels, the CIA, everybody, he was master of the world!

The insane cackling went on for a long time as the terrorist drifted farther and farther into deep space, disappearing into the infinite heavens.

Prime Base, Khulukrudu

"WHAT DID THEY DO?" Colonel Southerland demanded, his face a mask of feral rage.

"Destroyed the *Royal Prince,* sir. All hands lost," O'Hara replied dutifully from the video monitor, his foggy words visible for a few seconds before dissipating. "I don't have any hard numbers yet, but it seems that the U.S. Navy, along with a few ships from the Canadian, British and Russian navies, sent up over a hundred anti-satellite missiles, but only four ASMs were armed with tactical nuclear warheads."

"I see. So when those exploded, the blast destroyed the other missiles, sending a shotgun blast of shrapnel into orbit."

"Yes, sir. Although, I think it was the plasma cloud that did the real damage."

"Astounding. Simply astounding. This must have cost them millions, hundreds of millions of dollars!"

"Unfortunately, it worked." O'Hara sighed, leaning back in his chair. Reaching over, he turned the rheostat on the electric suit a few degrees higher. "And the American government can afford losses like that every day for months, while we're down to only two X-ships." The man shook his head. "I don't know how the Pentagon got permission from Congress that fast to launch nukes…no, they couldn't have. It must have been an illegal launch. Somebody's head is going to roll for this!"

"Yes, mine," the colonel retorted angrily. The only thing that stood a chance of destroying an X-ship was a tactical nuclear explosion, and America had used four of them to protect that satellite. For a split second the man's mouth was filled with the metallic taste of fear. My God, who were we fighting? he thought.

In the background, the hallway opened and Lieutenant Henzollern entered the room. Going to the wall, she hung the flag of South Africa from a couple of steel rings set into the concrete, then stepped back and smiled. A little bit of home to brighten their underground dungeon! Turning around, the woman smiled at the colonel, then saw who it was on the monitor and her face went wooden.

"Hello, hacker," she said, sneering. "Grow any new pimples on your fat ass?"

"Sure," O'Hara shot back, "and they're almost as big as your fake tits, whore."

"Enough of this childish sniping!" Southerland bellowed. "I have no time for such nonsense! Both of you shut up and pay attention!" As the woman and image of the man subsided, the colonel continued. "All right, until further notice, there will be no additional missions into orbit. From now on, we stay low and fast, as in the original plan."

"Yes, sir!" O'Hara replied crisply. "Anything else?"

"Accelerate the schedule," the colonel added, thoughtfully stroking the scar on his cheek. "No more halfway measures to force media attention. Now we strike hard, smashing the seats of governments until the world collapses into chaos."

"Then we can return home," Henzollern whispered, glancing longingly at the flag on the wall.

"And there will be nobody to stop us this time," Southerland stated confidently. "America, NATO, and all of the other mongrel groups will be too busy trying to maintain their own borders to even notice our new government take power in the motherland. But first…" Tapping a macro key on the control board, the colonel brought up a vector graphic of North America, then zoomed in tight on one particular city in the south. Yes, they will do nicely. "But first we need to requisition some new supplies…."

CHAPTER FOURTEEN

Berlin, Germany

It was long after midnight and the sprawling city was asleep. The maze of roadways was dark, the streets empty and deserted during this time of emergency. The only signs of life were a sprinkling of neon lights from the infamous after-hours clubs, the glowing edifice of the rebuilt Reichstag, and the great cargo ships moving along the quiet Spree River like electrified phantoms.

Stepping to the edge of the roof, the soldier shrugged his G-36 assault rifle into a more comfortable position, and looked down into the darkness from the windy top of the Fermsehturm building. The air was clean and crisp. The new ordinances about industrial pollution seeming to have already started to take effect. From somewhere in the city, a dog barked just once, and a woman briefly laughed. Then there came the clatter of old-fashioned metal garbage cans from an alleyway, and a drunken man began to sing, only to abruptly taper off as if falling asleep. The soldier trembled as a little shiver ran down his back. There was a strange calm in the air tonight, as if a storm was rapidly approaching, but not quite here yet.

Shaking himself to dislodge the unsettling premonition, the soldier turned to continue his patrol along the roof of the building, watching out for nesting pigeons. Pausing at the corner, he scratched a match alive with his thumb and lit a cigarette to contentedly drag the sweet smoke deep into his lungs. Ah, the rest of the world was mad. Mad! Smoking helped ease a man's nerves and took the chill off his bones on nights like this.

Starting to cast aside the match, the soldier was astonished when the glow seemed to somehow expand and fill the night, banishing the darkness. How was that possible? Unless…

Looking straight up, he cursed bitterly at the sight of something large moving across the sky, blocking out the stars. It was them! The sky terrorists!

Ignoring the assault rifle, the young man clawed for the fat pistol at his side and fired it straight upward. The flare sizzled out of sight, then exploded into a brilliant wash of blue-white light. Instantly, from a dozen other rooftops there came a ragged series of flashes, closely followed by clusters of light burst from Red City Hall. Seconds later the soldier could see the fiery exhaust of a hundred Stinger missiles streaking toward the oncoming enemy.

Suddenly a massive fireball filled the sky, the rumbling detonations sounding again, and again, as the transport tore itself apart. A hit!

The soldier started to whoop in victory when a burning rain of debris tumbled into the river, the ragged chunks of the fuselage clearly discernible as an ordinary commercial jetliner.

"No…this cannot be happening…" the private whispered, going cold, the sensation having nothing to do with the evening chill. He had been told that speed was essential to protecting the city, so he'd reacted as fast as humanly possible. But this was monstrous!

As the broken tail section plummeted into view, the soldier recoiled at the brutal understanding that he hadn't just saved the city, but slaughtered hundreds of innocent people. It hadn't been an invading X-ship, just a commercial liner full of civilians, tourists with their families and children…

Just then a soft wind reached him carrying the faint smell of aviation fuel and roasted flesh. Doubling over, he violently retched again and again until he thought the pain in his gut might break him in two.

The delayed boom of the detonation arrived to roll over the city, rattling windows, and setting off car alarms. In rapid stages, the city began to awaken in front of his tearing eyes, and the horrid magnitude of the mistake sunk in to shrivel his soul. He was a murderer, a mass murderer.

He'd be court-martialed, the young man realized in shock. His parents would have to change their name. He'd failed his country, and brought shame upon his family in the eyes of God….

The decision seemed only logical when it occurred. Very slowly, the weeping man withdrew his sidearm and placed the cold ring of gunmetal against his forehead. The click of the hammer locking into position was preternaturally loud, and the noise that followed shattered the universe, seeming to echo forever.

Washington, D.C.

LOCATED IN THE BUSY DOWNTOWN DISTRICT, the National Central Bureau was a rather drab building of tinted windows and gray concrete, the dull five-story structure barely noticeable among the sparkling office buildings and trendy hotels made of chrome and glass. But that was the whole idea. The NCB was the United States division of Interpol, and the last thing it wanted was notoriety of any form. Covert was their byword, clandestine their creed. There were no markings on the roof for a heliport, yet it could easily accommodate the weight of four Black Hawks if necessary. There were weapon scanners set just inside the front doors, but there were more buried inside the walls at the fire exits, ventilation shafts and garbage chutes. The rows upon rows of windows were cleaned constantly by a diligent maintenance staff. But behind the sheets of glass were thick slabs of bulletproof plastic, the space between the sheets a hard vacuum, making it impossible to hear any conversations held inside the building by bouncing a maser off the vulnerable glass.

Video cameras were set on top of the elevators, and biohazard filters inside the air shafts. Ugly mechanical grinders, very similar to a kitchen blender, were placed at strategic locations in the water and sewage pipes, and every computer was individually shielded against an EMP blast, just in case some terrorist group, or criminal cartel, tried to magnetically erase any critical records. The furnace burned all of the trash twice, chemical sensors checked the water, the mail was X-rayed, every door had a SOTA hand scanner, every land line was filtered for extraneous noise that might be a hacker, and every file cabinet was fireproof, water-resistant and airtight.

Safe inside the building, thousands of police officers and law-enforcement personnel went quietly about their daily work, filing reports and coordinating information.

To the casual viewer the NCB would merely seem like any other office building in the world. But down in the lobby, where everybody could see as they passed through the security checkpoint, was a counter that clicked forward to a new number with every terrorist arrest, every kidnapped child returned home alive, every drug cartel smashed.

Low-key, and unobtrusive, the drab NCB building was not the most secure location in the District of Columbia, but it was damn close.

It was early in the morning, and the traffic was sparse on the streets, with only a few cabs hauling drunk tourists home to their hotels, and a scattering of stretch limousines conveying their unseen passengers to unknown locales.

Sitting on a public bench, an old man was feeding popcorn to a flock of pigeons on the sidewalk. His clothes were rumpled, but clean, and a thick wooden cane lay nearby for ready access.

Whistling tunelessly, Dee tossed another handful of popcorn onto the sidewalk. The birds swarmed over the food, fighting among themselves to be the first. That almost made the Red Star operative smile. Wasn't it funny how animals often duplicated the actions of humans? In spite of being born and raised in Beijing, the man had always loved pigeons. Roasted in orange sauce, as the old joke went. Bah, the filthy things were little better than rats with wings, he thought.

After escaping from Central Park, the five intelligence operatives had combined their resources and as subtly as possible gone on a manhunt for the enemy mole. The Washington, D.C., branch of the NCB was the end of the information chain. The traitor had to be here, a member of Interpol. Unfortunately, they did not know who it was among the staff of eighteen hundred people. They had briefly discussed bringing in the U.S. Army and surrounding the building, then questioning everybody individually. But that would only give the mole enough time to destroy any incriminating documents, kill himself or herself to avoid capture, or worse, summon an X-ship. That could lead to the fiery deaths of nearly two thousand Interpol agents, along with most of the civilian population in downtown Washington. If they moved too slow, the mole might escape. If they moved too fast, an X-ship could kill thousands of innocent people, along with the mole. However, Brognola had come up with a third option.

Just then, the watch on his left wrist vibrated. Zero hour, Dee noted calmly, inverting the bag to shake out the last few crumbs. Time to see how good humans were at duplicating the actions of animals. Almost smiling, the Red Star agent looked skyward.

STANDING IN THE OPERATIONS ROOM, the executive staff of the NCB watched the clock on the wall and nervously checked their assorted weapons.

Interpol agents had always been allowed to carry weapons for self-protection. However, ever since 9/11 their power had been vastly enlarged so that now they could take active part in the field missions, personally arresting the animals that fed on the blood of humanity, people who once had been safe and secure before the immaterial shield of diplomatic immunity. But no more.

It was a new world, the NCB commander thought,

making sure the safety was off his old-fashioned Walther PPK .38. "Wait for it…." he muttered out loud. "Wait…"

Nobody spoke, intently watching the video monitors on the roof trained on the empty sky.

"Get ready, just a few seconds more…."

Suddenly a double flight of USAF jetfighters appeared in the sky and swooped down to all hit their afterburners in unison. Seconds later a titanic sonic boom hit the city, rattling windows for a dozen blocks and setting off hundreds of car alarms.

"Now," the NCB commander said calmly.

Waiting eagerly at the banks of controls boards, the staff lurched into action, flipping switches and spinning dials.

Marker charges hidden on the rooftop ignited and harmless white smoke started pouring down the outside of the building. Every air vent started blowing out torrents of hot air, and warning sirens cut loose, filling every inch of the complex with a strident howl.

"Emergency, this is not a drill. Repeat, this is not a drill," a computerized voice announced over wall speakers. "We have an emergency. Will everybody please immediately leave the building."

On every internal monitor, startled people looked up from their work, then noticed the hot air and instantly made the connection. Sonic boom, billowing clouds of smoke, heat wave…this was an X-ship attack. The sky terrorists were here!

As the clerks and secretaries stuffed documents into automatic shredders, hundreds of people pulled out handguns, while a chosen few rushed to hidden weapons cabinets set along the hallways and started passing out assault rifles and bandoliers of ammunition.

The heat from the vents was becoming rapidly worse and dull booms could dimly be heard coming from the roof. Was an X-ship landing, or dropping bombs? Nobody knew, but it added fuel to their work, and the split second their files were safe, or destroyed, the people flooded out of the offices and poured down the stairwell heading for the nearest exit.

On the way, they saw squads of grim law-enforcement agents heading up the stairs carrying heavy ordnance and wearing full battle armor, while more took defensive positions in front of specific doors. The staff knew that anybody coming near one of those locked doors would be gunned down on the spot, without pause or question. These were the nexus junctions for the computer lines, and deemed by some to be more vital to the safety of the world than their own lives. There were always a few newcomers who assumed that directive was some sort of a joke, until the NCB commander personally informed them it was dead serious. There would never be a drill conducted involving those doors, or any kind of a loyalty test. They were to avoid the doors at all cost, unless they saw somebody—anybody—trying to get inside, then blow off their heads without attempting an arrest. Kill on sight was the rally cry. End of discussion.

The crowds of cops stayed well clear of the forbidden doorways as they proceeded toward the nearest exits. The heat was much worse now, the windows impenetrable with thick curtains of smoke, the building itself seeming to vibrate slightly, but that might just be from the impacts of thousands of running shoes. There came the soft chatter of an assault rifle, closely followed by the dull boom of a grenade. That settled the matter, and the Interpol redoubled their speed to get outside and run for their lives. What else could they do against an X-ship?

Standing quietly at one of the nexus doors located in the lobby near the main intersection, Hal Brognola hefted the assault rifle in his grip and carefully studied the streaming crowd of people. So far, nothing, and he had been absolutely positive that this trick would work!

"This is starting to look like a failure, Hal," Debra Stone subvocalized into her throat mike, even though the Israeli agent was less than a yard away.

"The hell it does," Brognola whispered back. "Check four o'clock!"

Trying not to be obvious, Stone only shifted her eyes and looked in that direction. Among the grim throng of men and women, only one person was walking without apparent fear. Clutching a thick sheath of manila folders, the woman stayed in the thick of the crowd, almost as if she was trying not to attract any attention. Short and slim, she was wearing a long skirt that hid her legs, flat shoes and a bulky sweater that masked any hint of a figure. Long bangs hid her face, along with horn-rimmed glasses. Those seemed a tad incongruous, until Stone noticed it was nearly identical to what a score of other female cops were wearing. The traitor wasn't in disguise, just the civilian version of a ghillie suit; trying to blend into the herd, so to speak.

"Is it a terrorist attack?" somebody yelled.

"No, it is them, my friend!" another cop answered from within the crowd, his Russian accent pronounced. "We got an X-ship on the roof disgorging troops!"

The whole crowd grimaced at the news, except for the file clerk, she merely raised an incredulous eyebrow for a second, then hunched her shoulders as if trying to protect the files in her arms, and managed to look very frightened.

"So that is our traitor," the Israeli agent muttered. "Well done, my friend."

"Learned this trick from an old Army buddy," Brognola said honestly. "What he doesn't know about psyche warfare hasn't been invented yet."

"A good man to have. Is he one of your field ops?"

"He was FBI," Brognola lied, and forced a look of sadness on his face for moment, then stood tall denying the fake memory. "Okay, let's move, nice and quiet." As always, the abrupt switch in topics worked to derail the unwanted line of conversation. Get sad, then get mad, that was how soldiers remembered fallen comrades.

"Confirm, I have your back," Stone replied, minutely adjusting the direction of the assault rifle. Since this was U.S. soil, Brognola was in charge. In Tel Aviv, she would have been the leader. This was more than basic courtesy; a mission could easily go sour with one wrong move, and no outsider could ever know all of the idiosyncratic details of any culture like a home-grown cop.

As the timid-looking file clerk approached the reception desk, Brognola and Stone moved away from their door, just as Korolev come out of the men's room brandishing a .357 Magnum Rex revolver, and Braith-Waite stepped into view from the weapon scanner at the front entrance.

"Hey, lady, what the fuck is that?" he asked pointing at her feet, one hand resting on the holstered pistol at his side.

But the woman didn't even glance down, instead she

kicked the man ahead of her, making him tumble into Braith-Waite, and then vaulted over the conveyor belt to dash for the revolving door. Extracting himself from the tangle of limbs, the Scotland Yard inspector grabbed her arm. The manila folders went flying, and the woman jerked her free hand toward the man. There was a loud explosion, and he dropped back, blood spraying into air, gray smoke rising from her sleeve.

"Somebody take her!" Brognola snarled, swinging up his M-16, but there wasn't a clear shot with all of the people moving in the lobby.

Without a word, Stone fired. The 40 mm gel bag from the grenade launcher hit the clerk in the back, but only shoved her forward to hit the revolving door and impel her outside even faster.

"She's got a vest under that sweater!" Korolev barked, shoving people aside in a mad rush for the exit. Most of them bridled at the rough contact, then saw the gun in his grip and backed away fast.

Tracking the clerk on the other side of the window, Brognola risked a short burst from the assault rifle, but the hardball ammo only slammed into the bulletproof glass to sit there like flies in amber.

Surrounded by running people, Dee looked up from the bench, his expression radiating total confusion as the woman sprinted past. "Sweater and big glasses?" he asked without any preamble.

"That's her!" Brognola replied over his com link. "Don't let her reach the parking lot!"

"Done," the Red Star agent stated, dropping the popcorn bag and grabbing the cane to fire without taking aim. The 12-gauge shotgun blast blew the pigeons apart, the hail of bloody feathers and beaks smashing into the woman's back and sending her to the pavement. But she came up in a controlled roll and fired her trick gun again. Dropping the cane, Dee double over to clutch his stomach, blood gushing from the hideous wound.

By now, several of the Interpol agents on the sidewalk had drawn their own weapons, but not exactly sure what was happening, they could only move away from the combatants to give them room. A couple headed for Dee, while a host of others flipped out cell phones and called for local assistance and an ambulance.

Seizing her chance, the clerk nimbly hopped over a decorative hedge and pelted across the parking lot, zigzagging between the vehicles as if her life depended on it. Putting a large SUV between her and any possible snipers on the roof, the Dark Star mole whipped out a garage door opener and pressed the button twice. Instantly, every car alarm started howling, the headlights flashing, then two of the vehicles unexpectedly hissed out clouds of tear gas. Avoiding those, she kept low and headed for the far corner of the lot.

Moving through the chaos as if they did it every day, Brognola, Stone and Korolev charged boldly after the enemy, maintaining a constant barrage from their assorted weapons. The hail of rubber bullets ricocheted harmlessly off the sides of the cars, only to do it again and again, spreading out fast. Windows cracked, hub caps popped off to clang musically on the pavement, and two more cars began venting tear gas.

Pausing in the lee of a massive Hummer to catch her breath, the clerk flinched as something smacked into the side of a car a few yards away, only to come back and catch her on the shoulder. The rubber bullet hurt, but did no real damage. Then she saw a distant windshield shatter, a round object land on the hood, a cut in the soft cloth oozing a clear gel as if it were a wound in living flesh. Stun bags! In horror, the Dark Star operative realized the Interpol agents clearly wanted her alive for questioning. That meant torture, a rape room, red-hot pliers, knives and hammers. She knew all about such things. The colonel had shown her secret CIA videos of the atrocities. Her stomach rebelled at the thought of her being violated in that way, and she resolved to die before being taken alive by the dirty mongrels.

Reaching a light-blue SUV, the clerk jerked open the unlocked rear hatch, yanked up the carpet and lifted a South African Army MM-1 8-shot grenade launcher. Clicking off the safety, she savagely turned and sent three fast rounds arching across the rows of cars. The fat canisters ignited in the air and a rain of burning napalm fell upon the vehicles. Instantly the cloth roofs of a dozen convertibles burst into flames. Caught in the wash, an Interpol agent shrieked as his hair and clothing caught fire. Unable to move from the incredible agony, the poor man simply stood there howling in unimaginable pain, burning alive.

Stopping behind a Volkswagen to reload, Brognola saw the man, then caught the telltale scent of napalm. Knowing there was no help for the poor bastard, the chief of the Sensitive Operations Group sent a fast flurry of mercy rounds into the man to end his unimaginable agony.

"She's trying to delay us by attacking the others," Korolev said over the com link. "Ignore any victims! Concentrate on capturing her!"

"Before she has a chance to call for help from above," Stone added. "Harold, can you have somebody jam the airwaves?"

"Not without revealing what we're doing if the *Skywalkers* are keeping tabs on their spy!" he retorted, firing a couple of rounds into a car window. The safety glass shattered into hundreds of tiny green cubes, and then again in the next vehicle beyond. For a split second Brognola obtained a direct view of the surprised clerk. Swinging her massive weapon in his direction, they fired in unison.

With a cry, the clerk jerked backward, blood spraying from her shoulder, and something punched a soup-can-size hole in the SUV behind Hal. Fueled by pure adrenaline, the middle-aged man dived for cover and the car erupted, the windows shattering. The fuel tank ignited in thunder, lifting the vehicle high off the ground, sending it crashing down on top of an expensive sports car.

Scrambling to her feet, the clerk triggered five more 30 mm rounds in a fast arc, then took off at her best speed for the nearby Potomac River. Escape was only a block away. Hidden in an old boathouse she had rented under a series of assumed names was a cache of supplies, more weapons, full body armor and a homing beacon radio. One push of the button and thundering help would arrive from the sky in only minutes. All she had to do was to press the button, then dive into the river and swim away to the other shore, to be rescued, then sit back and watch as the X-ship burned the city to the ground.

By now, there were a couple of helicopters overhead, the PA system booming out commands to surrender, but she ignored that nonsense. American police helicopters were not allowed to carry deadly weapons, a foolish policy in her opinion, and there had not been enough time for the commander of the NCB to summon military assistance from any of the local bases. Actually, the helicopters were aiding her escape by raising the level of noise and confusion. The only real threat were the people chasing her through the parking lot.

Painfully rising from behind a old Chevy, Brognola beat out the flames on his pant leg, then took off after the clerk again, ignoring the sensation on his cheek that could only be trickling blood. Thankfully, the wound throbbed with pain, which meant it was only a flesh wound. Anything major would have gone numb from shock. So the big Fed kept running and firing sprays of rubber bullets. But this was his last clip. After that, he only had M-203 slaved to his M-16, and his Beretta, which was loaded with steel-jacketed, hollowpoint rounds, perfect for an execution, but lousy for a capture.

The smoke from the burning cars was intensifying, windows shattering loudly from the growing heat, people shouting incomprehensible things, and those damn sirens still howling away to announce the fake X-ship attack. On top of everything, Brognola could hear police sirens coming this way, and knew if they tried to arrest her, that would only get everybody killed. The balloon had gone up. He was out of options. They had to capture or kill her in the next few minutes, or else all hell was going break loose! "LeRoux, now!" Brognola bellowed into the throat mike.

There was no response, but suddenly he heard the powerful roar of a speeding motorcycle.

Turning at the unexpected sound, the clerk gasped at

the sight of a man streaking between the parked cars at breakneck speed, tilting dangerously as he nimbly avoided a burning chassis or a pile of sparkling glass.

Triggering her last few rounds, the clerk threw hellfire and iron death at the speeding man. He managed to dodge the first two discharges, but the third hit him in the chest, blowing him off the machine. The bike continued on for several yards, before tilting over and skidding across the pavement throwing off a geyser of sparks before whoofing into flames.

As the fireball streaked past the clerk, she saw the airborne rider land on top of a Cadillac with a tremendous crash. Incredibly, the man struggled to get up, the tattered remains of his leather jacket ripped asunder to reveal the dented steel plate underneath.

Cursing at the sight, the clerk turned and ran. The sons of bitches had to have assumed she would have some heavy ordnance, the clerk thought, and sent in a sacrificial lamb to take the brunt of the attack, leaving her unarmed. Unfortunately, the trick had worked.

Suddenly she could hear the murmur of the Potomac River. Freedom was only a few yards away. Casting aside the useless grenade launcher, the woman fumbled for the derringer tucked up her sleeve, when she caught a reflection of her pursuers in the window of a sports car. They had climbed on top of a Hummer for clearance and were pointing their assault rifles in her direction. Frantically diving for cover, the two M-16s spoke in unison, the twin streams catching her on the fly. The rubber bullets hammered her to the ground, pain filling her world as she actually heard the bones break. Landing hard on the pavement, she lay panting for an unknown length of time, then came alert at the sound of running shoes.

They were coming for her now, she realized, clawing for the watch on her left wrist. The chase was over and she had failed. Out-fought and out-maneuvered by the dirty mongrels. But I will never go down into their torture room alive! she vowed.

Raking blood furrows in her skin, the snarling woman got the watch off her wrist, turned it around, and started to shove it back on again when Brognola appeared. He had no idea what she was doing, but he fired from the hip, the 5.56 mm hardball rounds stitching a line of holes through her raised arm. The watch went sailing as she shrieked in pain and clutched the wounded limb to her heaving chest. A few seconds later the timepiece landed with a splash into nearby river. Instantly there came a dull thump and a steaming column of water rose upward, throwing out gobbets of red mud.

Distracted for only a moment, Brognola turned to face his prisoner, and saw that the woman was desperately clutching a fountain pen. Knowing the trick pens that many people in the intelligence community carried, he raised the assault rifle to fire again just as a needle-thin blade stabbed out of the pen and she buried it deep in her throat.

Moving fast, Brognola kicked away her hand and yanked out the pen, planning to press a handkerchief to the wound. But he spotted an orange gaze along the edge of the blade, and the clerk suddenly went into a violent spasm, thrashing and kicking, then she went still and deeply exhaled, making a sound that could be duplicated by a living human being.

"Did it work?" Stone asked over the com link. "I heard the explosion in the river, did we take her alive?"

"No, she's dead," Brognola said wearily, rising to his feet. "Took her own life rather than be captured."

"Then we failed," LeRoux panted in their earbuds. "In spite of everything, we failed!"

"Maybe not," Brognola replied slowly. "I watched her as she ran. This wasn't a blind panic, but a planned escape route, and her goal seemed to be the river."

"So there must be some sort of cache nearby," Korolev added over the radio. "Perhaps a boat or more weapons."

"Or a radio," Dee wheezed, obviously in terrible pain. "L-locate it, and we can…find the *Skywalkers*. We're n-not…not b-beaten yet. Find that cache!"

"And fast," Brognola added grimly, involuntarily glancing upward at the fleecy white clouds dotting the beautiful azure sky.

CHAPTER FIFTEEN

Atlanta, Georgia

It was midnight, and all the world seemed asleep. There was little traffic on the complex maze of concrete ribbons that ensnared the great southern city, and the rolling landscape twinkled with a blanket of electric stars.

Deep in the rolling hillside, the sprawling complex of the CDC dominated the pastoral landscape with gleaming buildings of glass and steel, the ultramodern structures just far enough away from each other to create a sort of parkland feel to the manicured lawns and neatly trimmed hedges. Ever since its creation in 1946 to battle malaria, the Centers for Disease Control had waged a grim war against the infectious ills that plagued humanity since time immemorial, and had conquered many foes, improving the life of millions.

But these days the work of the CDC had taken on a more sinister aspect as it became the nation's bulwark against bioterrorism. Special field units raced to locations where it was believed some terrorist group had unleashed a viable toxin.

Far under the ground, bare steel tunnels and terrazzo walls connected the massive medical research facility. Hundreds of technicians, doctors, chemists and instrumentation specialists scurried around intent upon their vital tasks. These days it seemed like there was always some new infectious disease coming out of Africa or the slums of some great metropolis. Massive conduits were filled with bundled cables connecting the banks of Cray supercomputers that barely were able to handle the load of data needed by the diligent medical staff. And even farther underground was the little known vault composed of layered metal several yards thick. It was sunk into a sea of concrete and protected by armed guards stationed inside and out.

This was where America stored the last-known vials of disease that had been wiped off the face of the Earth. These were not mere scientific curiosities, but vital sources of research data used to template the advance of medical defenses. Many times some antitoxin seemed to be perfect on paper, and functioned beautifully in a computer simulation, only to fail miserably in a laboratory test against the real thing. Science had taken humanity into space and split the atom, but the invisible world around us was a thousand times more complex and infinitely more deadly.

The threat of bioweapons was fast becoming the bane of the twenty-first century. Military hardware had evolved to the point if every nation launched their entire nuclear arsenal it would be a total gamble, a crap shoot, if any of the ICBMs ever made it to their targets. There were too many anti-missiles, antianti-missiles for anybody to know who might win a nuclear war anymore.

However, a biological attack could easily wipe out the enemy population, leaving the buildings, factories and precious farmland completely unaffected. Then your own population could simply walk in and take over. A win-win situation, if people weren't disturbed by the slaughter of a hundred million people. Money and talent poured into the CDC in a Homeric effort to stem the tide of a biowar. So far, the technological dam was holding, but it was anybody's guess when it might crack and unleash a plague of biblical proportions.

But there, nuclear bombs offered an odd hope of survival. A disease fully capable of killing a billion people could be stopped dead in its tracks if the car full of terrorists was hit with a tactical nuke in the desert. The ultimate weapon of destruction could be converted into a surgeon's flame to cauterize a wound, if the CDC knew about the attack early enough, when, where and what it was. The nuclear arsenal of the CDC was even more heavily protected than the artificial plagues, and much more secret. Or so it was believed.

Far outside the city limits of Atlanta, a janitor slipped into a flowery grove of trees and bushes. Glancing around in every direction, he decided the coast was clear, and pulled out a cigarette to carefully light it with a contraband butane lighter. Smoking was strictly forbidden at the CDC. Almost everybody had kicked the habit by now, but a small handful of scientists, guards and one janitor were still struggling to slay that particular dragon.

As he took the first deep drag, the warm breeze from the west abruptly changed direction. Puzzled, the janitor looked up quizzically as the air suddenly became oppressively hot. Was there a fire somewhere in the installation? There were no alarms, and he couldn't see…

Then the janitor blinked, the precious cigarette dropping from his slack mouth. Holy Hannah, he could see!

The night was definitely brighter with some sort of a reddish tint. One of the buildings had to be on fire! Unless…no, it couldn't be!

He looked skyward just in time to utter one brief scream before the drive flame smashed the bushes flat and tore his body apart, limbs and head sailing away before the 100-ton X-ship landed directly on top of what remained, proving once and forever that smoking was very bad for your health.

Masked in rising clouds of smoke, the side hatch opened and two Dark Star agents assumed positions with Armbrust rocket launchers, and started laying down a barrage of high explosives across the medical complex. Water tanks were blown open, releasing a deluge across the lawns and sidewalks, and cars violently exploded in the parking lot, blocking the entrance. Tossing aside the spent Armbursts, the terrorists armed two more of the silent rocket launchers, the metal room behind them frosty from the backblast of nitrogen gas and snow. Now they ruthlessly took out the radar globe, the main search lights, the auxiliary power plant and finally they put a few rockets into random windows just to spread the confusion.

Slamming the hatch shut once more, the X-ship took off just as a pair of searchlights crashed on, the bright beams sweeping the sky for the invaders. A dozen deadhead missiles launched from hidden bunkers, streaking across the black sky and disappearing into the distance. More than a simple research lab, the CDC was fully capable of defending itself from enemy invaders or local mobs. What good was a tanker truck full of serum, if the doctors couldn't get through the howling mobs of terrified civilians to administer the cure? The outbuildings

were full of heavy ordnance, armored personnel, a score
of APCs and even more Apache gunships.

Charging out of the darkness, a Hummer full of troops
stopped for only a second at an electrical substation to un-
load two men, and then hurried away. Nervously, the soldiers took their assigned positions in front of the
burnished steel doors.

"The bastards aren't getting past us," a burly sergeant
stormed, working the heavy arming bolt of a M-249 SAW
machine gun, a golden belt of linked ammo dangling
from the side.

"Not without saying hello to ol' Barry here," the private agreed, hefting a 25 mm Barrett rifle.

On the rooftop, the hedges slid aside on greased rail-
ings to expose a SAM bunker, a dozen needle-sharp tips
jutting out, ready for instant launch. As a last resort, the
nuclear vault was set to detonate to stop an invader from
obtaining the supply of tactical nukes. The so-called clean
nukes were small, but in the right hands fully capable of
sowing tidal waves of destruction.

As the sirens wailed on, the U.S. Army soldiers
watched the sky and the searchlights continued sweeping
back and forth. Small fires were raging across the complex, but crews of specialists in biohazard suits were already battling those with antiseptic foam. Just in case
something got loose from the upper labs.

Nervously, the men touched the three plastic tubes
snug in their shirt pocket. Each was designed for speed
and simplicity. All they had to do was to bend one of the
tubes in two, as if activating a chemical glow-stick, then
shake it hard to make the stubby needle protrude and jab
it into the carotid artery on the side of their neck. One was

an antidote to most types of nerve gas, the second a broad-spectrum protection against most types of germ warfare, but not all, so the third brought instant, and absolutely painless, death. The civilian doctors and technicians were terrified of the three tubes, but the military personnel jokingly referred to them as the Holy Trinity: Faith, Hope and Charity.

Suddenly there was an explosion of light from the other side of the complex, their view partially blocked by the Visitor Center, then something rose quickly on a rumbling wash of fire and vanished among the stars.

"Double C, this is Unit Alpha, what the hell is going on?" the sergeant demanded. "Did they just leave?"

"We have a confirmation on that, Alpha," a crisp voice replied. "The invaders have left the complex."

"But, sir, that doesn't make any sense!" the private muttered. "Everything deadly is located deep underground. It'd take us hours to reach those vaults! Besides—" His next words were lost as a dozen SuperCobra gunships appeared overhead, the deadly military gunships spreading outward in a combat formation in a definitive seek-and-destroy pattern.

"Yeah, I know," the grizzled old veteran said, tightening his grip on the SAW. "Doesn't seem to make any sense, does it?" If the terrorists had dropped off a virus to kill all of the doctors at the CDC, it would not work. That was an old idea and had been incorporated into the safety plans decades ago. There was always a full staff of medics safe and secure inside an airtight bunker, ready to rescue everybody else. Okay, they couldn't steal any virus that fast, or kill the doctors, and they hadn't gone anywhere near the nuclear bunker, so what…

"Oh, shit," the private whispered, his hand automatically slapping his shirt to check for the tubes. But it kept going and he grabbed the microphone hanging off his shoulder. "C and C, get me the executive director! This is a class-one emergency! We have to warn the Pentagon immediately! I know what the sons of bitches stole!" Looking to the east at the twinkling lights of downtown Atlanta, the man felt a shiver run down his spine. "And may God help us all."

Stony Man Farm, Virginia

"YES, THE HOMING BEACON arrived safely," Barbara Price said into the phone receiver, resting an elbow on her desk. Then she smiled, even though the person on the other end could not see her. "Damn, it's good to hear your voice again, Hal."

"You almost didn't," Brognola said, exhaling wearily. "I've tangled with mobsters who weren't as tough as this file clerk."

"The female of the species is always deadlier than the male."

"So I've heard. Something to do with protecting the young."

"Bet your ass. So, where did you find it?"

"An abandoned boathouse. The door was locked and lined with enough Claymore mines to blow the Statue of Liberty back to France. We got in through the roof."

"There was a hatch?" she asked skeptically. "That seems like a rather basic mistake to make."

"No hatch. We simply removed the roof."

She chuckled. "Yep, that would do it, all right." Price tapped a few keys to check on Kurtzman's and Wethers's progress. They were carefully disassembling the beacon to extract the frequency chips without altering the settings. A job equivalent to replacing the pistons in a car engine while it was driving down a highway. "Well, I have to say, for a bunch of intelligence ops who never worked together before, the five of you did a pretty damn good job. Was there any breakage?"

"Nothing serious, just cuts and bruises. Dee will make a full recovery and LeRoux will walk again, although he may have a limp."

"Pretty tough for a bunch of old folk."

"Hey, some spies are milk, while others are whiskey," Brognola stated. "Some go sour after just a few days, while others only get stronger with every passing year."

"Yeah, keep telling yourself that," Price snorted, reading the scroll on a monitor. "Okay, Akira finally got an ID on the clerk. Her name was Dorothy Swanson. She was an unpaid intern at the NCB, getting extra credit for her classes at Georgetown university. Her major was law enforcement."

"That's what the NCB says. Anything else?"

"Not really. According to Akira, her major at college was going to be political science, but after a trip to Europe, Swanson changed it to law enforcement."

"Europe," the man muttered. "Any chance she went to Belgium?"

"Checking…yes, she did. That must have been where Dark Star recruited her."

"Makes sense," Brognola agreed. "Any word from Aaron yet on where she was supposed to rendezvous with the X-ship that was going to take her away?"

"Absolutely. Roosevelt Island."

"Where? Never heard of the place."

"It's smack in the middle of the Potomac River, right

on Route 66," Price replied. "Used to be a swamp, but now it's a national park. I pulled up a map of the place, and it could not have been better suited for the *Skywalkers*. All of the trees were planted in circles around a memorial for Teddy Roosevelt. Two wide marble strips that connect to a statue of him and a couple of water fountains, marble pillar covered with his most famous quotes."

"Circles of trees and two intersecting marble strips… Jesus Christ, that would look like a bull's-eye with an X in the middle from high altitude!"

"Even when navigating with a GPS, never underestimate the value of a visual reference to a pilot," she added. "Ten feet in the wrong direction, and you just crushed the person you were supposed to rescue."

"True enough. An island, eh?" Brognola mused. "Before, you said that her major was law enforcement, and that got her into the NCB. Any chance her minor was physical education?"

"Good guess. Specifically, long distance swimming."

"These people don't miss a trick," Brognola growled in grudging admiration. Just like that set of rigged dogtags on the corpse from Spain. If Hawkins had not removed them on the beach to store the tags away, when they exploded the shrapnel would have reduced Phoenix Force by two or three people. As it was, their Hercules suffered some serious damage while in flight. Grimaldi had managed to land the huge plane in an olive grove and they'd obtained a replacement from a NATO base near Madrid.

"Where is David McCarter at the moment?" Brognola asked.

"On route to South Africa. Colonel Southerland has something big planned for that country, probably a military junta. Having our people there in advance might tip the scales in our favor, and could save a lot of lives."

"That's over five thousand miles away, they won't arrive until late tomorrow in a Hercules! It could all be over by then."

"Actually, according to my timetable, they'll be there in a few hours," the woman corrected, glancing at her watch. "I had them dump the Herc at Tel-Aviv Airport and obtain a Learjet 60. It is twice as fast as a C-130."

"They stole a twelve-million-dollar aircraft?"

"Paid for in cash. Thanks to the late Emile San Saun. David is a big fan of Sun Tzu."

"'A pound of supplies taken from your enemy is worth ten pounds of supplies carried from home,'" Brognola quoted.

Price smiled. "Exactly." Just then, her desktop computer beeped with an incoming message. "Good news, Aaron and Hunt got the codes and have already sent them to Schwarz," she stated. "Once Able Team is in position, they'll start broadcasting."

"What did they choose as a combat zone? If anything goes wrong, we don't want that X-ship anywhere near civilians."

Briefly, Price checked a picture-in-picture monitor to make sure the land line was secure. Everything was in the green, there were no spikes or other irregularities. "They're at an abandoned amusement park, right off a railroad track that services the D.C. area."

"I see," Brognola mused. "This way it looks like Swanson left downtown to find a nice secluded spot for a rendezvous. Wait a second. Didn't an X-ship refuel at an

abandoned amusement park in western Maryland yester-
day morning?"

"Yes, and since the *Skywalkers* never land at the same
place twice, that makes it the perfect location for a pickup."

"Reasonable, and believable. This may just work."

"Absolutely. That is, if the terrorists think it's legit, and
still want to recover their spy instead of simply burning
her down," Price added grimly. "There's a good chance
this could go sour. Able Team is setting a trap for terrorists who hold all of the cards, every aspect is in the favor
of the *Skywalkers.*"

"Except for one," Brognola retorted. "And his name is
Ironman…."

Flintstone, Maryland

DESERTED FOR MANY DECADES, the Flintstone amusement
park was a forgotten relic of its glory days when people
poured in from across the state to visit the water slide,
roller coasters and famous haunted house. Live actors in
heavy cosmetics used to hide among the stage exhibits
and grab the patrons, scaring them into hysterical laughter. Young girls clung tightly to the arms of their escorts,
and giddy children squealed in unabashed delight at the
twisted faces of the living monsters.

But that was all long gone now, erased by the slow passage of time. Nearly overgrown with weeds and small
tress, the amusement park stood like a crumbling mau-
soleum in a forgotten graveyard. The front gates were
firmly closed, draped with a thick chain, and the turnstiles
at the ticket kiosks were half buried in windblown trash,
impossible to open without heavy machinery or explo-

sives. But the hurricane fence surrounding the park was streaked with red rust, and sagged in many spots low enough to touch the ground, offering easy access.

Torn banners announcing prizes and fun fluttered impotently in the breeze, the noise oddly sounding like an ancient sailing ship on the high sea. The rainbow paint was peeling on every building and hut, and their glass windows were smashed. The pavement was badly cracked, and assorted piles of rotting debris jostled for supremacy with the mounds of corroded machinery that was all that remained of the rides. Even the haunted house was decomposing into the earth, the hidden loudspeakers exposed, the trapdoors ajar, the brick walls vandalized with graffiti, as the structure slowly began to resemble a real Gothic mansion of yore.

Only in the center of the once glorious midway were the weeds gone, burned out of existence, the cracked pavement pitted with slagged holes deep enough to bury a grown man. The ground was spotlessly clean, everything loose, leaves, dead rats and petrified ticket stubs had been blasted a score of yards off by the fiery exhaust of the X-ship. Trailing away from the landing zone was a burn mark on the ground leading directly to a jagged blast crater, bits and pieces of curved metal lying about, one of them still bearing enough lettering to show it had once been a refrigerated container of liquid hydrogen.

Overlaying everything was a forensic grid erected by the FBI and local police. Steel pegs had been hammered into the pavement, brightly colored twine strung between them to a section off the area into square yards. Methodically, the FBI had vacuumed the blast zone, collecting everything, searching for anything that might possibly be a clue to the identity or whereabouts of the *Skywalkers*.

They took a thousand photographs and even dusted the rocks for fingerprints, accumulating the grand total of absolutely nothing of importance. The volcanic drive flames of the X-ships utterly destroyed any possible DNA trace from cigarette butts, discarded chewing gum or dropped human hair. Once filled with happy throngs, the barren midway was now as lifeless and sterile as a morgue freezer.

Outside the fence, a parking lot stretched for a hundred yards to end at a small building constructed to resemble a Wild West saloon. On the other side, a set of railroad tracks ran through a pass in the rolling hillside, disappearing in both directions. Once there had been a platform for passengers to disembark, but that had been removed. Now there was only the ramshackle saloon, the windows covered with sheets of plywood, a bird nest blocking the chimney and a thick blanket of ivy covering everything else in sight.

However, inside was another matter entirely. Lyon was studying the amusement park through field glasses supported by a tripod; Blancanales was eating stew out of a steamy MRE envelope, and Schwarz was wearing headphones, hunched over a sonic oscillator, trying to fine tune the piece of equipment to even greater sensitivity. Blankets of ballistic cloth were hung over the walls, offering the men some small degree of protection, open crates of heavy ordnance lay on the floor for easy access, and industrial carbon dioxide fire extinguishers were in every corner, but those would only give the men a few second of protection if hell arrived from the heavens.

"Any sign of them yet?" Blancanales asked, licking the

spoon clean and dropping it into a plastic bucket along with the empty MRE envelope.

"Nothing so far," Schwarz replied, adjusting the controls on the oscillator. "But then, it's only been twenty minutes since I turned on the beacon." Several shotgun microphones and a long-range dish mike were hidden among the ivy outside, but Schwarz was pinning his hopes on the oscillator. It should detect an X-ship descending from the sky long before he could hear anything on the headphones.

"Are you sure it'll work?" Blancanales asked.

"Absolutely. They can hear us. Whether they wish to respond is another matter."

"Pity we couldn't put a dish mike on the roof," Lyons said, switching from normal vision to Starlite. Everything went black and white, but got noticeably sharper in detail. "If we did, then we might as well put a giant 'this is a trap' sign on the roof."

"I hate to think of Toni out there all by herself," Schwarz muttered, shifting uncomfortably on his box.

"She's not alone," Blancanales replied. "We're here."

His sister was wearing the clothes taken from Swanson's work locker, stitched together where they didn't quite fit over the woman's figure, especially as it was augmented by NATO body armor. Unless the X-ship saw their spy in person, they might not land. The danger was that they might not land anyway, preferring to kill her rather than endanger the ship by sitting still for even a single minute on the ground.

"Damn, it's cold," Toni said over a speaker on the audio amplifier. Unlike the rest of the team, the woman was not wearing a throat mike and transponder. One of the shotgun microphones was pointed in her general direction, relaying everything she said. "Thanks for tucking the chemical pocket warmers into my body armor, Carl. They help a lot."

"Been on enough stakeouts to know what to bring," Lyons replied as if she could hear him.

There was the rumbling of cloth, closely followed by scratching. "Although, they are making my breasts sweat like crazy," Toni added. "Itches a bit, too."

"I didn't need to hear that," Blancanales said with a pained expression.

"You know she's doing this just to torture you, right?" Lyons asked, almost smiling.

"Sisters," Blancanales replied with a sigh, as if the single word explained everything.

Softly, the team could hear steps mixing with the snap and flutter of the old banners. "Hey, you guys want to hear about the time I caught Rosario and his prom date swimming naked in our swimming pool?"

"Gadgets, does that thing have an off switch," his teammate growled, glancing sideways.

"Sorry, no." Schwarz chuckled, covering the aforementioned item with a palm. "Hey, Carl, five will get you six, they were drunk."

"I'll take ten of that," Lyons said over a shoulder.

"You're covered. Blancanales?"

"Listen, asshole…aw, what the hell, I'm in for five that she says it was wine."

"Was it?"

"Ask her."

"So, it was after midnight, and our folks were asleep," Toni started. "I got up to get a glass of water, and they were splashing and swimming about in the moonlight. Buck-naked, naturally, and waving around bottles of— Hey."

At the word, the men were suddenly alert, the joking banter instantly gone.

"I think there was just a…" Toni's voice paused uncertainly. For a moment there was only the rustling of the windblown trash. "Nope, I'm certain, it just got noticeably warmer out here."

Lurching to his feet, Blancanales rushed into the next room and there came metallic clicks and clacks.

"Outside temperature is up two degrees," Lyons reported, checking the gauges. "Three…four… Get hard, boys, they're here!"

"And coming fast!" Schwarz announced, flipping the kill switch on the oscillator and ripping off the headphones. Going silent, the sine wave pattern on the glowing green screen was peaking like crazy, the valleys getting smaller and sharper every second. Set off by itself, the portable radar unit was humming smoothly, the grid perfectly clear.

Suddenly they heard dim thunder from the dish mike pointed at the stars. Then the men heard it through the roof, and the night brightened outside, a reddish light streaming through every small crack behind the ballistic cloth until it seemed they were incandescent.

"Height…one mile. Range…ninety-two yards!" Lyons announced, swiveling the field glass to track the descending vessel. "Okay, they're heading for the parking lot, not the midway!" There was a definite note of relief in his voice. "One thousand feet….five hundred feet—" The deafening exhaust of the X-ship cut the man off.

Some garbled words came from the speaker of the audio amplifier, but whatever Toni said was completely lost in the growing thunder of the arriving X-ship.

Lyons grabbed a HAFLA rocket launcher from a stack on a nearby shelf. Pulling the pin, he extended the plastic tube to its full length, the sights popping up and a cover sliding back to reveal a single red button.

Turning, he saw Schwarz already at the exit, the laptop slung at his side, both hands cradling an M-16 assault rifle. Blancanales stepped out of the back room carrying an FN 303. Resembling something from a sci-fi movie, the stubby weapon had an enormously wide barrel, a pistol grip and a small air tank connected to a drum magazine via a flexible hose. A purely pneumatic weapon, the 303 fired .63 plastic spheres, similar to ordinary paint balls, except that these went a lot farther, hit much harder and could be loaded with anything that was liquid at room temperature: tear gas, deadly neurotoxins or even acid. But since the team needed the terrorists alive, these projectiles were all packed with a narcotic sleep gas. There would be no mistakes this time. The Stony Man operatives were going for a capture, not a kill.

Resting the stock of the bulky weapon on a hip, Blancanales held up two fingers. The other men nodded in understanding, then Lyons kicked open the splintery saloon door and Able Team boldly stepped outside into the billowing clouds of smoke.

A hot wind buffeted the men, almost knocking them to the ground, windblown bits of trash and loose stones peppering them with stinging force. The air reeked of hot tar, and the noise level was deafening. Conversation was impossible, even with the throat mike and earbuds.

Balanced on a column of flame, the X-ship lowered to the ground, the legs automatically adjusting to keep the vessel on an even keel. Directly under the rocket engines, the pavement was gone, a ragged hole extending out of sight, the opening ringed with bubbling tar. Every trace of the weeds was gone, but the larger bushes and slender trees growing out of the pavement were on fire, adding a nightmarish effect to the scene.

Spreading out, Able Team took what cover was available, and patiently waited for the smoke to clear, all the while counting off the two minutes under their breath.

Dominating the abandoned amusement park, standing larger than the top of the roller coaster, the colossal X-ship visibly radiated heat, the air shimmering in waves, while the engine vectors started making sharp pinging noises as the hot metal contracted slightly at the touch of the evening breeze. Then a small hatch swung outward and a man in a military jumpsuit appeared. He toted an FN F2000 rifle and wore a respirator-style gas mask.

Muttering a curse, Blancanales tossed aside the fully loaded FN 303 and swung around the M-16/M-203 from behind his back, working the arming bolt and clicking off the safety. Okay, they had to do it the hard way, he thought.

Muffled by distance, a female voice yelled something indecipherable on the breeze.

Scowling, the terrorist standing in the hatch turned awkwardly toward the haunted house. A blond woman was in the third-floor window, waving and shouting. Touching his throat, the terrorist muttered something, then nodded in assent.

Already working at his laptop, Schwarz smiled coldly as the screen pulsed then scrolled with a line string of numbers. Gotcha! Okay, the first step was accomplished. He had the frequency the terrorists used to communicate with each other. However, the electronics expert could plainly see that the transmission was heavily encrypted, far beyond the ability of him to decode in the field. Grimly, he closed the laptop and locked the lid into place. Fair enough. He either needed one of the bastards alive and talking, or else he had to get inside that ship and find the communications board. However, for right now… Touching a switch on the transponder at his belt, Schwarz jammed the airwaves with impenetrable hash.

"Here we go," Lyons said under his breath, restraining himself from looking behind.

Exactly on schedule, the roof of the saloon was violently blown apart into splinters and shingles as a stuttering stream of bright streaks lanced into the sky to noisily explode. Hot shrapnel rained upon the X-ship as the automatic motor continued to discharge rounds nonstop.

Taking that as their cue, the men of Able team broke cover and raced toward the X-ship. The mortar was only a diversion, and throwing that much firepower skyward, the ammunition bins would be empty in only a few minutes. That was all they had to cover three hundred feet of open ground with nothing to use as cover aside from a few burning bushes.

Gasping in surprise at the bombardment, the terrorist on the ladder paused for only a heartbeat, then started frantically climbing back up toward the hatch. Raising the HAFLA, Lyons aimed on the run and pressed the button. Fire and smoke exploded from the aft end of the tube, and the rocket streaked away, crossing the intervening hundred yards in under a heartbeat. The napalm rocket hit, and the terrorist was blown off the access ladder, chunks of him flying away like flaming meteors.

Charging forward, Blancanales and Schwarz raced toward the X-ship, their assault rifles chattering steadily away, the 5.56 mm HEAT rounds sizzling through the air to impact on the armored hull and cling there like droplets of burning honey. The miniature thermite rounds were experimental, something new created by Cowboy Kissinger just for this mission. Their purpose was not to destroy, but merely to weaken the hull until the SSO was no longer capable of flight.

However, each man had only one clip of the specials, and as they became exhausted, the two commandos switched to conventional HEAT rounds. They looked almost the same as the handmade Cowboy specials, but did no damage whatsoever.

Riding the streams up the hull, the two Stony Man operatives reached the open hatchway and poured in hot lead, the hardball ammo and perfectly imbalanced tumblers ricocheting madly inside. But there didn't seem to be any results. No explosions or showers of electrical sparks. They had been worried about this. The entrance point was just as well armored as the exterior hull.

Without warning, the automatic motor in the saloon stopped and an eerie quiet covered the wartorn landscape.

Unexpectedly, a squat machine appeared in the open hatch. It had a burnished metal shield and a short ventilated barrel. Recognizing the weapon, Blancanales and Schwarz dived for cover, and a split second later the 20 mm Gatling began to hammer loudly, the big HE shells streaking down to chew up the cracked pavement, throwing around chunks like black confetti.

Swinging up the Atchisson, Lyons paused to brace himself and stroked off an entire drum of 12-gauge deer slugs. The recoil was brutal, almost knocking the man backward, but the DU rounds hammered the hull with ringing force. Casting away the spent drum, Lyons slammed in a fresh one, and saw with some satisfaction that the X-ship now had a series of small dents along the fuselage, the first real sign of weakness any of the giant machines had ever shown.

Destroying the machine once it was on the ground would have been easy; simply bring in a Vulcan minigun or a pod of 7.8 mm Hellfire rockets and it would have been twisted metal trash in less than a minute. But the man needed the people inside the ship alive and unharmed. Intel from the crew of the X-ship was vital to locate their base and take out Colonel Southerland.

There was a flash of light from the haunted house. A missile flew over the amusement park and slammed into the pavement under one of the support legs. The X-ship trembled, but corrected itself with a hiss of powerful hydraulics.

Switching tactics, Blancanales and Schwarz sent 40 mm shells into the hatch. At first it seemed they had both missed, but the shells detonated inside the ship and the 20 mm Gatling gun hurtled free, still firing randomly as it tumbled to the ground and smashed into assorted pieces, the linked belt of shells coming apart. Only a thick teleflex cable remained to dangle impotently from the hatch.

Three bright flashes winked from the haunted house

and a trio of missiles appeared out of the night. One of them struck the nose of the X-ship and burst into a napalm firestorm, but the other two went past, missing the vehicle by only inches.

Suddenly there came a bright spray of sparks from the rocket engines as the preburners were ignited.

They were getting ready to run!

Out of DU rounds, Lyons shoved in a drum of stainless-steel fléchettes, chose a mark and poured everything he had into the deepest dent.

Circling the X-ship, Blancanales and Schwarz joined their team leader and added the destructive power of their grenade launchers.

A powerful whine came from the engines as the pumps revved to full speed, then a maelstrom of plasma bellowed from the vessel, the exhaust hitting Able Team like the concussion of a blockbuster bomb. Their boots came off the pavement and they went sailing backward to painfully crash down once more. But the team was still holding weapons as the X-ship began to rise.

Another missile was launched from the haunted house as Able Team shot at the transport while lying down. They couldn't see a thing, and were totally relying upon their combat senses.

However, the X-ship began to rotate, moving the target area away from them. Inserting a fresh drum, Lyons bitterly cursed. Obviously the pilot was no fool and had deduced their plan of attack. Then something cool touched his face. Swatting it away, the man felt moisture and looked to see snow in his palm. For a split second, he thought the pilot was venting liquid nitrogen, but when he didn't die, Lyons knew the truth. This was not a deliberate release, but a leak! Oxygen? Hydrogen? It didn't matter, as long as it was enough to stop the ship from taking off!

In a rush of power, the X-ship flashed upward and was gone from sight. Grimly, Blancanales and Schwarz continued to fire at the vessel, even though they knew it was almost certainly out of range.

"Cease fire," Lyons said into his throat mike. The combination of exhaust gases and vaporized tar actually reminded the man of when he was a smoker. "Save your ammo for when they come back."

"Come back…think we did some damage?" Schwarz asked, using the M-16 to lever himself upright. His left arm hung limply, red blood dripping off his fingers. There was a dark stain at his shoulder, but the area did not seem to be increasing in size.

Concerned, Lyons looked in the face of his friend and saw the truth. Whew, just a flesh wound, nothing important. Good. They would need the technical expertise of the man very soon. Just then, a beautiful glistening snow fell from the sky. Most of it vanished before reaching the pavement, but the few flakes that drifted near the burning tree puffed out of existence in small explosions.

"They must be leaking fuel like crazy for it to reach us down here!" Blancanales cried in delight, pulling out a med kit. "Come on, I can fix Gadgets while we race to the next battleground."

A deep throb sounded in the night and a moment later bright lights appeared over the amusement park. Sweeping low and fast, a Black Hawk helicopter came toward the three men, a blond woman at the controls.

Good. Time and the elements were against them. The

crew of the X-ship had to know they had a leak by now, and were making some fast decisions. If they kept flying, it could get worse and they'd drop from the sky, out of fuel. Or worse, it might reach the engines and ignite, turning the ten-story-tall space ship into a bonfire. No, they had to land, and fast. But far enough away so that the attackers on the ground couldn't reach them in time with bigger weapons capable of finishing the job of crippling the X-ship. Some place where they would have cover, some place that could hide a 120-foot-tall machine that generated more noise and light than the battle for Bunker Hill.

As the Black Hawk landed, the men bent low to avoid the spinning blades and rushed forward. Yeah, Lyons knew the perfect location, tailor-made for the terrorists, and it was only twenty minutes away by air. That had to be where the *Skywalkers* were going. The big question was, would the X-ship still be there when they arrived? Or was this ambush just about to turn into a full-fledged slaughter?

CHAPTER SIXTEEN

Brussels, Belgium

With a loud squeal of brakes, the speeding Hummer pulled to the curb in front of the brick building, narrowly avoiding a LAV 25 Armored Personnel Carrier.

"That was fun," the new lieutenant from Greece said mockingly, waiting for the military vehicle to stop rocking back and forth. "What's the matter, incapable of reaching warp speed?"

"I was thirsty!" the French major replied with a chuckle, stepping from the vehicle and closing the door. "Come on, you're the new fish here, so the first round is on you."

"Thought I'd be treated to a drink," the lieutenant said accusingly, climbing to the curb with wobbly legs.

Spreading his arms, the major smiled. "Welcome to NATO."

"Thanks," the Greek officer said, reading the sign on the wall. "Club 13? As in, a baker's dozen? A sign of good luck?"

"No, it's some kind of an American joke," the Frenchman replied. "Never quite understood it myself."

Pushing open the weathered door, the two officers entered the club and a steamy wall of music, cigarette smoke, chatter, fried food and beer hit them in the face. Smiling broadly, both men looked around for an empty table, then hurried over, trying to beat anybody else interested in the precious rarity. There were no reservations held at Club 13; there were hardly any rules. Officers and enlisted personnel sat together, nobody saluted anybody, and a score of civilians mixed freely with the off-duty military. Originally, the club had been a WWII Quonset hut erected by a couple of Army Air Corps and British RAF pilots as a place to relax between flying missions into Germany. But it soon became so popular that the club grew exponentially, the building changing and expanding over the decades until it reached the present incarnation of a two-story brick building containing a hundred tables, a fifty-foot-long bar, two jukeboxes and a grand piano for anybody with musical talent or just drunk enough to give it a go anyway.

A Turkish waitress nearly as weathered as the front door took their food and drink order, slapped the major on the back of the head for patting her ass, and strolled away shouting English to the Japanese cook busy frying something in the steamy kitchen.

Vastly amused, the Greek lieutenant looked around the establishment, drinking in the relaxed atmosphere. Everybody seemed tense, yet no one was talking about the *Skywalkers,* but that was the only iron-clad rule of Club 13: no business. At least, the lieutenant thought they weren't discussing the problem. There were at least a dozen languages being spoken in the club. He had expected something like this, but the reality was nearly overwhelming.

"So, have you been fully briefed?" the major asked, snagging a handful of popcorn from another table.

"Of course," the Greek replied crisply, assuming this was a friendly test. "Although the rest of the world calls us NATO, we call ourselves the Alliance. We do all the fighting, while our political division, SHAPE, the Supreme Headquarters Ailed Powers of Europe, does all the talking."

"Yes, that's nice," the major said, munching on the snack. "But I meant, have you been briefed on truly important things? Such as, don't date any of the female Swedish fighter pilots, they'll kill you in bed, and that's a Frenchman giving you that warning."

"I see." the Greek chuckled, taking some of the popcorn. "That's highly useful intel to have. Anything else?"

"Sure! Never let the Italians talk about fashion, they'll never shut up, and shooting them is against the rules. Always accept a drink from the Portuguese, they have a white wine that is so good it should come from France. But if an American invites you to a game of 52 Pickup…"

Suddenly there came a low rumble of thunder from outside, the noise level rapidly escalating until it swamped the Russian jazz playing on the jukebox. Every conversation stopped for a moment, then there came the rattle of heavy machine guns.

Instantly the NATO soldiers kicked back their chairs and charged for the nearest exit. Bursting into daylight, the major saw that the sky was filled with chaos, tracer rounds stabbing upward from numerous locations, the smoky contrails of a dozen missiles crisscrossing above the military base, heading in various directions. Sirens were howling from every building, and people were dashing in every direction.

"Good God," the major whispered.

"It must be them!" the lieutenant growled, clenching a fist. "The *Skywalkers!* Are they insane to attack the Alliance?"

"And why not?" the major snapped. "Nothing has stopped them yet."

"But surely our new THOR missiles…"

"Are heat-seekers and radar-guided, both of which are useless against an X-ship. Useless!"

Just then a ragged delta of jetfighters rose from the airfield and arched upward, launching Sidewinder missiles from their wings, the 30 mm nose-cannons flashing brightly.

"Ah, the Swedes have arrived!" the major cried, raising a fist. "And the Russians, too! Now the bastards are in for a real fight!"

"Do you think…" the lieutenant began when a NATO jet came tumbling back into view, the entire fuselage covered with flames. It exploded before reaching the ground, and seconds later, several more half-melted wrecks plummeted through the thinning clouds.

Every weapon on the base moved toward that area of the sky, but the X-ship dropped into sight faster than the gunner on the ground could track. Gushing white clouds from a ring of vents set along their middle, the X-ships moved sideways over the base, pumping out flares and metallic chaff. The rising swarms of SAM and THOR missiles ignored the giant machine as if it did not exist, and instead locked upon the countermeasures, detonating far away from the descending terrorists.

Sweeping the airfield, the exhaust of the X-ship destroyed a dozen more jetfighters on the ground. Dripping flames, an Italian Ashanti gunship made it aloft only to drop back once more onto the tarmac, smashing into a million pieces, the blades spinning off into the distance.

Appearing on the roof of Club 13, a soldier lifted a LAW and braced for the recoil. Smoke shot out of both ends and the rocket streaked across the military base, missing the X-ship by the thickness of a prayer.

Shouting something in what sounded like Norwegian, a big woman shoved a couple of assault rifles at the lieutenant and major. Thankfully grabbing the weapons, the officers worked the arming bolts and started firing at the enemy. The range was extreme, but if he could help take them down even a little bit, it would be more than worth the effort. The machines could not be invulnerable. They had to have a weakness. They had to!

By now a hundred other soldiers in the street were also cutting loose with assault rifles and even sidearms at the X-ships. LAW and Stingers launched from every rooftop and more NATO jetfighters appeared on the horizon.

As if responding to the renewed threat, the machine vented more white mist, then rose upward, stopping just below the cloud layer. A small hatch opened on the side, something fell out, and then the X-ship shot skyward at incredible velocity, disappearing in only seconds.

"A bomb?" the Greek said, sneering, lowering his weapon. "After all of this they drop one bomb…saints alive, it is a nuke!"

"No, it's worse," the major said, watching the object fall. An expert in nonnuclear munitions, he recognized the device instantly as an FAE, fuel-air explosive, the most powerful, nonnuclear weapon in existence. There was still the taste of popcorn in his mouth, and he thought longingly of the Turkish waitress.

"What could be worse than a nuke?" the Greek demanded.

But before the Frenchman could reply, the falling object seemed to softly explode, a gaseous cloud shooting outward for hundreds of yards in every direction, then the sky burst into flames.

The searing flash temporarily blinded everybody looking in that direction, then the physical shock wave arrived. Missiles and rockets detonated in midflight and bullets were deflected. A water tower burst apart, the rooftops of a hundred buildings buckled and a thousand windows shattered. Anybody standing directly below the titanic airblast was crushed into pulp. Everybody else was roughly thrown off their feet to fly backward for yards, often to crash into the trembling brick buildings with sickening results.

A split second later the thermal wave arrived. The people on the street burst into flames, weapons detonating in their hands. Cars exploded, the pavement buckled…then all of the flames went out and everything loose was sucked into the sky with hurricane force by the hard vacuum created by the FAE.

Badly cooked, but still alive, the soldiers inside the armored personnel carriers and battle tanks suddenly could not breathe as they were slammed against the tiny air vents. Their eyes popped, blood gushed from their noses, then the choking soldiers began to convulse as their lungs ripped lose inside their laboring chests and were literally sucked out of their open mouths.

The swirling maelstrom of debris and bodies rose above the decimated NATO base, then the titanic forces in the atmosphere equalized in a crashing peel of thunder and the grisly objects fell back to the burned ground in a hellish rain.

Long minutes passed. There were no sounds, no cries of pain, or crackling fires, only the unearthly still of battlefield where the fighting was over and there was nobody left alive.

Flintstone, Maryland

IN A RUSH OF WARM AIR, the Black Hawk landed in a soybean field and the side hatch was slammed open. Jumping to the ground, the four Stony Man commandos charged toward the distant trees, hoping and praying that they were not too late. But after a few yards they stopped and turned around as the Black Hawk revved its engines to take off again.

"Toni?" Blancanales asked, looking back over a shoulder.

"Sorry, big brother, but we each have a job to do," Toni replied over the com link, the helicopter rising off the ground slightly. "Carl, let me know when to move, and I'll be there."

"Confirm," he replied with a curt nod. "Okay, guys, let's move!"

"Is Toni going to do what I think she's going to do?" Schwarz asked, running alongside the others.

Hopping over a fallen tree, Lyons made no reply, and Blancanales's face was a hard, expressionless mask.

"Gonna take that as a yes," Schwarz muttered, dodging a tree stump. He always knew the woman had guts, but this was off the chart.

Darting into the woods, the men of Able Team didn't slow until light dappled the darkness as they approached the end of the grove. Staying low, the team maintained the brisk pace, ducking under branches and plowing through bushes until reaching the edge of the forest. Dropping low, they crawled into the moonlight until reaching the end of a cliff.

Ahead was only a vast empty space, the darkness oddly distorted by the moving shadows on the rock walls of the huge quarry. Long ago, the name of the town and county had not been a humorous reminder of a classic TV show, but a simple declaration of why the town was created. The flint in the ground, a much-needed commodity to operate the muskets of the time period, along with starting cooking fires. But that was more than a hundred years ago. Now the sprawling quarry was crumbling along the edge, the sharp outlines of the interior softening with the advance of greenery, ivy and kudzu seeking out any tiny purchase in the cracked facade.

There should have only been inky blackness at the bottom of the deep quarry, the moon at the wrong angle to shine inside. But instead something large could dimly be seen in the stygian gloom, a gigantic, ten-story shape roughly outlined by the tiny handheld worklights of people inspecting the outside, moving the beams up and down the vessel. Nearby was a shimmering pool of rainwater reflecting the moving points of illumination and causing the distorted shadows.

The team eased closer. The top of the X-ship was easily a hundred feet below the level of the ground, making it practically invisible to anybody passing on the road or flying overhead Unless you already knew it was there.

Suddenly the lights winked out. Instantly the team readied their weapons, braced for the X-ship to take off once more. But instead some hatches swung open in the dented hull, light pouring out, then there came ringing tones of metal hitting metal and the blue-white sputter of an electric arch welder.

"Hallelujah." Lyons exhaled, voicing a rare chuckle. "They're doing the repairs right here."

Reaching up, the man touched his throat mike. "Lady Bird, this is Jungle Cat, time to bung the barrel."

"Roger, JC," Toni replied crisply. "ETA sixty seconds!"

"Confirm."

For a few moments there was only the soft murmur of the breeze through the trees, the sounds of nature oddly mixing with the mechanical noises from below. Then the night came alive with a dull beat that quickly escalated to the powerful throb of the Black Hawk. Moving fast and low, Toni streaked over the treetops and dived down into the quarry. The sound of the repairs stopped. Then she turned on a halogen searchlight, the bright beam playing over the X-ship as she began to fly around it. From the other side, where the men could not see, there came some virulent cursing, followed by several pistols shots. Sparks showed on the armored hull of the helicopter, but the pilot ignored the incoming rounds and moved over the X-ship to hover directly above the rounded nose cone, less than ten feet away.

Immediately the gunfire stopped and there was more cursing. Lyons grunted at that. Okay, the bastards knew they were trapped. If the *Skywalkers* tried to take off now, they would have to plow through the Black Hawk. The X-ship could easily smash the much smaller helicopter aside, but the impact would deflect them just enough to crash into the flinty stone walls and tear the spaceship apart. A mouse standing defiant in front of an express train.

"This is the Maryland State Police," Toni boomed over the external speakers of the helicopter. "You are all under arrest! Come out with your hands raised!" But only silence answered the challenge.

"Jesus, that's smart," Schwarz said in frank admiration. "Now they think it's only the local PD and not the lunatics from the amusement park."

"Hell of a woman," Lyons agreed, opening a HAFLA for combat.

"You don't know the half of it, amigo," Blancanales replied, a marked trace of a brother's pride in his voice.

Shouting down more commands for surrender, Toni continued to make as much noise as possible. The pistol shots returned, closely followed by the sustained yammer of an assault rifle. But the belly armor of the military transport was designed to take that sort of punishment, and there was no result other than more ricochet sparks. Then there came a double thump and two explosions blossomed on the side of the Black Hawk. The helicopter shook slightly from the 30 mm rounds, but did not move from its position.

"Showtime," Lyons declared, standing to swing up the HAFLA and fire. The napalm rocket streaked across the stone quarry and just missed the X-ship. It slammed into the opposite rock wall, spraying out a chemical inferno, the hull of the X-ship tanging sharply with the arrival of hundreds of rock chips.

With the X-ship perfectly silhouetted by the writing flames, Schwarz unleashed a LAW and hit the machine amidships just alongside the access ladder. The quarry magnified the echoing blast until it sounded like doomsday, and when the roiling smoke cleared, there was a ragged hole in the hull that exposed a complex maze of wiring, pipes and cables.

Moving fast, Blancanales aimed and launched his Stinger, the missile locking on to the heat signature of the explosion. The warbird lanced straight down from the cliff and slammed into the small breach, detonating deep inside the vessel. Smoke and broken machinery thundered out of the hole, tumbling into the dark waters with countless little splashes. Visibly, the entire X-ship shook from the hit and started to tilt slightly when the hydraulic jacks built into the legs came alive and the damaged vessel righted itself once more.

Able Team grimaced at the sight. Even trapped motionless on the ground, their weapons could do nothing more than damage the monstrous machine. However, there was now a gaping hole in the armored hull large enough to drive a Hummer through. Even if the *Skywalker* got off the ground, any attempt to fly full-speed would split the vessel apart. Casting away the spent launchers, the team took off at a full sprint down the sloping access ramp. The terrorists couldn't reach space anymore, but the aircraft wasn't grounded yet. The X-ship could still turn on the engines and easily burn them out of existence. That was, unless the Stony Man team kept the crews too busy fighting for their lives.

Pausing on a natural ledge, Lyons fired off an entire drum of double-aught buckshot from the Atchisson while his teammates raced ahead. When the drum ran empty, Lyons took off at a run, hastily reloading as he sprinted past Schwarz who was standing at the next ledge down, hammering the damaged hull with 5.56 mm tumblers from the M-16. When the clip was finished, he dropped it and reloaded on the run, moving past Blancanales doing the same thing, and adding the destructive power of a 40 mm AP grenade. The hole did not get any bigger, but more broken machinery came flying out, along with a steady trickle of hydraulic fluid.

Maintaining the three-on-three formation, Able Team poured death and destruction at the X-ship, while Toni kept loudly demanding the surrender of the terrorists. Reaching the bottom of the ramp, the men separated and zigzagged across the bare stone floor of the quarry, utilizing what little cover there was, a block of stone, a lump of ancient machinery, a clump of weeds. The air was warm and carried the bitter stink of ozone, a by-product of oxidized fuel. But there was also the tang of hot metal and something else they could not quite identify. Sort of a metallic smell...

"Venting!" Lyons shouted, dropping to roll behind a pile of loose stones.

A split second later the X-ship began to hiss and a terrible white mist gushed from a ring of hidden vents. Instantly the air chilled to arctic temperature. The team's breath started to fog and every inch of exposed skin felt as if it were being stabbed with steel needles. This was a tactic the team had no defense for, no countermove to implement. They could only ignore the terrible pain and keep fighting.

Forcing themselves to stumble forward, the Stony Man operatives took new positions closer to the X-ship, when there came a hard thump from high overhead and something shot away from the ship to explode in midair, sending out a sizzling cloud of rolling flames. Sweet Jesus, that was white phosphorous! The team recognized it as a real danger. There was nothing they could do to stop the descent of the fiery cloud. Stoically, they rose and moved onward again, trying to get underneath the engines of the X-ship before death arrived.

Revving the Black Hawk's big diesel engines to full power, Toni banked sharply and flew straight toward the chem. storm, the wash of the spinning turbo-blades scattering the burning chemical until it dissipated. Then she raced back into position, the landing rails of the helicopter edged with bright yellow flames.

"Thanks, Lady Bird," Schwarz panted, breaking cover and charging forward once more. The terrorist had made a beginner's mistake with that double attack, the heat of the willie peter countering the cold of the liquid nitrogen. They might be hot-shot pilots, but on the ground they were a bunch of rookies compared to the seasoned veterans of Able Team.

Apparently figuring that out for themselves, the terrorists tried a new tactic. There came the sound of an assault rifle firing, a hail of bullets smacking into the floor of the quarry. The combined noises almost enough to mask the sound of metal on metal. One of them was trying to hold off the invaders, while the other made hasty repairs.

Firing controlled bursts in response, the team got closer to the X-ship when a 30 mm shell landed in a pile of rubble behind them, the blast sending out a halo of loose stones. All three of the men were bowled over and fell gasping for breath. The NATO body armor had prevented their spines from breaking, but the pain was nearly overwhelming. Nearly, but not quite. Rising once again, they kept going, unstoppable, grimly determined to reach the ship at any cost.

"Lady Bird to Jungle Cat," Toni said over the com link. "I saw what happened. Are you injured? Do you want an extraction?"

"Negative!" Lyons snapped, jutting to the left and right to make himself difficult to target. "Do not move from your position! Keep them on the damn ground!"

"Consider it done, Jungle Cat," the woman replied. "Call when you want me."

"Roger, Lady Bird," Lyons replied, forcing himself to keep going. There was a numb spot on his hip that spoke of a serious injury, but there was no time for that now. They had to keep going, get close, get inside, find that transponder and end these murdering bastards!

A terrible fury was welling up inside the man, and this time the former police officer did nothing to hold it in check. Shouting defiantly, he strode directly for the X-ship, the Atchisson booming lead and steel. He had no idea how much liquid nitrogen that big ship could carry, and if they vented again with the team this close, it was all over. But Aaron Kurtzman had theorized that the X-ships had to have a very limited supply. Just enough for each mission, and no extra. The huge spaceships were the ultimate gas guzzler, and every ounce of weight limited their flight time. So there would be exactly enough for them to conduct a specific task, and maybe a touch extra for emergencies, but no more. With no way to confirm that, Able Team was risking everything on the guess of their chief hacker.

The classic sound of an M-16 came from the darkness to his left, and then another from the right. The others were on the move again, closing in around the X-ship from different angles. Firing off a full drum of fléchettes toward the unseen enemy above, Lyons broke into a full run, covering the remaining hundred feet in breathless seconds. Then turning fast, the man slammed his back against one of the landing legs, the metal oven hot even through his clothing and body armor. But he made it, he was at the ship! Now, to get inside.

"Six o'clock!" Schwarz said over the com link.

Lurching into motion, Lyons headed that way fast, and soon saw the other man already climbing up the access ladder set into the next leg.

Just then, there came an odd revving noise from the rocket engines and hot sparks began to spray out from vector nozzles. The terrorists had turned on the preburners! A shower of white-hot sparks covered Lyons, but he ignored the new pain, concentrating on just reaching the ladder. Then the agony abruptly ceased and he found himself in the protective lee of the wide leg, the hot sparks splaying out on either side.

"Senator, give me your location!" Lyons gasped, shouldering the Atchisson.

"I'm trapped behind a leg on the other side," Blancanales answered. "No way I'm getting through this shit without asbestos underwear."

"Then stay there, and try to keep their attention for two minutes!"

"I'll buy you five. Good luck!"

Grunting in acknowledgment, Lyons grabbed the rungs and started climbing, putting everything he had in getting as far away from those titanic engines as possible. Which meant that he was now heading straight for the nitrogen vents, but there was nothing to do about that, except climb faster.

Crouching in the protective lee of another leg, Blancanales touched his belt to count the ammo clips, making a plan. "Give me some midnight, Lady Bird," he said urgently into his throat mike.

There was no reply from Toni, but the halogen searchlights blinked out. Instantly he broke cover and charged into the darkness. Hopping over a yawning crack in the ground, Blancanales landed in a shoulder roll and took position behind a rusting mound of unidentifiable mining equipment. Even if the X-ship started to launch, it should buy him a few seconds of protection. Before I fry like bacon in boots, he thought.

Concentrating on the open hatch, the Able Team warrior poured in clip after clip to make sure it stayed open. "Come on, guys, haul ass!" he muttered under his breath, slapping in his next-to-last reload.

As if suddenly aware of the danger on the ground, he heard a hard thumping sound from the engines, and then they ignited, a tidal wave of flame thundering across the floor of the quarry. Dropping as low as he could, Blancanales braced himself for the onslaught, but nothing happened aside from the deafening splay of fire. The terrorists were merely performing a controlled release! Not trying to launch, just trying to kill the attackers.

"Bad move, assholes," he growled, thumbing a fat 40 mm round into the grenade launcher and waiting impatiently for the ocean of fire to die away.

On the access ladder Schwarz was almost at the hatch when a man appeared carrying a FN F2000 assault rifle, and wearing body armor. Jerking a hand forward, Schwarz buried his Gerber between the legs of the terrorist. Rocked by pain, the man lost the rifle and grabbed for the bloody knife with both hands. Still holding on to the handle, Schwarz yanked hard and the off-balance man went out of the hatch and over his head to fall away into the night.

"Incoming!" Schwarz said, crawling into the hatch, his Beretta sweeping for targets.

"Yeah, I saw. He landed near me," Blancanales answered. "I don't think we can interrogate this one without a Ouija board."

"So go buy me a Ouija board," Lyons muttered, climbing into the hatch.

Standing alongside each other, the two Stony Man commandos studied the metal room, noting the lack of video cameras or anything else that might prove dangerous. Clearly, the *Skywalkers* had never thought anybody would get this far, and they had almost been right.

Going to either side of a ladder welded to the wall, the two men hefted their weapons and listened intently for any sounds to betray the location of the rest of the crew. They had no idea if the X-ships carried ten or ten thousand people. Price thought it would be no more than three, and she had been right so far. Which meant there was only one man left. Probably, the captain of the craft. Unfortunately, the engines were making so much noise, they couldn't have heard a grenade in their shorts, which also meant the terrorists could not hear them climbing up the ladder.

Arriving at the same conclusion at the same time, Lyons grabbed the rungs to charge up the ladder, with Schwarz only a step behind.

There was an open hatch at the top, and the Able Team leader rose into view with his Colt .357 Python at the ready. The circular room was lined with banked controls and there were three cushioned seats, two of them empty. The third held a man in a jumpsuit, intently hunched over a set of joysticks, minutely adjusting them constantly.

Easing to his feet, Lyons crossed the room in two steps and shoved the big barrel of the Colt hard against the neck of a terrorist. "Spend your life in a comfortable jail cell, or die here and now." He spoke in his best cop voice, putting the full weight of brutal honesty into every word.

Laughing contemptuously, the terrorist shoved both joysticks all the way forward. "Die, mongrel!" Captain Fawcett screamed, half the controls becoming illuminated as the rocket engines surged in volume and power to a launch.

Without hesitation, Lyons shot the terrorist dead. Dropping the Colt, the man reached past the corpse to grab the joysticks and savagely jerk them backward as hard as possible.

Already starting to lift, the X-ship seemed to pause as the engines cut off. There was a brief instant of what almost seemed like weightlessness, then the spaceship dropped back to the stone ground with triphammer force. A video monitor shattered, rivets popped from wall seams, the lights died and a terrible groan permeated the entire vessel as if it were dying.

Slowly, ever so slowly at first, the X-ship started to tilt. In pounding response, the hydraulics tried to compensate, but that proved impossible, and the X-ship kept going, rapidly accelerating. Then there came an unexpected crash and the ship came to rest at a sharp angle. Struggling to stay on their feet, Lyons and Schwarz looked at each other, unable to comprehend what had happened.

"The damn thing is too big to fall over!" Blancanales said over the com link. "You're wedged against the cliff face!"

"See? Size does matter," Toni added with a strained laugh.

Smiling in relief, Lyons and Schwarz turned to the controls and started ripping off the thin plastic covers in search of the transponder, when one of the monitors that was still intact came alive and out stared a broad man with a military-style crew cut.

"Report!" the stranger barked. "Telemetry is going crazy over here. What has happened to the *Oriental?* Are you under attack again?"

"Not exactly, Colonel," Lyons said, looking directly into the tiny video camera set above the monitor. For a long moment the two men stared at each other, then Schwarz flipped a switch and killed the transmission.

"So that was Southerland," he said, removing the panel just below the monitor. "Well, it was mighty nice of him to tell us where the transponder was located….damn, loan me your knife, Carl."

Lyons passed it over and, reaching into the jumble of wires, Schwarz slashed around, then whooped in victory as he withdrew a small black box. This was the goal of the whole mission. The circuits in the transponder contained everything they wanted, everything the terrorists did not want them to know.

Realizing what that meant, Schwarz raised both arms high and threw the box at the deck. It shattered into a score of pieces, including a large wad of C-4 plastic explosive. Snatching the C-4, he threw it at the hatch and it dropped from sight an instant before loudly detonating.

The concussion violently shoved both men against the control board, the X-ship trembling to the internal blast and sliding down the cliff a few more yards with a terrible grinding noise.

"What the hell was that?" Blancanales demanded in their earbuds.

"Th-the…sound of victory," Schwarz said, lifting a microprocessor from the tangle of wires and chips.

CHAPTER SEVENTEEN

Prime Base, Khulukrudu

"Gone," Colonel Southerland said, as if unable to believe the word. "A second ship, gone."

"Did they get the transponder?" Henzollern demanded, scowling fiercely at the image of Eric O'Hara in the video monitor. "Do they know our locations?"

"Of course, not," O'Hara lied. "I blew the circuits long before anybody could find and extract the right ones." Actually, the hacker had no idea if the people onboard the *Oriental* had acquired the microprocessor. But he'd decide to play it safe, only recently the man had discovered, and disconnected, a large cache of remote-controlled TNT hidden under the floor of his computer rooms, more than enough to reduce the entire bunker into memory. Whether it was the colonel, or Zolly, made no difference. O'Hara had sworn absolute allegiance to the beloved motherland, but he no longer trusted the colonel. Which was why he had turned off the scrambler circuits in every X-ship. Just as a precautionary measure.

"Well, you better be correct," Southerland growled

menacingly, tapping a hand on the console alongside a small keypad. "Because if they did, you die."

"There is no problem, sir." The monitor flickered, then went dark.

Throwing a switch, Southerland cut the circuit to the video camera and microphone. "I think he knows about the TNT," he muttered thoughtfully.

"Then we should remove him immediately," Henzollern replied eagerly. "Everything leads to him. We have carefully planted a dozen clues that show he was the mastermind behind the X-ship attacks. And the last ship can carry out the final bombing runs without additional guidance or assistance. The hacker is of no more use. Why not kill him now?"

"Because he may still prove highly useful," the colonel replied. "I have looked into the face of the enemy, and there is no stopping such a man once he comes after you. I understand this white American. He dies, or I die. There is no third option."

"Agreed. Kill the hacker."

"Oh no, this blond man must be allowed to remove Eric. Remember, my dear, that the scrambler circuit would have blurred my image on the monitor in the *Orient,* so the American has no idea what I look like." Leaning back in the chair, Southerland stroked the keypad that could detonate all four of the boxes of TNT hidden in different locations throughout the Georgia base. Things were starting to unravel fast, but the master plan was still in operation. In just a little while, he would be able to leave this pitiful excuse of an island and triumphantly return home to start the great purge. The execution dock at Johannesburg would be busy for years once I'm back in power, he thought. Not yet. Oh no. But soon. Very soon…

Stony Man Farm, Virginia

BARBARA PRICE HURRIED inside the Computer Room. "Well?" she demanded. "Did they get it?"

"Of course," Kurtzman replied, typing furiously at his console. "We should crack the encryption in just a few more minutes."

"Good." Thoughtfully chewing a lip, Price studied the wall screen at the far end of the room. "Exactly how many FAE bombs did the Dark Star people get?" she asked.

"Four," Wethers replied from around his pipe. "More than enough to flatten Manhattan."

"Unfortunately, I think they have bigger goals than that," Price said grimly. "What I want to know is, how did they steal the bombs? Those monsters weight five hundred pounds each, and an X-ship needs to be as lightweight as possible."

"And I may have the answer to that," Delahunt said from behind her mask. "I ran some figures and think they might have stripped off some of their armor, or reduced the crew. That X-ship Able Team fought in Maryland had a 20 mm cannon. That's impossible, unless something else had been removed to lighten the ship beforehand."

Yes, she had been wondering about that herself. "So they can only carry one thing," Price said. "An offensive cannon, or a bomb, but not both."

"The math is incontestable."

"Then how did they steal four of them in the first place?" Kurtzman demanded.

"The ship must have been stripped to the bare essentials," Tokaido replied thoughtfully. "And had no liquid nitrogen on board. That dense a material weighs a tremendous amount."

"How much?"

"At an educated guess, two tons."

Deep in thought, Price nodded. Yes, that sounded right. Just enough for them to haul away the bombs. Pity nobody shot at them with a live heat-seeker at the CDC instead of deadheads. The missiles would have blown the damn thing out of the air. But who knew at the time?

This was exactly like the AutoSentries in Barstow, she realized. The computerized guns had started by firing live rounds, then switched to blanks to delay the fight for as long as possible. Now the terrorists were doing the same thing with the X-ships, depending wholly upon their reputation of invulnerability as protection.

"But this means they're now vulnerable to heat-seekers," Kurtzman said excitedly. "They'll probably keep a little liquid nitrogen on board, just in case. But certainly not enough to withstand a sustained barrage!"

"Akira, inform the Pentagon and NORAD," Price ordered. "Carmen, tell NATO and Chief Greene. We need to rearm some of our own Stingers immediately."

She paused, then added, "Hunt, have Cowboy check into getting a MetalStorm. He'll know who, where and how."

"Done!" the former Berkeley professor replied curtly. He had only recently heard of the bizarre weapon during a briefing with Brognola the previous week. The Metal-Storm Project was an Australian invention that had been quickly purchased by the Pentagon. Instead of having a complex firing mechanism, each tube in a MetalStorm was the entire weapon. Inside each tube was a stack of 40 mm shells that were fired electronically from an induction coil embedded inside the barrel. As each one detonated, a ring set around the neck of the shell behind the first expanded for a microsecond to vent all of the propellant gases forward, and even before the first high-explosive shell left the barrel, the blowback ring collapsed and the second round was triggered. Fully capable of unleashing 4000 rounds a second, the MetalStorm was the most potentially devastating weapon this side of a FAE. The one major drawback was that it took nearly an hour to load the 40 mm version, and much longer for the bigger models, an unacceptable delay to soldiers in the thick of combat. But under certain circumstances, it might just give the nation the tactical element of surprise against the X-ship. If they could get their hands on one.

"Done!" Tokaido announced, removing his headphones. "I've deciphered their codes. Damn, their hacker is good."

"Start talking," Price said brusquely, taking a chair and turning it to sit with her arms folded across the back.

"After picking up Swanson, the X-ship was supposed to drop her off in Hawaii, then proceed to get a dragon egg from the *Navicula*. I assume the reference to the dragon egg is code for the stolen FAE bombs."

"Obviously," Price replied. "Is *Navicula* the name of an X-ship, or one of their bases?"

"Unknown. Hunt is checking it out."

Bent over his console, the professor waved at the sound of his name but did not look up.

"Good enough," Price acknowledged. "However, I'm puzzled over this reference to Hawaii. These did not seem like the sorts of people who would retire their agents to a tropical paradise. More likely it was some vague reference to killing the spy, and hiding the body."

"A reasonable assumption."

"Do we know the origin of the transmission?"

"Yes, it was from deep inside the Okefenokee Swamp, the section in Georgia, not Florida. Able Team is already on the way. ETA is two hours. There was a response from…" The man blinked. "Wait a minute, let me double-check that."

"Something wrong?" Price asked.

"Their main base…the headquarters for Dark Star," Tokaido muttered in disbelief. "It's…Robben Island."

Swiveling around sharply at his console, Wethers arched an eyebrow. "Is that possible?" he demanded.

Tokaido gestured at the monitor. "See for yourself!"

Scowling, the professor linked their two consoles together and checked the coordinates. "It seems that you are correct," he demurred. "What clever little racists they are."

"Robben Island," Price said slowly, tasting the words and trying to invoke some memory about the place. Clearly, it meant a lot to Akira and Hunt. "Just a second, wasn't that where Nelson Mandella went to jail?"

"Yes, a brutal prison facility a hundred times worse than Devil's Island," Kurtzman stated, brushing back his crop of black hair as he read off a monitor. "The guards liked to refer to it as Khulukrudu, but everybody else called it Hell. When the white regime fell, everybody in Robben Prison was set free, and the whole place closed down to eventually become a museum."

"A museum?"

"We did the same thing to Alcatraz and Andersonville, as did the Germans to Auschwitz and the other death camps."

Grudgingly, Price accepted that. To forget history only meant you were doomed to repeat it endlessly. Even the bad had to be remembered to protect the future. "Okay, so this is the HQ for the X-ships. Southerland must have established a sort of facility there years ago when he was in charge," the woman theorized. "Then he was kicked out with the rest of the racists, but came back to use it as the base of operations for his planned retaking of the nation." She snorted. The colonel was staging a coup right under the nose of the South African government, less than a dozen miles from Johannesburg. Determined was not a strong enough word, she realized. The man was a fanatic.

Tapping a few keys, Kurtzman threw a map of the small island on the wall. "Okay, Robben Island is located right off the southernmost tip of South Africa. Beyond is only open water all the way to the polar ice cap. It is literally the edge of the world."

Picking up a light pen, the chief hacker put a red dot on the wall map. "The whole island is surrounded by unclimbable cliffs, one of the main reasons it was made into a prison. There's a natural harbor incapable of taking oceangoing ships, only small surface boats, and the water is too cold for swimming during most of the year, you'd be dead in less than a minute." The dot moved. "As for the rest of the place, there are only a handful of buildings and tents. The place is practically deserted. Over there is the old prison, and that's the new one. That's the limestone quarry, and this is a World War II gunnery implement, long abandoned. Now over here is the leper church—"

"Lepers?" Delahunt asked, turning her helmet.

"Long gone," Kurtzman assured her. "The place is clean by now,"

"Damn well hope so," Price called uneasily. The place had been a combination prison and leper colony. Nice. "Okay, what's that big structure, another limestone quarry?"

"Plain rock this time, and over here is the graveyard." Kurtzman clicked off the pen. "That's the biggest place on the island, damn near the same size as the farmland. Nobody knows how many people are buried there. There are no records, and we can't even hazard a guess."

Crossing her arms, Price studied the map. The island was fourteen miles in diameter, that was twice the size of Manhattan. "What's the population?"

"Roughly a hundred. There are a few caretakers for the museum, and a couple of guides, former prisoners who now give inspirational walking tours."

"Inspirational?" Tokaido asked, looking up from his work.

"A lot of uneducated people went into that prison. Folks forbidden to go to school, or read a book. While slaving in the limestone quarry, the few educated prisoners taught the others how to read and write, gave lessons in law, philosophy and politics. Secretly, the quarry was called the University. A lot of the present-day leaders of South Africa came out of that as learned men."

The University. Where prisoners taught each other how to read and started a chain reaction that toppled the white regime and freed them all. Her respect for the South Africans went up considerably. "And somewhere in there is their base," Price said softly, drumming fingers on her arm. "It must be underground. There's nowhere else to hide a base with tourists coming and going."

"Agreed. Unfortunately, the colonel ruled the island for

years, so it could be anywhere, under the prison, buried in the stone quarry, anywhere at all. It would take a U.S. Marine battalion a week to search the whole place."

"And we only have a few hours before Able Team reaches Georgia," Price added. "All right, send Phoenix Force to the island and have them do a covert recon. They're to locate the base, then hold until Able Team finds the American base. This has to be a coordinated strike. We have to keep them off balance until locating the last X-ship."

"And to make sure he doesn't have any more stashed away somewhere," Kurtzman added. "He'd be a fool not to have an escape plan, and unfortunately, the colonel is not a fool."

"What we need is a diversion to keep his attention while our teams get into position," Price mused. "Any ideas?"

"Can we repair the X-ship in Maryland, use it as a Trojan horse?"

"No, the engines are cracked. At the moment, it is a hundred million dollars of finely crafted junk."

What about using the original *Delta Clipper?* It's a lot smaller than the X-ships, but they looked nearly identical."

"And it has a range of a mile. We'd have to haul it there by truck."

"Damn!"

"Now, I may have something for you," Wethers said, removing the pipe from his mouth. "The word 'navicula' means small boat in Latin. Knowing the military's penchant for crude humor, I did a modified Boolean search for anything large with the name—a person, or a town.

After removing the obviously useless results, I was left with three possibilities—a massive outdoor restaurant in Tunisia that specializes in seafood, a gigantic children's theater located in Blackpool, England…" The man smiled. "And a reconditioned oil tanker now registered in Belgium, but originally built in South Africa."

"An oil tanker," Price mused. "That's more than large enough for an X-ship to simply land on the main deck. Where is it now?"

"Unknown," Wethers replied, gesturing with the pipe. "Their GPS suspiciously broke just before the first attack on Compose Island." He tapped a button on his console, and the wall screen changed to a view of the Pacific Ocean. "However, this was their last known location…." A red star appeared on the map. "And this is how fast they can travel without a payload." A large circle appeared around the star.

"Roughly a million square miles of open sea." Price sighed. "Aaron, is there any chance we could track them down using the thermal pictures from a Keyhole satellite, the way we did in India?"

"Let you know in a minute," the computer wizard replied, already typing away.

The view on the wall screen started flipping through a fast series of oceanic views until suddenly stopping.

"Found it," he said, and the picture zoomed in to focus on an oil tanker moving at a brisk clip. "They're roughly two hundred miles off the Aleutian Islands, smack-dab in the middle of nowhere."

Which would give them all of the privacy needed, Price noted. "That must be where they're storing the FAE bombs," she said. "They cannot take a chance of any one

X-ship carrying all of them. If it got shot down, or crashed, they would never be able to get their hands on more."

"So this is a combination refueling base and armory," Kurtzman said, cracking his knuckles. "That gives us two good reasons to blow it out of the water. Akira, does the U.S. or Russia have anything nearby that we can commandeer? A missile cruiser or nuclear attack submarine?"

"Not really, no," the young man replied, as if expecting that question. "But Alaska is nearby, and Eielson AFB is the home for a B2 stealth bomber. They could scramble a wing, and blow that tanker out of the water in five minutes."

"Unfortunately, this is all guesswork," Delahunt stated, pausing in her work. "And we might be wrong. It could be a perfectly innocent oil tanker, simply in the wrong place at the wrong time."

"Besides, we want them calling Southerland for help," Price added ruthlessly. "Aaron, contact Hal. We need the commander of Eielson to prepare a squadron for a fly-by, not a bombing run, just to fly over the tanker to test the reactions of the crew."

"If they do work for the terrorists," Kurtzman said, "all hell will break loose. What then, sink her?"

"Hell, no. They're to board the *Navicula,* and try to take as many of the crew alive as possible," she replied. "If I read Southerland right, he'll immediately send an X-ship there to remove the danger. That will give the teams a chance to enter the bases unobserved and capture Southerland, along with his computers."

"Alert! I have an incoming news flash from the White House," Delahunt said, tilting her head. "Just a few minutes ago... Oh my God! An X-ship dropped an FAE bomb near the Vatican! Hundreds are feared dead. And that's not the worst part!

"How could it possibly be worse?" Price demanded, her heart hammering in her chest. The Vatican bombed... it was monstrous!

Removing her helmet, Delahunt looked at the others with a pained expression. "There was a crescent moon painted on the side of the X-ship," she said softly.

A stunned silence ruled the room for a minute.

"That could start a worldwide religious war!" Kurtzman exploded, thumping a fist onto his console. "Are these people insane? What in hell are they trying to achieve?"

"My guess would be World War III," Wethers declared.

Glancing at the wall clock, Price weighed a thousand variables before coming to a hard decision. "In two hours I want everybody in position," the mission controller ordered. "Then no matter what else is happening, we strike!"

CHAPTER EIGHTEEN

Robben Island, South Africa

With a sputtering engine, the skiff moved steadily across the cold Atlantic. Only fifteen feet long, the craft was barely able to hold the five men and all of their equipment, and seemed constantly on the verge of swamping.

The morning air was chilly, and a fine mist sprayed up from the bow soaking their windbreakers and hair. Dressed in bright-yellow rain slickers and heavy boots, the men of Phoenix Force each had a camera hung around his neck, and the name of a famous nature magazine was emblazoned across his back, and painted on the skiff.

At the bow, Encizo was dipping the long telephoto lens of his camera into the water, the EM scanner inside sweeping for proximity sensors and or mines in the thick water, while pretending to take underwater photos. Sitting in the middle of the skiff, James was typing on his U.S. Army laptop, the slim military model neatly inserted into the bulky waterproof case of a civilian version. The device was attached to a small sonar array hurriedly bolted to the bottom of the skiff. The passive sensor had a tremendous range, and could give them advanced notice of anything dangerous deep below the surface. But so far, there were no torpedoes, submersibles or submarines. There were only huge schools of fish and a few dolphins. At the stern, McCarter was checking a compass in one hand, the other tight on the tiller of an old outboard engine that trailed blue smoke behind the little skiff.

"We're smack on course," McCarter announced, closing the compass with a snap and tucking it under his slicker.

"We're only going twelve miles," Hawkins muttered, his camera pointing at the sky and taking pictures of the squawking seagulls.

"Which is quite a bloody distance for some civilians," McCarter reminded gruffly. "As soon as they lose sight of land, some folks get mighty tetchy."

"Tetchy?"

"That's what I said."

"These damn kids with their weird slang," Manning said with a straight face.

Only a few days younger than the big Canadian, McCarter snorted in reply.

"How much longer?" Hawkins asked, shielding his eyes and looking upward at the dim sun.

"Able Team should be reaching the swamp right about now," Encizo replied, pretending to stifle a yawn so that his hand blocked his mouth from any possible lip-readers watching them through binoculars. "We should be getting the go-code any second."

"Then we better haul ass."

In mute agreement, McCarter opened the throttle of the outboard. The sputtering increased to a steady roar of controlled power, and their speed noticeably increased.

As covertly as possible, the rest of the team armed its weapons under the cumbersome slickers, knowing full well they could be under direct observation of the terrorists and walking straight into another trap.

Crossing the intervening miles, there was only the sound of the sputtering engine, the gulls overhead and the dull slap of the waves against the wooden bow. Reaching the lee of the rocky island, the team headed toward Longbeach, a narrow strip of sand situated on the north side of the island. There was no direct way to get from the beach to the top of the sheer cliff overlooking the sea. In the past, prisoners had dived off, but most of them did not clear the jagged rocks lurking just below the freezing water, their broken bodies sinking to join the others at the bottom of the sea. A few professional mountaineers had climbed the vertical rock face using only their bare hands, just to show that it could be done. However, the task took them the better part of a day, and the climbers reached the top utterly exhausted. Time and energy, the men of Phoenix Force did not have to spare.

A dozen sea lions lounged on the black rocks edging the small beach, a few of them sunning their pale bellies. Protected by international law, they were not afraid of the humans, and greeted the arrival of the skiff with snorting disdain. Off somewhere in the distance, there came the snorting explosion of a whale clearing his blowhole, but when the team looked around there was nothing in sight but the endless choppy waves.

"It was a whale, not a submarine," James reported, closing the lid of the laptop. "We're safe now. The water is too shallow for anything dangerous."

"But the sky is wide open," McCarter stated, turning

off the engine so that the skiff crossed the last few feet in silence until they heard the sound of the keel scraping on the sand below.

Hopping over the gunwale, the man waded forward to grab the tow line and drag the boat securely onto the beach. Most of the sea lions completely ignored the intrusion, only one young pup barking at the strange creatures.

"Looks like love to me," Encizo said to Hawkins.

"Must be your animal magnetism," Manning added.

The big Texan shrugged. "When you got it, you got it. What can I say?"

"Okay, let's unpack!" James suggested loudly, swinging around a device that resembled a light meter. In reality it was a small EM scanner, a special built by himself and Gadgets Schwarz.

As the others got busy, James walked along the beach, the sand crunching under his boots. There were a lot of cracks and crevices in the weathered cliff face, some of them puffing out with dried grass and sticks from old seagull nests. But one in particular caught his attention, and the man walked past it to not draw special notice, but he dragged his feet in the sand to mark the location.

Noting the location of the hidden video camera, McCarter kept his expression neutral. He had expected something like this. Colonel Southerland would be a fool to not cover the beach, even though it did not offer access to the island. But a soldier always prepared for what an enemy could do, not merely for what they should do.

Hauling dozens of plastic boxes from the skiff, the rest of Phoenix Force started making random stacks, one of the piles accidentally covering the marked nest. Not completely, just blocking the west side of the beach, but leaving a clear view of the skiff to help reduce any suspicions. Completely blocking the camera would have been a red flag that could not have been ignored by anybody. A partial would raise suspicions, but hopefully not enough for the colonel to send in the troops. This was the tough part of the mission, getting onto the island in broad daylight, but without being seen.

Talking about the weather and work, the Stony Man commando continued working for a few minutes, as James laid his laptop on top of a flat rock near the camera and tapped a macro key.

"Okay, let's make some coffee and wait for twilight," his voice said from the stereo speakers of the device. The other voices of Phoenix Force replied, and they started chatting about sea lions, penguins and then the local women.

Quietly opening some of the equipment boxes, the men occasionally walked back into view on the side to maintain the illusion, and McCarter actually opened a can of sterno to start a pot of water boiling for coffee. Sure enough the smell startled the sea lions just as it said in all the documentaries. The animals voiced their strong disapproval and dived into the sea, swimming away with remarkable speed and grace. On land, they were lumbering behemoths, but in the water they moved like panthers.

The cliff was only fifty feet high, an easy climb with a rope. The team was in position and ready to move, but couldn't go just yet. For now, they had to exercise patience and wait for the go-ahead.

Aiming a grenade launcher at the top of the cliff, McCarter glanced sideways at his watch. Five minutes to go, and counting…

Okefenokee Swamp, Georgia

MAKING MORE NOISE than the end of the world, the battered aluminum airboat streaked across the marshy water, brushing aside the tall grass and punk-tail weeds as if they were loose papers lying in a street. Behind the speeding airboat, a fine spray was highlighted with a beautiful rainbow, which counterpointed the pungent reek of fetid mud and rotting vegetation permeating the millennium-old fen. The sodden landscape was a mixture of soupy mud almost thick enough to walk on, endless fields of weeds and small islands of banyon trees covered with Spanish moss.

Dressed as duck hunters, the men of Able Team were wearing rubber waders that rose to their chests, and carried bolt-action Remington .357 rifles. The big-bore weapons were beyond useless for duck hunting. There wouldn't be enough meat left from the largest canard to make a decent canapé. But the main attribute of the bolt-action Remington was that it looked absolutely nothing like a military assault rifle. The AR-15 was legal in Georgia, and at first glance would strongly resemble an M-16. The weapons for this mission were tucked into rolled-up sleeping bags, loaded and primed for combat.

Bright-yellow hunting permits hung around the necks of the Stony Man commandos on chains, and they were wearing orange safety vests, so that they wouldn't get shot by any other hunters who mistook them for alligators or deer. Their hands were stripped with bandages, their faces oddly shiny in spots from the plastic surgical film sprayed over the numerous cuts received in the stone quarry.

On the deck of the speeding boat were several large coolers and assorted camping gear, some of it brand-new and still bearing the sales tag from a local store. Many hunters in the swamp these days were business executives who had never done it before, and the tags were a subtle touch to add a dash of realism.

Nestled among the plastic boxes and foam coolers was a squat fiberglass cylinder with a domed top. In an odd quirk, the state-of-the-art device resembled an antique portable hair dryer. There was no brand name to be seen, or a model number, bar code or sales tag, and a thick electrical cord ran from a squat dome to a purring Honda generator working at maximum output, every gauge and meter quivering at just below the red zone.

Opening a can of beer, Lyons took a long drink from the warm water inside, the tiny hole in the side where the alcoholic beverage had been drained, and then replaced, neatly covered with a price tag.

"Almost there!" he shouted over the loud engine. The team members all wore throat mikes, but the time to use those hadn't come yet. For the moment they had to appear perfectly ordinary as they headed toward the terrorist base.

The encoded signal from the X-ship had been expertly defused to blur the precise location of the installation. But a thermographic scan of the national wetlands from a NASA satellite revealed a large warm spot deep in the heart of gator country. That had been a big mistake on the part of the Southerland. The two massive supercomputers hidden in the swamp needed to be kept as cold as possible. However, a huge cold spot in the middle of a swamp would have been a dead giveaway. So they were cleverly pumping out warm air to mask that. But a swamp was a living organism, and the balance between the two was not perfect. Unless somebody was smart enough to look for a hot spot, the terrorist base would have remained invisible. But now it was pinpointed exactly. But that yielded a new and different problem.

Unlike Phoenix Force, the men of Able Team knew exactly where the enemy was located. Unfortunately they had no idea where the entrance was located, or how to get inside. Under the water somewhere was the most likely approach. It would be the easiest to conceal, although a lot worse for moving any equipment. However, performing an underwater search meant using active sonar, which would reveal their presence faster than arriving in a U.S. Navy gunboat.

"Anything?" Blancanales shouted hopefully.

"Nothing so far!" Schwarz bellowed in return, wiping the sheen of moisture off his face with a hand. "But at least this isn't salt water!"

"Yeah, great!" his teammate replied sourly. "So instead of it stinging our dozens of cuts, we're getting a bazillion diseases from this sweet toilet of nature."

Bursting out of the tall grass, the airboat skimmed across a wide patch of open water. Several of the floating logs ahead of them unexpectedly lurched into motion at their noisy approach, the gators bawing in rage, slipping into the murky water to vanish from sight.

"How do you kill an alligator anyway?" Blancanales asked, working the bolt on his Remington .357 rifle. He took a shot at the animal, deliberately missing by several feet. The discharge of the hunting rifle was barely discernible above the deafening airboat engine.

"From a very great distance!" Schwarz shouted. "And with high explosives, if possible!"

"Thanks for the info!"

"Always glad to help!"

"Shoot them in the head!" Lyons added, swinging around a jumbled collection of fallen trees. "And don't stop firing until they roll over! Gators like to play dead to lure in food!"

"Like I said, from a very great distance!" Schwarz yelled with a smile, then the grin vanished. "Heads up! I just got a major spike on the EM scanner!"

"Is it their base?" Pol asked hopefully, tightening his grip on the Remington.

"Too small! Almost looked like a… Carl, turn left now!"

Responding instantly, Lyons swerved the nimble airboat in that direction, and a split second later the water behind them violently exploded in a boiling column of lily pads and mud, a swarm of fléchettes hissing skyward. Several of them smacked into the layer of bulletproof vests lining the bottom of the airboat, making the garments jump slightly.

"Land mines!" Schwarz added unnecessarily, crouching over the device and adjusting the controls. "Left again…now right!"

Following the man's directions, Lyons zigzagged the craft across the swampland, and two more explosions churned the murky waters, mud and blood spraying over the craft, along with steaming chunks of a monstrously large snake. But in truth the ragged pieces were so small it could have been anything.

"We must be getting close!" Lyons shouted, dodging a sunken airboat. The bottom of the craft was riddled with dozens of tiny holes.

"Close enough for this?" Blancanales asked, crouching to place a hand on top of the softly humming domed cylinder.

"Not yet!" Schwarz answered, his full attention on the scanner. "Go, left! Now, left again! Left! Damn, we're boxed in! Stop the boat!"

Fluttering the engine to try to make it sound damaged, Lyons turned off the big fan at the rear of the craft and waited a precious few seconds for spinning blades to stop, before throwing the engine into reverse. The fan strained at the abrupt shift, and for a moment the former cop thought the blades were going to snap off and go flying, then the fan engaged and a powerful rush of air hit the three men, almost knocking them over the sides. But the forward momentum was countered, and as the craft came to a halt, Lyons cut the engine again and Blancanales tossed out an anchor to keep them from drifting back into the mine field.

Standing with their hunting rifles ready, the other men tensely waited as Schwarz turned slowly, sweeping the dark water with the scanner. "Mine…mine…mine…this way!" the man shouted, his ears still loudly ringing from the proximity to the air fan.

Dropping the hunting rifles, the rest of the team grabbed their real weapons and hopped overboard. The swamp rose to their chests, nearly topping their rubber waders, and the men slogged forward as fast as possible to a small island of banyon trees. Climbing out of the sticky mud, they took refuge among the hanging curtains of Spanish moss, and waited. A tense minute passed and nothing happened. As their hearing cleared, the buzzing of a million insects returned. A vulture flapped lazily across the blue sky, and from somewhere distant, a wood-pecker hammered on a tree.

"Now?" Blancanales asked tersely, a remote-control device tight in his fist.

"No, they have to come after us," Schwarz said. "They have to open up, and come after us!"

"Well, it better be soon," Blancanales observed. "Because the air boat is sinking fast." Already the craft was listing hard to one side, the swamp water lipping over the low gunwale.

"Then let's give them a reason to hurry," Lyons growled, pulling out a grenade. Yanking the ring free, he flipped off the arming lever and threw the military sphere toward the wall of underwater mines. The grenade splashed out of sight, then the swamp heaved upward from the triphammer blast. In response, several of the hidden mines ignited, blasting swarms of deadly fléchettes upward. Blancanales tossed a canister in the other direction, and there came a dull whomp from below the surface, closely followed by a bright light that increased in power until the muddy water began to boil from the hellish output of the thermite charge.

From within their waders, the men drew more grenades and threw them randomly, the explosions churning the dark waters.

"Okay, here they come," Schwarz said with a hard smile, looking up from the scanner.

There came the sound of squealing metal from a rush of weeds on the other side of the mines, and a man rose into view wearing a radio headset, NATO body armor and cradling an FN F2000 assault rifle.

"Freeze, this is the FBI!" Blancanales shouted.

Swiveling at the hip, the man fired a burst of 5.56 mm rounds in their general direction, and Lyons coolly responded with a single shot from the Remington. The .357 Magnum Maximum hollowpoint round plowed into the terrorist's face and blew out the back of his head, chunks of hair and gray matter smacking into the dirty water a dozen yards away.

Nearly headless, the corpse toppled over and Blancanales savagely pressed his thumb hard on the remote control.

Nothing seemed to happen.

"Did it work?" Blancanales asked.

"Seems to have," Lyons replied, pointing with the Remington.

Near another island of banyon trees, wisps of smoke rose from among the branches, and dimly they heard distant angry voices.

"Got them!" Schwarz declared triumphantly, tucking away the scanner. There had been no way for the team to find the underground base in time, so they'd had to make the terrorists come to them. The two supercomputers used by the enemy hacker had to be deep underground, cushioned against surface explosions, insulated from the killing Georgia heat, and protected from any sort of electrical interference by a Faraday shield. But when the *Skywalkers* opened up a hatch to come outside, that would create a small breach in the shield, not much, but it made the supercomputers vulnerable to an EMP blast if the team was close.

Resembling a hair dryer, the machine used ordinary current to slowly store a massive charge, and then released it in a single microsecond burst of concentrated magnetics. Silent and invisible, the electromagnetic pulse was nowhere near as strong as an EMP from a nuclear bomb, and it had a very limited range. But now every piece of advanced electronics in the immediate vicinity was dead, permanently fried, and that included radios, cell phones, proximity sensors in land mines, video cameras, digital watches, even multimillion dollar supercomputers.

Returning to the airboat, the men of Able Team reclaimed their military weapons, then rushed over to the weedy island. As they approached, a second man in body armor stood, firing an FN F2000 assault rifle. The Stony Man pros ducked low and shot back in unison. Still firing his weapon, the terrorist was thrown backward by the hammering barrage of soft-nosed lead, raking gunfire through the Spanish moss before tumbling into the mud.

Briefly checking the island for mechanical land mines or tripwires, the Stony Man team clustered around the open hatchway and looked inside. A ladder descended several yards down a metal shaft, ending at a concrete tunnel. Suddenly an arm came into view firing another assault rifle, the tracer rounds wildly ricocheting off the sides of the shaft. The Stony Man operatives rocked back out of the way, and as the firing ceased, they advanced, sending down a sustained volley from their weapons. A scream of pain announced a kill, and the arm flopped back into sight, the FN F2000 falling from limp and bloody fingers.

Aiming at an angle, Lyons fired two booming rounds from his Atchisson, the fléchettes and steel buckshot invoking additional cries of pain, while his teammates pulled out gas grenades and heaved them down the shaft. The canisters hit the bottom and bounced away, spewing thick volumes of black and green smoke. Curses and coughs were followed by the clatter of dropped weapons, then the dull thud of falling bodies.

Shouldering the Atchisson, Lyons joined the others in tossing down more gas grenades, the team grimly trying to saturate the entire underground with sleep gas before donning gas masks themselves and heading down the ladder to finally confront the enemy in direct combat.

SITTING AT THE DEACTIVATED control board of his dead supercomputers, Eric O'Hara could only stare in horror through the Lexan window at the armed men stumbling through the swirling clouds of smoke filling the corridor. What in hell was going on here? Reaching out, the man flipped a switch to close every hatch, hermetically sealing the base, and activating the AutoSentries hidden outside in the swamp. Nothing. No response.

Softly, there came the sound of automatic gunfire from the corridor outside the computer room. As the hacker watched, a coughing guard appeared out of the smoke to paw feebly at the entrance to the room. But the keypad was also not working and the door remained closed. Exhausted, the solder collapsed limply to the floor.

Thinking furiously, O'Hara chewed a lip. The keypad wasn't functioning. How was that possible? Unless this wasn't a cybernetic attack on his computer but the effect of an EMP bomb! Which meant U.S. Special Forces were already in the base.

Launching out of his orthopedic chair, O'Hara raced across the room. Yanking down the South African flag, he revealed a safe set into the concrete wall. Twirling the mechanical dial, he yanked open the steel door, breaking the seal on the small Faraday shield. Tossing aside the stacks of cash and a loaded 9 mm Viktor pistol, the terrified man pulled out a cell phone, powered it up and hurriedly tapped in a memorized number. The situation was completely out of control, and the base was lost. Obviously it was time for him to call the colonel and summon the X-ships!

CHAPTER NINETEEN

North Pacific Ocean

Majestically steaming along, the massive oil tanker, *Navicula,* continued on its carefully plotted course to nowhere. Too massive and wide to be affected by the chop, the surface waves, the wide metal bow of the tanker easily smashed them aside.

On the main deck, armed sailors were coiling insulated hoses, preparing for the next refueling. There was no bright work like on most vessels, nobody scrubbing rust spots with pumice stone. The tanker was dirty and ill-kept. The only truly clean area was the center of the main deck where the steel plates were spotlessly clean of any paint, as if it had been removed with a blowtorch, the bare metal circle marred by four big dents as if something extraordinarily heavy had been set down there.

Carving an apple with a pocketknife, a bosun was eating the slices and strolling along the deck when there was a low rumble in the clear sky and something dark appeared on the horizon.

Still calmly munching, the bosun arched an eyebrow

in surprise. Strange, nobody was cleared to come back yet. He hoped there wasn't anything wrong. For a moment the sailor debated waking up the captain, then decided against it. The captain had a mean temper when he was drinking, and he'd been knocking back the sauce all day in a sort of precelebration of their glorious victory against the mongrels. Personally, the bosun didn't give a damn about that sort of nonsense. White, black, red, yellow, it made no difference, he hated everybody. Pay him enough and the Dark Star merc would happily kill anyone.

The rumble got louder and the speck grew larger with every passing second, then the angular shape of a B-1 stealth bomber shot past the *Navicula* at just below Mach speed.

The wash of the jet bomber churned the sea to a frothy white and buffeted the crew on deck, knocking them down and hurling several of them overboard.

Banking sharply, the B2 started to turn for a second pass. That was when the bosun noticed a host of ships on the horizon heading their way.

The fire alarm started to howl, that being the only real danger to a vessel the size of a small island, and the captain appeared in the bridge wearing only shorts and a sleeveless T-shirt, binoculars clenched in both hands. A hatch was thrown open and a group of sailors charged across the deck. Several of them raised Stinger missiles launchers and fired at the B2, while the rest ripped off a sheet of canvas to expose a 20 mm Vulcan minigun and a black launch platform containing four French-made Exocet antiship missiles.

As the Exocets came on-line and started swiveling toward the distant armada, the Stingers leaped away in a tight formation. Climbing fast, they raced toward the big

B2, then suddenly one of the missiles simply detonated in midair for no visible reason, and the rest began to separate, heading in different directions as if no longer able to lock on the big Air Force bomber. Sizzling magnesium flares shot out of the angular wings of the B2, then a cloud of twinkling chaff, closely followed by a swarm of tiny shapes that lanced out faster than lightning to slam into the Stingers with devastating results.

Cursing at the sight, the bosun cast aside the apple and drew his sidearm. Antimissiles! He hadn't even known a B2 carried such advanced defensives.

Now there came the sound of working hydraulics, and a dozen lifeboats spun up on hinges to show that they were actually made of riveted steel and reveal a score of torpedo racks. There came the soft explosions of compressed air, and Russian made rocket-torpedoes were tossed into the sea to vanish below the waves and then streak off toward the approaching American Navy.

Just then, three larger missiles dropped from the belly of the B2, and headed straight for the *Navicula*. Instantly, the Vulcan whined into action, flame jutting out from the eight rotating barrels, and an icy cloud hissed into existence around the Exocet launcher. One of the Sidewinders was torn apart by the wall of stainless-steel buckshot thrown out by the strident Vulcan, and the other two missiles flashed past the Exocet to splash harmlessly into the sea.

Dashing across the deck, the bosun heard his own heart pounding, then realized it was the big guns of the approaching American Navy opening fire. Shells started to rain down around the *Navicula*, throwing up huge geysers of water, but none of them came close to hitting the slow-moving tanker.

As the B2 strafed the main deck again, the bosun was slammed aside, his sidearm flying away from the turbulent shock wave dragging behind the big jet. Oddly, this time it didn't start to curve around again. Instead the belly hatch opened and out dropped a couple of huge missiles much larger than the Sidewinders.

As their aft ends extended daggers of flame, the two Tomahawk missiles flashed upward to spiral and then come at the *Navicula* like avenging angels. A dozen Sidewinders rose to meet the threat, and the Vulcan whined into action. But the Tomahawks dropped below the attacks until almost touching the ocean waves, then they sharply rose again at the very last moment to just clear the deck, one of them hitting the Vulcan, the other taking out the Exocet launcher.

A double explosion shook the stern of the tanker, the vibrations felt all the way to the bow through the metal deck.

As more torpedoes were launched and Stingers climbed upward from all over the tanker, the bosun stood calmly amid the chaos thinking furiously. This whole attack was bullshit. The Americans could take the *Navicula* any time they wanted. The main defense of the ship had always been anonymity, the simple fact that nobody knew they even existed. Once that was blown, the mobile Dark Star armory was dead meat.

Were the Americans playing some sort of game with the crew, the bosun wondered, some kind of subtle revenge? Or were they stupid enough to think the tanker was full of flammable liquids? *As if anybody would be insane enough to land an X-ship on top of a hundred million gallons of crude oil!*

That was when comprehension hit, and the bosun turned to charge for the nearest deck hatch. There was an arsenal of weapons stashed all over the tanker, but he was heading for the captain's quarters to activate a beacon and ask the colonel for help. This battle hadn't even begun yet.

"Death to America!" the bosun screamed defiantly before diving into a hatchway and scampering down a long flight of metal stairs.

Robben Island, South Africa

WALKING ALONG THE BEACH, McCarter tossed some scraps of bread to the seagulls, then strolled back out of sight behind the stacks of plastic crates.

The recorded voices on the laptop were still chatting away about nothing special, while the rest of Phoenix Force stood with weapons in hand, ready to move at a second's notice.

"I think it's working," James whispered into his throat mike, listening to a coded transmission from the Farm. "Both Georgia and the oil tanker have asked Southerland for help. We should have his exact location in just a few... he's under the south wing of the new prison, Block C, about fifty yards down."

Silently, McCarter thrust a finger at the others.

Instantly the men fired the grappling hooks over the cliff, and when the lines grew taut, started climbing fast, their bodies festooned with weaponry. Reaching the top, the Stony Man commandos crawled onto the flat land and swung up their silenced MP-5 machine guns, bright laser beams stabbing out from small boxes under the main barrels. The ruby-red dots danced across the chests of two startled men leaning against a small VW tour bus.

"What in the world...." a young a man gasped, then

threw both hands high. "Don't shoot! We're just tour guides!"

"Who are you people?" the older man demanded, suspiciously looking over the vast array of military hardware. "We were told by the Ministry of Defense to park these cars here!"

Actually, by the nimble keyboards of Aaron Kurtzman and his cadre of trained hackers, McCarter corrected mentally. "Alcatraz," he said out loud, a finger tightening on the trigger slightly.

"Devil's Island," the other man responded, sounding as if he was not sure that would satisfy the heavily armed strangers. "How did you get up the cliff? That's fifty feet!"

Easing his grip on the machine gun, McCarter ignored the question. "Is the prison empty?" he demanded, lowering the weapon. "Are there any visitors or maintenance staff still inside?"

"No, everybody is gone," the tour guide answered slowly. "Why, what's going on here? Does this have anything to do with those X-ship people?"

Tossing a C-4 satchel charge into the rear of the tour bus, Hawkins paused at that remark. Tour guides, my ass, he thought. "Jesus, I bumped the detonator!" he barked. "Quick, somebody hand me an MRE before it explodes!"

Terrified, the younger man looked around helplessly, unsure of what to do, while the older man scowled in disbelief. Then he realized what had just happened and grimaced.

"Okay, you got me," the man stated, crossing his arms. "I'm from the ministry. The prison is clear of all civilian personnel, there should be nobody inside." He squinted. "But somehow I think there is. Correct?"

"Sorry, I have no idea what you're talking about,"

McCarter replied, getting into the vehicle. "We never met, and you have no idea who stole your bus. In fact, this whole thing never happened."

"Hey, I'm at home watching cricket with my wife," the man said smoothly, then threw a salute. "Stand where they aren't flying, son!"

Almost smiling at that, McCarter crisply returned the gesture, and Hawkins stomped on the gas pedal, the old VW roaring off in a cloud of dust.

Driving away at the top speed of the tour bus, the team tried not to curse at the plodding civilian vehicle. If this had been a half-track, or even an ATV, they could have gone directly to the prison over the rolling farmland. But in this bucket of bolts, the Stony Man commandos were forced to follow the paved road that skirted along the cliffs edging the entire island, going miles out of their way and wasting precious minutes.

"There it is," McCarter subvocalized, pulling out his Browning Hi-Power to work the slide before tucking the gun back into the holster. "Gary, on the hump!"

Reaching the turn-off, Hawkins slowed a moment as Manning jumped from the moving bus to hit the ground rolling and come up at a full run heading for the highest point of Minto Hill. Pressing the gas pedal to the floorboard, Hawkins tried to get as much speed as possible from the laboring four-cylinder engine. Straight ahead of the team was the prison. The walls were thirty feet tall, the front gate banded iron that looked strong enough to stop a tank.

"We have a confirm from Bear," James said, touching the transponder at his belt. "CIA spy satellites confirm the prison is empty, but there are thermal hot spots showing live people."

"Then hit it!" McCarter ordered, bringing up his MP-5 and thumbing off the safety with a hard click.

There was a flash of light from behind the bus, and then something streaked past the team to hit the front gate with triphammer force. The iron barrier was blown to pieces by the LAW rocket, and went tumbling across the punishment yard as the rattling tour bus plowed through the roiling smoke cloud.

Dodging around a concrete whipping post covered with chains, Hawkins hit the brakes and shifted gears at the same time, the transmission tearing itself apart as he forced the vehicle to a full stop directly in front of the main entrance.

As the men scrambled from the bus, Encizo paused to fire a 40 mm grenade launcher. At the arrival of the HE shell, the massive wooden doors exploded into a maelstrom of splinters. Charging into the building, Phoenix Force assumed a standard two-on-two formation, their weapons sweeping for targets. Ahead of them was a long concrete hallway edged with cells, and framed photographs of former prisoners adorned the opposite walls. But a hundred feet away was a second hallway, a neatly painted sign at the intersection showing the way to Cell Block C, also known as death row.

Suddenly they heard the sound of a slamming door and running boots. Taking defensive positions, the Stony Man team rolled flash-bang grenades down the corridor just as a swarm of men appeared around the corner, each of them wearing civilian clothing, military body armor and carrying FN F2000 assault rifles.

As the terrorists raised their weapons, the stun grenades cut loose and the men screamed from the blinding light burst. Ruthlessly, Phoenix Force stitched the enemy with a hail of 9 mm rounds, their lifeblood spraying onto the walls. But from the floor, one terrorist feebly raised his FN F2000 and fired the grenade launcher. Dropping fast, the team dodged the round that went straight out the front door to slam into the tour bus. The VW left the ground, flipping over as the gas tank erupted to come back down like a flaming meteor demolishing the inhuman whipping post forever.

Already running down the next corridor, Hawkins took the lead and stopped at the riveted iron door set into the wall. A small sign claimed this section was still under renovation and was closed to the public.

Kicking open the door, he sprayed his MP-5 back and forth in a classic figure-eight pattern. Two armed men crouching behind a sandbag nest died on the spot, their startled expressions clearly showing disbelief that their vaunted armor had not helped protect them in the slightest.

"Gotta love these case-hardened Penetrators," James snorted, moving ahead of Hawkins, then pausing to let McCarter get ahead of him.

"Better than Christmas," Encizo subvocalized, tossing another stun grenade down the next turn of the maze. The charge detonated, and men screamed, one of them stumbling into view, clawing at his eyes. Dispassionately, the Stony Man operative removed the killer from the world and kept going, clearing a path for the others with lethal accuracy.

Reaching a section of the corridor made of fresh concrete, McCarter noted this was new construction. They had to be close now, he thought. That was when he noticed a reflection from inside an air vent. Firing a burst from the MP-5, the man tore off the louvered cover, briefly revealing a video camera before it smashed into junk.

"Visors!" McCarter barked, flipping down his IR goggles.

A split second later the corridor crashed into complete darkness.

Moving steadily, the team pressed forward, shouldering their machine guns and pulling out silenced pistols. The red blur of a man appeared ahead of them, and Encizo smoothly dispatched the terrorist with a single .38 round from his Walther PPK, the discharge no louder than a subdued cough.

More figures moved stealthily in the blackness and were quietly taken out of commission.

Encountering a branching corridor, McCarter paused for only a moment to double-check and make sure that it was not on his mental map of the prison. This was it, the enemy base.

Pulling the ring on a HE grenade, Hawkins waited until the big Briton did the same, then they tossed the explosive charges down each branch. The double explosion buffeted the men hard, billowing smoke and plastic shrapnel ricocheting off the smooth walls. Human screams of pain came from the left, and the mechanical yammer of an AutoSentry sounded from the right.

Without hesitation, the team poured into the left corridor, their silenced weapons coughing high-velocity death at anything that moved.

CHAPTER TWENTY

Prime Base, Khulukrudu

The sounds of machine guns and explosions were coming from all over the base, Colonel Southerland noted dourly from the secure control room. Plus, half of his video cameras were dead, along with most of the AutoSentries. The invaders were consummate professionals, covering their flanks, bold when necessary, ruthless and virtually unstoppable. In spite of the fact that his troops were being slaughtered, the colonel grudgingly had to admire the unseen enemy. So far, he had not even gotten a glimpse of them on the video cameras. Just for a moment, the man wondered if the hacker's joke about the Ghost Police was a lot closer to the truth than he had ever dared to imagine.

"Yes, of course I'll help you, Eric," Southerland said soothingly into the cell phone. "Are you at the master control board right now?"

"Yes, but it's dead!" the hacker replied, panic ripe in his voice. "Everything is dead!"

"Not quite everything," the colonel replied calmly.

"Reach under the right side of the console, and you will find a small plastic lump. Push that aside, and press the button inside."

"What will that do?"

"Just do it, unless you're eager to learn what the food tastes like in the Pelican!" Henzollern snapped in bad temper.

There came a mumbled reply from the cell phone and suddenly the video monitor came to crackling life on the control board.

"I'm online!" O'Hara gasped in astonishment, closing the cell phone. "When did you install a second communications system?"

"From the very beginning," the colonel said, laying aside his own phone.

"Amazing! Can we get the computers back online?"

Breathing in deeply, Southerland let it out slowly. "Sadly, no, my friend," he said, reaching into his shirt to pull out a black key. "I just wanted to say farewell to your face. You have served the motherland faithfully, and deserved that much respect at the very least." Inserting the key into a slot on the control board, the chief terrorist twisted it hard and a small panel slide back on the board, exposing four red buttons.

"What are you talking about?" O'Hara demanded, comprehension slowly dawning on his sweaty features. "No! Don't do it! I can still escape! I can run and—"

Without a word, Southerland pressed the first button and the video monitor promptly went blank once more.

"So much for the fat little hacker," Henzollern said with a sneer, working the bolt of an Atchisson autoshotgun. Usually, she used an FN F2000 like the rest of the troops—it was good for morale—but special circumstances required special tools.

"Now to see about the good doctor," Colonel Southerland said, turning on the second screen.

"Where have you been?" Dr. Ingersol yelled from the monitor, blood smeared across his face, a pistol in his hand. "The goddamn Americans are all over the *Navicula!* I need an X-ship to come to get me at once!"

"That will not be necessary," the colonel said sadly, activating the second key.

The inventor of the X-ships scowled in disbelief. "Are you mad? I'm certainly not going to surrender to the mongrels!"

Just then, a powerful explosion shook the base and cement dust sprinkle down from the ceiling.

"Good to hear, but I would never ask that of you, Doctor," the colonel said in an even tone, placing a finger on the button. "Goodbye, old friend. Hail the motherland."

Briefly, the scientist registered surprise, then outrage, and started to raise his pistol when Southerland pressed the button and once again the screen went blank in a crackle of static.

"So much for the loose ends," Henzollern snorted, hefting the Atchisson to a more comfortable position. "Now what's the plan? Do we stand and fight, or head for the *Belle* and leave this cursed hunk of rock forever?"

"Don't worry about it," the colonel said softly, drawing a 9 mm Viktor pistol and working the slide.

At the metallic noise, Henzollern started to turn and Southerland fired twice. The hollowpoint slugs plowed into her face and blew open the back of her head, brains and blood splashing against the far wall. Sighing softly as if going to sleep, the corpse leisurely eased to the floor, twitched once and went still.

"Sorry, my dear," Southerland said, holstering the pistol. "But it was necessary. For the motherland, eh? I'm sure you would understand." Sadly, there really had been no other course of action available to the man. Prime Base was lost, or soon would be, and with it went the fight to free South Africa. As a soldier, Southerland was trained to accept defeat, then rally back and turn it into a victory. The battle was over, but not the war. He had millions stashed in a Cayman Island account under his great grandmother's maiden name, instead of a numbered Swiss bank account, and knew how to make more X-ships. The blueprints were on a microchip buried under his skin. All the colonel needed was to get away alive, and in just a couple of months, he could rebuild the fleet, bigger and better than ever before. Then the mongrel nations would pay for this defiance in an ocean of blood, he thought.

Swiveling back to the control board, the colonel activated the com link and contacted the last remaining X-ship. "Prime Base to the *Lady Colette,*" he said hurriedly, putting a lot of stress into his voice, trying to sound tired and harried. "This is a priority-one command. Authorization code Tango, Alpha, Zulu. Emergency! Do you copy?"

"Confirm, Prime Base," the captain responded promptly. "What are your orders, sir?"

"The *Navicula* has been compromised and destroyed. Finish your last bomb run and return immediately to Prime Base for my extraction. Please confirm."

"Finish the run and return to Khulukrudu," the captain repeated obediently. "Don't worry, sir, we won't let you down. Hail the motherland!"

Dutifully, the colonel repeated the oath, then cut the microphone. Pausing for a moment to listen to the sounds of battle coming ever closer to the control room, he then activated the third and fourth buttons, pressing them in quick succession.

On the monitor, the terrorist watched as the roof exploded off the old church for lepers, revealing the rounded nose of the *Bellelarthon.* Bright lights played around inside the church as the preburners started, then the engines ignited and the vessel rose quickly on a thundering column of flame.

But just as it cleared the stone block wall of the church, there came the unexpected sound of a large-caliber rifle, and a dent appeared in the side of the unarmored *Belle,* closely followed by two more. Hydraulic fluids gushed into view and the engine fluttered, nearly stalling.

"Damn fine shooting, soldier," the colonel muttered, tapping the third switch again, and the X-ship violently exploded, leveling the church. The *Belle* had never been his preferred escape route, simply one of the many available. There was even a carefully preserved corpse on board whose dental records were those of Southerland, but the hands and feet were hopelessly pulped to make recovering any prints impossible. *As the old saying goes, to achieve success, plan for failure.*

Tapping the fourth button a second time, the colonel felt a rush of warmth from the satchel charge of thermite under the console. Now he had only seconds in which to act.

As he rose from the chair, another explosion shook the base. Southerland walked briskly to the far corner and placed his palm on a smooth section of the concrete wall.

The warmth of his body activated a buried sensor, and the thin layer of concrete covering the exit cracked apart as a door swung open to expose a long tunnel.

Quickly stepping inside, the colonel felt a rush of warmth from behind as the thermite charge filled the control room with a searing heat, the temperature rapidly increasing until the room was a blazing inferno that completely annihilated any possible forensic evidence. Then the fierce wave of heat stopped as a massive slab of concrete dropped from the ceiling, completely sealing off the passageway.

Breaking into a run, Southerland dashed along the tunnel, activating two more sliding walls, then filling the space between them with loose rubble. By the time anybody breached this tunnel, it would be all over.

Reaching the end of the subterranean passageway, Southerland emerged into sunlight near the top of the western cliffs. Without a pause, he took a deep breath and launched himself off the island to expertly dive into the choppy sea and disappear from sight.

BATTERED AND BLOODY, the few remaining Dark Star agents gathered together at the end of a long corridor. Behind them was the door to the control room, and it seemed oddly warm, but there was no time for that now. The invaders were coming fast and hard. Hastily building a grotesque barricade from the bullet-riddled corpses of their fallen brethren, the terrorists readied their weapons and braced for the coming attack.

"They don't get past us, ya hear?" a sergeant shouted, pulling the pin on a grenade. "We protect the colonel at any cost. At any cost!"

The battered men growled their assent, all the while wondering where their leader was, and what he was doing about this group of unstoppable demons. Bullets, bombs, blades, nothing slowed them down. It was like trying to hold back the sea with bare hands.

"The Ghost Police," one man muttered, working the arming bolt on his FN F2000.

"Cut that shit!" the sergeant barked, sliding a fresh clip into his 9 mm Viktor pistol. "They're just men, nothing else! Just a bunch of guys!" Just then a ragged hole appeared in the middle of his forehead, and the terrorist jerked back to slam against the door to the control room. Limply, he slid down to the floor, leaving a long red smear behind on the burnished steel.

Stunned for only a moment, the remaining five South Africans spun around firing their weapons on full-auto, unleashing a 5.56 mm storm of hot lead.

Coming out of the swirling smoke and flames, Phoenix Force moved swiftly along the wall, their MP-5 machine guns chattering steadily. Encizo and McCarter each got hit, but the soft lead rounds were completely unable to penetrate the NATO body armor. Then James staggered, blood spraying from his arm.

Switching the MP-5 to his other hand, the man continued firing just as the others dropped to the dirty floor and swung up their acquired FN F2000 assault rifles. Long out of their own explosives, the team was now looting the dead. In unison, they sent off a barrage of 30 mm shells that missed the nightmarish barricade completely, going over the top and hitting the stone wall behind the terrorists. The explosion of shrapnel hit the Dark Star soldiers from behind, all of them crying out from minor wounds.

Suddenly the barrels of the MP-5s crested the wall of bodies, and the men of Phoenix Force gunned down the wounded terrorists without hesitation.

Quickly reloading, the team moved past the dead and warily approached the steel door. Less than a yard away they could feel the awful heat coming from the other side, along with the unmistakable reek of burning human flesh and a very familiar metallic tang.

"Seems like Southerland decided to die rather than be captured alive," Hawkins said in disdain, working the arming bolt on his MP-5 to clear a jammed round from the ejector port. "Smart move. We had no intention of sending him to jail."

"Which he damn well knew," McCarter replied uneasily.

Resting his weapon on a shoulder, Encizo gave a sniff. "Smells like thermite."

"No, it smells like bullshit," James muttered, clumsily tying a field dressing around the wound. "Southerland was insane, but he was no coward. No way he took the easy way."

"Agreed," McCarter said, touching his throat mike. "Firebird to Zeus, has anybody recently tried to leave the prison?"

"Affirmative," Manning replied over the com link. "There have been four attempts, but none of them got very far."

"Glad to hear it. Any of them look like Southerland?"

"Possibly," Manning hedged. "Can't tell for sure. A small X-ship launched from inside the old leper church, but I took it out with the Barrett. Could have been anybody inside."

"You took one of them down with a rifle?" Hawkins said suspiciously. "But these things are armored like tanks!"

"Well, this one was a lot smaller than the others we've seen," Manning stated. "So maybe it had less armor. All I can report is what happened. The roof blew off the church, an X-ship rose into view, I hit it with four shots and it did a Hiroshima."

"How badly did it explode?" McCarter demanded. "Could somebody have survived?"

"That blast? Hell, no. There's not enough of the ship left to stuff into your hip pocket."

"Now that's mighty convenient," Hawkins drawled thoughtfully.

"Too damn convenient," McCarter agreed, hefting his weapon. "Rafe and Calvin, stay with me to recon this hell-hole and make sure we got everybody, and watch out for any hostages! Southerland is a tricky bastard, and might try to pose as his own prisoner to escape."

He turned. "T.J., join Gary and recon that crash site. See if there was anybody on board, and bring me back whatever you can find."

"Check, fingers and toes," Hawkins replied, and took off at a run into the thick clouds of bitter smoke.

"Hold it, everybody freeze!" Encizo said, his face contorting into a grimace. The man touched his throat mike. "Bullfighter to Zeus, you said this was a small X-ship?"

"Confirm, less than a third of the size of the others."

"Are you sure? There wasn't some trick of the light off the water, or anything?" Encizo asked.

"Not through a Zeist telescopic sight," Manning replied. "Trust me, this was something new, and entirely different from all of the other X-ships!"

"Yeah, I was afraid of that."

"Which means there's still one, full-size X-ship out in the world somewhere," McCarter growled, glancing upward. Along with a host of these new versions. Briefly, the man wondered if Southerland could be on the remaining X-ships? But that made no sense. If he was, then why would the others have fought so hard to keep the team away from the control room? Thankfully, the small X-ships were no threat to the world, they seemed easy enough to destroy. It was the last big vessel that he was worried about.

Looking at the metal door visibly radiating waves of heat, the former SAS operative could feel it in his bones that something was terribly wrong here. They were being played. And if Southerland was retiring from the fight, and was trying to escape, he would need to stage a diversion to keep the entire world busy elsewhere until he could effectively vanish. The last ship would have to hit something big, some place important.

"Fire Bird to Rock House!" McCarter spoke quickly into his throat mike, his heart pounding. "Send an alert to Brognola, we only have a few minutes, but I know where the last X-ship is going to strike next!"

Washington, D.C.

IN TERRIBLE THUNDERING majesty, the last X-ship dropped swiftly through the rumbling storm clouds covering the capital city. Prime Base was invaded, the *Navicula* was not responding, and the computers were off-line, possibly destroyed. The mission was over, and they'd failed. The mongrels were still in control of the motherland. But the South African terrorists had a task to finish before they could retire from the field of combat, one last blow to the very heart of the hated Americans.

Coming to a halt above the White House, the lambent drive flame of the powerful rocket engines washed over the rooftop, throwing aside a dozen Secret Service agents, their burning bodies flying through the air to land with meaty thumps on Pennsylvania Avenue, the Rose Garden and the OEM Parking lot.

For a few moments the X-ship hovered in place above the executive mansion, the pilot and crew supremely confident that the LOX-LOH engines were completely annihilating the unseen building below, the structure completely blanketed in the roiling sea of chemical flames.

If the X-ship had attacked sixty years earlier, they would have been right. But during the onset of the cold war, President Eisenhower had directed that the two-hundred-year-old wooden building should, somehow, be made strong enough to withstand the physical shock wave of an atomic blast. So slowly over his term of office the work was done quietly, covertly, section by section and room by room. From basement to the roof, the entire structure had been painstakingly replaced with an exact duplicate of ferro-concrete, massively reinforced with steel beams more suitable for the foundation of another Empire State Building than a mere three-story, Colonial mansion. President Kennedy added a bomb shelter; Nixon put in the first subbasement; Johnson, the next ten; Carter added a U.S. Navy nuclear power plant and a Faraday Cage; the first Bush had the entire structure hermetically sealed against nerve gas. Serenely beautiful, the White House still looked exactly the same as it did since the halcyon days of Thomas Jefferson, but in cold reality it was a military hardsite that rivaled the Rock of Gibraltar for sheer brute strength.

Far down in the bottom-most level of the bomb shelter, the President and his staff watched the attack on a wall monitor, the picture sent from a video camera on top of the Old Executive Building across the street. A dozen Secret Service agents stood behind them armed with a wide assortment of weaponry, and a hundred U.S. Marines filled the corridors outside.

"My God," a man whispered, going pale. Another man turned away unable to look any more; a woman covered her mouth as if about to be physically ill. But the rest glared in open hatred at the sneak attack.

"Ready all guns." The President spoke calmly into a microphone clipped to his collar. "Take your time, people, there's no rush…and…fire."

On the side monitors, the staff watched as a dozen searchlights winked on, pinning the X-ship in a deadly halo of clear illumination. Then an army of U.S. soldiers stepped out of every civilian car parked on the streets around the White House. Each raising a Stinger launcher, they aimed and fired, the rockets creating a smoky umbrella of contrails as they raced toward the colossal X-ship.

As expected, the heat-seekers were unable to get a thermal lock on the target and continued on toward the Atlantic Ocean. But now, a thousand heavy machine guns began shooting from the top of every downtown building, the barrage of tracer rounds stretching across the nighttime sky in a burning spiderweb of destruction.

Nonstop, the deafening assault brutally hammered the X-ship, denting the armored hull from the sheer volume of steel-jacketed lead. Moving quickly, the X-ship slipped sideways from the White House and a dozen MRL trucks commenced launching deadhead rockets at the machine, forcing it farther away from the civilian population until it was over the woodsy park surrounding the Eclipse.

That was when the treetops exploded upward as a dozen of the brand-new U.S. Army PEP lasers cut loose, the scintillating power beams stabbing upward in hellish beauty. Wherever the beams touched, the armored hull erupted into puffs of superheated plasma. Whole sections came loose, hydraulic fluid gushing out like watery blood.

Spinning fast to escape the weapon, the X-ship spiraled into the sky on an steep angle, then paused amid the stentorian assault, the side hatch briefly opened and out dropped the last remaining FAE bomb.

Primed and ready for that very event, the tarpaulins covering a dozen Mack trucks positioned strategically around the city disintegrated from the mind-numbing maelstrom of 40 mm fléchette rounds thrown skyward by a hundred MetalStorm cannons mounted on the flatbeds. In unimaginable numbers, the stainless-steel fléchettes flowed upward like a black river of death and tore the FAE to pieces. Propelled by the millions of fléchettes, the highly volatile gas spewed out ragged cover as the bomb continued to fall, then the vents opened and the canister sparked. But thrown completely out of sequence, there was no thunderclap explosion, merely a loud boom and an irregular zigzag of fire across the sky, most of the FAE fumes were driven too far away from the canister to even ignite.

Defused and impotent, the empty bomb canister fell onto the White House and crashed on the bombproof roof to bounce off and land amid the rosebushes, crushing a wrought-iron statue and a few decorative chairs.

Now the PEP lasers came again, full-force this time, closely followed by hundreds of deadhead LAW rockets from the rooftops and streets. Thousands of 7.5 mm Hellfire rockets arched from the battalion of Apache and SuperCobra gunships coming in from the horizon. Shouting the names of their fallen brothers, a Marine battalion from Fort Bragg cut loose with swarms of LAW rockets, Stingers, SMAWs, Carl Gustaves, every weapon the grim commander had been able to borrow or steal, the soldiers filling the sky with a sustained outpouring of armor-piercing death. Then the second wave of MetalStorm cannons awoke, finishing the bloody job.

Literally torn apart, and leaking fuel from a score of rents, the dying X-ship struggled to escape, then detonated, vanishing in a staggering explosion that banished the darkness and momentarily brought an artificial dawn to the nation's capital.

As the ragged pieces fell into the Potomac River to hiss out of existence, the soldiers bellowed a victorious cheer that the civilian population soon echoed in joyful triumph, the noise seeming to build until it shook the pillars of the world.

EPILOGUE

Perth, Australia

On the outside, the warehouse looked decrepit, the brick-work crumbling and covered with lewd graffiti. However, the interior was bright and clean, the cinder-block walls reinforced with concrete pylons. Racks of automatic rifles lined the walls, with stacks of military ordnance piled high in the corners. In the center of the warehouse was a large wooden desk, a hundred folding chairs facing it as if this was an audience chamber. Hanging from the ceiling directly above the desk was a huge British flag decorated with an iron eagle holding a Nazi swastika in iron claws.

Talking in hushed tones, two middle-aged men were bent over the desk, studying a mechanical blueprint. Watching them closely were several dozen men and women sitting in the orderly rows of folding chairs. Each person's head was shaved bald, their necks and arms heavily decorated with garish tattoos. A few carried bolt-action hunting rifles, but most of them held Steyr machine pistols in their laps, the handles of knives jutting up from their combat boots.

"So we have an agreement?" Colonel Southerland asked, gesturing at the technical specifications for an X-ship spread across the desk.

"Absolutely!" the other man replied with a broad grin. "I believe that we can accomplish great things together, Colonel!" Heavily muscled, the leader of the Neo-Nazis was also shaved bald like the others, but instead of jeans and a black T-shirt, he was wearing a black suit with a matching designer shirt, almost as if the civilian clothing was a military uniform. A 9 mm Luger rode in a shoulder holster under his loose jacket, a snub-nosed S&W .38 Police Special tucked into his belt behind the buckle.

"Thank you…ah, General," Southerland replied, trying to keep the contempt he felt for self-appointed officers out of his voice. For the moment, he needed these lunatics, but afterward… Well, there was always an afterward.

"Combining your amazing invention and our manpower," the leader continued, facing the much younger people filling the folding chairs, "together, we will be able to free England, forge a new world order and save the white race from extinction!"

"Here's to the future!" Southerland smiled, extending a hand.

As the two men shook, the audience cheered loudly, several of them standing with excitement.

"Heil Hitler!" a woman shouted, giving a stiff-arm salute. "Today, the new leader is born!"

"Or maybe not," a heavily accented voice said from nowhere.

Instantly the applause died away and everybody nervously glanced around, but there did not seem to be anybody else in the warehouse.

"The bank account in the Cayman Islands was hard to find, I'll grant you that, Colonel," the voice continued. "But after that, it was easy to trace you to Perth."

Stepping out from behind a stack of crates, Phoenix Force and Able Team revealed themselves.

"You!" Southerland cried in shock, recognizing Lyons from the *Royal Prince* in Maryland.

"Take them!" McCarter snarled, firing an MP-5 machine gun from each hand.

The crowd of Neo-Nazis clawed for their guns, but the combined firepower of the two Stony Man teams removed them from the world in a concentrated barrage of hot lead, steel fléchettes and exploding HEAT rounds.

Ducking behind his desk chair, the leader of the Neo-Nazis got off several shots from each of his guns before Lyons took him out with a single booming round from his Colt Python. The man's head literally exploded from the .357 Magnum round.

Leveling the Barrett, Gary Manning fired a 750-grain manstopper straight through the wooden desk, and Colonel Southerland fell into view, bleeding profusely from a ruined leg and firing a 9 mm Victor pistol. Lyons and Encizo were both hit in the chest, but their NATO body armor easily deflected the incoming rounds.

Converging on the snarling colonel, both teams cut loose with everything they had, and when the thundering assault finally ceased, what lay sprawled on the bloody warehouse floor was certainly dead.

ROOM 59

THE HARDEST CHOICES
ARE THE MOST PERSONAL....

New recruit Jason Siku is ex-CIA, a cold, calculating agent with black ops skills and a brilliant mind—a loner perfect for deep espionage work. Using his Inuit heritage and a search for his lost family as cover, he tracks intelligence reports of a new Russian Oscar-class submarine capable of reigniting the Cold War. But when Jason discovers weapons smugglers and an idealistic yet dangerous brother he never knew existed, his mission and a secret hope collide with deadly consequences.

Look for

THE ties THAT BIND

by

cliff RYDER

GOLD EAGLE®